5.75

(

mount joy

daisy newman

mount joy

ATHENEUM   1968   NEW YORK

FOR

ELLEN AND IRVING,
KATHLEEN AND NICHOLAS
SUSAN, JAMES, NANCY AND CAROL

Frontispiece:
STATUETTE OF ST. JAMES. *15th-16th Century Spanish*
Courtesy of Museum of Fine Arts, Boston

The Way
of Saint James

O MILES 50　　100　　150　　200　　250

Santiago de Compostela

Vigo

Mount Joy

Lugo

MINO

SIL R.

PORTUGAL

CANTABRIAN MTS.

Leon

S

P

A

I

N

Valladolid

Salamanca

Segovia

Madrid

TAJO RIVER

Burgos

Santo Domingo

Logroño

Eunate

Santander

St. Jean-Pied-de-Port

Roncevalles

Puenta la Reina

Pampeluna

Zaragoza

EBRO RIVER

Bayonne

ATLANTIC OCEAN

GUY FLEMING

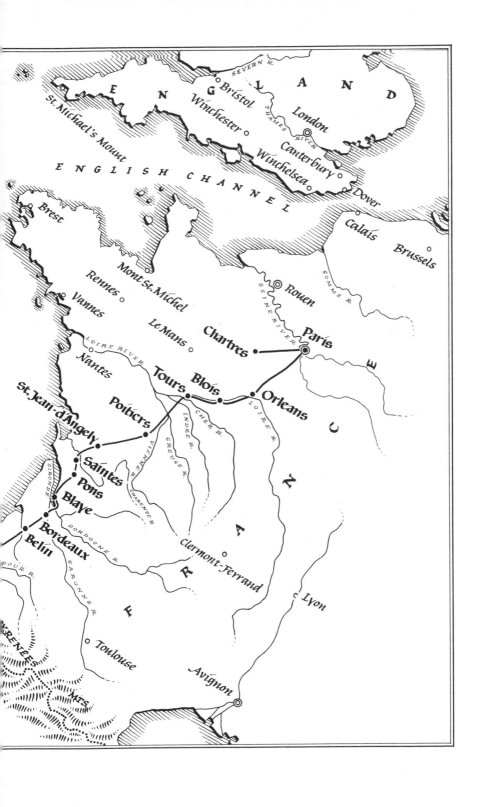

pART 1

Between two rivers, one of which is called the Sar and the other the Sarela, lies the town of Compostela. The Sar is in the East, between Mount Joy and the town; the Sarela is in the West.

Pilgrim's Guide, XII CENTURY

I

Sitting in the Gym amongst the unwanted girls, Maris thought, No one knows how humiliating it is, to be waiting for some boy —

This was the second Mixer she was sitting through without dancing.

By now, all she cared about was running back to the dormitory. But she was trapped. The music had stopped. Couples were leaving the dance floor. Someone she knew would surely notice if she tried to escape during the intermission. She'd have to remain on this hard folding chair, which was bolted to those of the other unwanted girls, so that they sat strung out in a row. She must keep looking as if she were enjoying herself, give the impression that her partner had just gone over to get her some punch.

Lonsie had been dancing with one boy after another.

The moment the music started again, Maris would slip out. Back in the room, she'd curl up on the window seat, where she had spent much of her first term at College, watching the students on the Quad below pass through the arch of Founders Hall. Girls walked together, boys walked together. Mostly, a girl and a boy walked hand in hand.

Here in the Gym, with nothing to do, Maris pictured the everchanging scene beyond the window of that top floor room. On a sunny morning, the spire of the College Chapel loomed very white against smoke rising from the factories down by the river. In mist, the spire took on the color of the atmosphere.

It was nicest at dusk. Then, Maris easily persuaded herself that the graying spire topped some ancient French abbey; that the students moving under the dim Quad lamps were really medieval folk — minstrels and paladins, pilgrims and monks; that Founders Hall was a crenellated tower from which, toward nightfall, a portcullis was lowered against invaders and wolves.

At dusk, on the window seat, she recreated a world she loved, which her courses in the art and history of the Middle Ages made increasingly vivid.

The band was tuning up again. Soon, Maris promised herself, she'd be free to leave. She must tell Lonsie. There she was — talking happily to some boy, at the far end of the Gym. How could Maris get through to her?

When they'd entered College, frightened little Freshmen, assigned to share that top floor room, Maris and Lonsie had learned their way around together. They elected the same English course. They helped each other acquire the indispensable habit of drinking many mugs of black coffee, which neither had ever touched at home. Side by side for moral support, they went to their first Mixer.

That was the other one Maris had sat through.

But it had been a fun evening for Lonsie. From then on, she had been swamped with dates and had tried to divert the overflow toward Maris. Nothing had come of it.

What's wrong with me? Maris had asked the sky and the tops of the horse chestnut trees outside her window after the first Mixer.

Lonsie never looked out. She just sat at her desk with her

record player blaring and studied till the buzzer announced a caller.

The Senior on duty down in the Office used a code for callers: two buzzes, a boy; three buzzes, a girl.

For Lonsie, there were never more than two buzzes. After they cracked the silence, she started to dress, while the boy waited in the Parlor, leafing through those out-of-date magazines.

What's wrong with me? Maris had asked, the whole first term.

The sky gave no answer. But the stately horse chestnuts had reached out their arms in comfort.

Now, at Midyears, there was this second Mixer. Maris had intended to skip it. Lonsie wouldn't let her. "You never can tell," she said knowingly.

So, Maris had come. But in another minute, she'd be gone.

Dreaming of leaving, she scarcely noticed that a boy was there. He was actually there, standing before her.

He was tall. His dark hair was decently cut, he'd shaved, his tie was knotted close to his throat.

"Care to dance? Name's Jim Grant."

Getting to her feet, Maris mumbled, "I'm Maris Miller," certain she'd never think of another word to say.

But there was no need to. Jim launched right in. He came from Joshua, a small town, fifty miles north, on a lake. Wonderful sailing. Here at College, he lived in Stephens Hall. He was a Sophomore, majoring in physics.

A Sophomore! An Upperclassman!

"I'm taking a course in psychology, too. It's great," he went on. "You ought to sign up for it. Filed your next year's study card yet?"

"No. I can't decide on a major." Maris surprised herself by confiding in this stranger. "I'm having trouble with math — trigonometry."

She turned for an instant, as they started to dance, and

scanned the crowd. If only Lonsie would see that she'd finally
got a partner!

"Looking for someone?" he asked, sounding almost jealous.

"My roommate, Janet Lonsdale. There's another Janet in
our Hall so the girls call her Lonsie. Never mind, I'll find her
later."

Nodding, as if satisfied, Jim said, "Trig's fun, Mary."

"I'm not Mary." People were always making this mistake.
"Maris. It's my mother's family name. My Grandfather Maris
lives on a lake, too, down in Maine — Meddybemps. He loves
sailing. But, now that he's retired, he spends most of his time
with the Indians."

"In Maine? I thought they were out West."

"There are two or three Reservations near Grandfather's
place." Here, at last, was a topic for conversation! "Penobscots,
Passamaquoddies —"

Jim cut Maris short. He wasn't apparently interested in Indians. "Maris." he repeated in time with the music, "Maris.
I like it. Has a nice ring."

Ridiculous, how pleased Maris was that he should like her
name!

They talked when they sauntered off the dance floor; they
talked when they sat down, a long way from the unwanted
girls.

"Let's just sit. Okay?" Jim asked, when the band started up
again. "I like the way you look. That's why I came over. I
noticed you clear across the Gym." His voice, which had been
a bit gruff, became almost tender. He reached out and stroked
Maris's sleeve. "Neat color you're wearing. What's it called?"

Maris tried to concentrate. "I don't know. Maize, I guess."

She was glad she had on long sleeves; her arms were too
downy.

"No!" he exclaimed, withdrawing his hand. "Maize is cold.
This is a hot yellow, like your hair."

Embarrassed, Maris stared at her lap, pretending to study the color. Her hair fell past her ears, screening her cheeks. If he could see the "hot yellow" fuzz on her arms, he wouldn't like the way she looked.

"Something's bugging you," he said, in that tender tone. "Is it math?"

"I'm doing badly in French, too," Maris explained, facing him. "I've read so many romances in Old French, I get the obsolete forms mixed up with the modern. But in two courses I'm doing pretty well: History One Thirty, *The Middle Ages*, and Art One Sixteen, *Romanesque and Gothic*."

"You're a Freshman? Those sound like advanced courses."

"They are. I read so much before I came to College, the Dean let me take them. All my life, I've been crazy about the medieval. Knights and minstrels —"

"Knights? Minstrels? Are you kidding? How old are you, anyway?"

"Eighteen."

"And you're still moony about knights and minstrels? Kid stuff!"

"That's what my parents say," Maris admitted. "But the most interesting people lived in the Twelfth Century. They left their mark on stone and glass, in music. Last summer at Chartres — Have you seen the Roland Window?"

Jim shook his head. "I've never been to Europe. What I'd want to see is that tower in Paris, where Pascal made his experiment with the barometer. He proved that the height of the mercury column supported by the air decreases when it's carried upwards through the atmosphere. My research problem goes back to that."

Maris knew nothing about barometers. But she *had* been to Paris.

"The only tower I saw was the Eiffel Tower. Where's Pascal's?"

"Don't know. But think how important that experiment is. Your minstrel business — what good will it be when you graduate?"

This was just what Maris's father always asked. He wanted her to major in a field that would prepare her for some job. Nothing he suggested interested her.

"Well," Jim conceded, "you could teach. Otherwise, I don't see —"

Maris was afraid to argue. He might walk off. "Math and French aren't my only troubles," she confessed, trying to make a joke. "That ball I'm required to throw twice a week — what could be more futile than throwing a ball into a bottomless basket?" Giggling, she pointed to the net hanging from a standard at the end of the Gym. "Don't worry! For me, the ball never goes in."

"Listen," he said, glancing at her hopefully. "About that trig — I'll help you. Want to make a study date?"

If he only knew how she'd been waiting!

They talked till the dance ended, till they reached the Hall. They couldn't make friends fast enough. The freedom and intensity with which they spoke were new to Maris. She'd never shared her thoughts, not even with Lonsie.

But that night, Maris told her roommate everything. Lonsie was in bed.

"He doesn't have much use for the Middle Ages," Maris had to admit.

"Who does? You're the only person I ever met. What's he look like?"

"Tall and dark. Decent hair cut."

"His face, I mean."

Maris couldn't visualize it. "I think his nose ends in a sort of a ball."

That made Lonsie hoot. "You're sure snowed," she observed, "if you can't even remember what he looks like."

Long after Lonsie fell asleep, Maris lay awake. When the Chapel bell tolled four, she slipped out of bed and curled up on the window seat, peering at the February morning. The stars were brilliant.

For a minute she forgot about Jim.

Tracing the path of the Milky Way, Maris thought of Charlemagne standing on a peak in the Pyrenees and gazing through this same Galaxy, more than a thousand years ago. She, too, felt the mysterious tug, which had compelled him to make a pilgrimage, following this luminous band clear across Spain to Santiago the Field of the Star.

2

AFTER THREE STUDY DATES WITH JIM GRANT AND ANY NUMBER of social ones, Maris skinned through her mid-semester exam in math.

"If I pass the final," she reported to Lonsie, "I'll get credit for the entire course. If I don't —"

It was easy for Maris to put unpleasant possibilities out of her mind. She was so happy! Sitting on the window seat, looking out, she wondered how she could have known such despair, only a short while ago. Everything was perfect, except that she still had to choose a major.

"How can one decide Freshman year what one wants to do the rest of one's life?" she asked, turning to Lonsie. "Lucky you, knowing all along that you're going into biology. Daddy thinks I should take Nursery Training."

Lonsie flared up. "This isn't a vocational school. College is a place to learn, just for the fun of it. Sure, you have to be able to support yourself, but you have to be interested in your work, too."

"It doesn't really matter," Maris murmured, gazing out again. "All I'm ever going to do is keep house for Jim, cook, have babies."

10

She'd sing them the songs of the troubadours. She'd tell them about Roland and his friend Oliver, about Sara, the gypsies' black saint, about Aucassin and Nicolette, the lovers who were always finding and losing each other.

"Has Jim asked you? You aren't even pinned."

Maris wheeled around in anger. "Why should he ask me? It's obvious. Soon as he graduates — I hope Daddy'll support me while I'm in College. What difference does it make to him if I'm married?"

Shrugging, Lonsie turned her attention to her books.

And what difference did it make which courses Maris chose? The questions she wanted answers for — questions about life — no professor ever discussed. Only the girls spoke of these things, sitting around late at night, over doughnuts and coffee. Sometimes the Seniors put in a wise word. But they didn't help Maris.

What's right? she wondered, when her classmate, Joanie Jarvis, had to leave College in order to get married. If they loved each other, were they wrong?

The College certainly seemed to think so and some of the girls on the corridor. Others —

"It's their own business," most of them said.

In the Middle Ages things were different. People were preoccupied with these questions: right and wrong, the meaning of life. Their interpretations were rigid, superstitious, cruel. Yet, people *cared*. They died for their beliefs. Who, nowadays, would dream of making a pilgrimage, following the leading of the spirit, as Charlemagne followed the Milky Way and, after him, thousands traveled to the shrine of Saint James?

Maris didn't know what she believed. Her parents tried not to influence their children in this area. They never took them to church. They wanted them to keep an open mind, to formulate their own ideas, when they grew up.

That was one reason why Maris liked visiting her grandfather. She went to church with him. She didn't understand what went on, but she liked the place and the music.

After the service, when Maris was small, her grandfather used to take her by the hand and they would walk up and down the aisles, while he explained each stained glass window as if it were a page in a picture book.

"That's how the Bible came to life for me," she told Jim one evening, describing those visits to Maine. She wanted him to know all about her childhood.

"Rats!" he exclaimed, dismissing all religion.

During his Joshua boyhood, of a Sunday — no matter how fine the weather — he'd been relentlessly squeezed into his best suit. He was the naughtiest boy in his Sunday School. He couldn't wait to get out.

"I'm through with religion for good," he told Maris flatly. "This Protestant gentility —" He changed the subject. "Filed your study card yet? It's due next week."

"I think I'll take Nursery Training."

"Okay. That'll require psych. You may not like it, but it'll draw you out of your fantasy world. And when you graduate, you'll make good money."

"I need some right now," Maris confided. "The deposit for next year."

Money worried Maris. Not that her father didn't send her all she needed. She simply felt she was wasting his hard-earned money here without getting enough in return. She tried to economize. She even denied herself the Twelfth Century *Pilgrim's Guide*, which Professor Hammond urged her to order from Paris.

But time — she was spending more and more of that at the window. Whenever she expected Jim, she was there hours ahead, waiting for him to come charging up on the Honda. No buzzer ever summoned *her*. The minute she saw him rounding the corner of the Quad, Maris ran downstairs so fast that, before Jim could dismount, she was at the door, her face upturned.

She saw him every evening, except during the last week in April, when she was finishing her term paper. That took all her concentration.

For her topic she'd chosen the *Chanson de Roland*.

Last summer, on a bicycle tour of France, when her group visited the Cathedral of Chartres, Maris saw the whole story illustrated in stained glass. Hundreds of little pieces — emerald, scarlet, amber and bright blue — described each episode. Maris stood in the cool Cathedral, overwhelmed by the majesty and the silence, looking up in wonder at that radiant window.

Now, in high excitement, she wrote pages about the courtly Old French poetry, which transformed Charlemagne's defeat at Roncevaux — the death of Roland, Oliver, Anselm and the other brave knights — into an epic of triumph.

"What's so special about this Roland?" Jim asked plaintively, when he telephoned one night. "How come, you're so in love with him, you don't have time for me? You should be concentrating on your weaker subjects."

He talked like that these days, telling Maris what to do.

"Please be patient," she begged, sending a kiss through the telephone. "I'll be through soon. Then we'll celebrate. Jim, I hate to ring off now but I've got to get back to my paper."

Lonsie looked up from her book, as Maris put down the receiver. "He acts like he owns you," she observed.

"Well," Maris murmured, smiling with inward happiness, "he really does. I love it, when he's so possessive."

"What do you mean, he *owns* you?" Lonsie cried, retracting her pen. "Don't tell me —" She gave Maris a searching look, filled with alarm.

"Quit worrying about me. After all, he's a Sophomore. If he tries to teach me how to study, it's because he knows. That doesn't mean —"

Fortunately, Lonsie had a class, so the conversation ended. But it left Maris uneasy. She didn't feel like working anymore. She curled up on the window seat with her recorder and played the songs of the medieval pilgrims.

They sang as they trudged, staff in hand, through Poitou and Aquitaine, wearing their broad-brimmed hats and long cloaks, with a scrip for their bread and money slung over one shoulder. They sang all across Spain.

But when, at last, the weary pilgrims reached the Mount from which they saw, beyond the River Sar, the spires of Santiago, they turned to one another, shouting, "Joy! Joy!"

Maris sat there tootling until the sun went down and the window turned crimson, the color of Roland's nimbus at Chartres.

3

WHEN MARIS LOOKED OUT, EARLY ON THAT FRIDAY MORNING in May, the Quad was beautiful. Lilacs and fringes of wisteria adorned the Halls. But her heart was pounding. She'd had a bad dream.

There was a portent of death in the Roland Window. The night before the battle against King Agolant, Charlemagne's soldiers stuck their lances into the ground and fell asleep. During the night, the lances of those soldiers who were destined to die the next day burst into flower.

Maris had seen the flowering lances in her dream, just as plainly as she'd seen them at Chartres, ranged beside the unsuspecting soldiers who, with their heads on their shields, still slept. Although Maris herself was wide awake now, she felt threatened by impending disaster. Her term paper hadn't been returned. The other students in the course had got theirs back, graded. She'd surely failed.

The Chapel bell tolled six. Outside, the horse chestnuts looked festive, decorated with white candles, like huge Christmas tree lights.

Last May, when Maris was still in High School, the freshness of spring made her almost die of ecstasy. She felt all fresh and green herself, she'd been accepted at College! This morning, she seemed cut off from the new season, shut out by anxiety. Not just about her work; Jim — their relationship was changing.

Until a few weeks ago, they'd been so happy together! True, they argued incessantly. But just when it seemed as if they'd fly apart, Jim would take Maris in his arms and kiss her. Their differences would disappear.

She'd heard that it was this way with married people — they might bicker all day, yet the moment they got into bed, they were united.

Maris and Jim poked at each other's convictions. It was exhilarating, like riding the Honda. Then Jim decided their friendship should have no limit.

"Perfect oneness," he murmured, in that tender tone.

As Maris hesitated, he challenged her. "You love me; don't you?"

"Yes. Oh, I do!"

"Well then —" What he was suggesting seemed to follow naturally.

When they said goodnight, standing on the steps of the Hall, kissing, unable to part, she wondered why she refused to complete what was so nearly a fact.

But lately, she'd felt that she had to be a separate person first. She no longer wanted Jim to own her. She wasn't a thing. Shouldn't they be equal? Before she was joined to him, she wanted to see herself as one sees someone walking on a beach, outlined against the horizon, distinct, heading in one direction.

The beach! That reminded her: this was the day she'd been looking forward to. She and Jim were going to cut classes and go over to the Bay. He was coming for her right after breakfast. She must get her math done quickly.

Lonsie was still asleep, face down on the pillow.

Even Lonsie had troubles now. Stew Stubbs was pressing her to go steady.

"I don't want to," she kept telling Maris. "It's fun, playing the field."

Then Lonsie would see Stew again and she'd come back worried. She liked him best. If she kept dating other boys, she might lose him.

Maris's mother also advocated playing the field. Her last letter, lying open on the desk, made this clear.

We'd like to meet Jim, it said. *Invite him for a day or two this summer, if you still want to. But I wish you'd go out with many boys instead of just one. Get to know your own mind.*

I do know my own mind! Maris thought angrily, pushing the letter away. I'm not a child anymore.

She opened her notebook, took out a compass and read the problem. She could never do it. Jim would have to explain at the beach. But if she wasn't willing to go to his room when his roommates were by prior arrangement elsewhere, how could she ask him to do her trig?

That fear of impending disaster returned. It made Maris want to run. Instead of sitting here — She dug the point of the compass into the notebook. The compass stood up with its pivot pointing to the ceiling.

Pushing the notebook aside, Maris threw her arms across the desk and buried her head in them.

Escape! Where to? Not home, certainly. She'd have to explain.

She had no money, just change. She'd have to wait till Monday. If she drew her whole balance out of the bank, how long would that last? Could she work her way? She hadn't even been able to get a summer job.

She was dependent on Jim, on her parents, her professors — a prisoner in this narrow cell. Her helplessness made her both furious and frightened.

Tears began streaming down her arms. The buzzer put an end to them. This was the first time Maris had to be summoned.

Grabbing her bikini and towel, she started out the door. Something made her glance back. The compass was still standing, stuck in the notebook.

Shouldn't be surprised, she said to herself grimly, running downstairs, if the pivot of that compass bursts into flower.

The moment she saw Jim, Maris felt safe again. She climbed up behind him, clasped his waist for dear life and pressed her knees into his thighs, as they rounded the corner of the Quad. Her hair streamed after the Honda.

At the beach, they lay side by side, their stomachs in the sand, their bare shoulders touching. It was too cold to swim. A fisherman walked past them, solid in his big boots, silhouetted against the water and the sky.

Jim wanted Maris to come to his room later. His roommates wouldn't be there.

"Why not?" he asked, when she shook her head. He raised himself on his elbow to look into her face. "Why not?"

Not knowing how to explain, Maris turned from him. There, half-buried in the sand, lay a little scallop shell. She hardly had to move to pick it up. Shaking it clean, she held it on the palm of her hand, offering it to Jim.

"This is for you," she said solemnly, "the badge of Saint James."

"I'm no saint."

Maris laughed. "You're telling me! I didn't mean that. Every medieval pilgrim who reached the shrine of Saint James in Spain was given a scallop shell."

Jim pushed her hand away roughly. A minute ago, he'd been so tender.

Clenching her fist till the scallops dug into the flesh at the base of her fingers, Maris tried to answer his question. "First I have to see myself the way we saw that fisherman outlined against the sea and the horizon — clearly, knowing where I'm going. After that. It's my way of loving, Jim."

He didn't understand. She knew this when he asked, "Are

you scared?"

She opened her hand so she could look into the silvery cup. "No."

Suddenly, he grabbed the shell. He pitched it savagely across the sand. "I'm sick of being uncommitted," he cried.

"We are committed," Maris insisted, watching the shell fall. "Soon as I graduate, we can get married. Maybe even when you —"

"Three years! By then, I'll be committed to Uncle Sam. I want to live now. All we ever do is talk." He stroked her arm, rubbing the golden down the wrong way. "This is make-believe to you. To me, it's an explosion that rocks the universe."

Maris closed her eyes. How could she keep refusing? He wanted her so —

Then, in a matter-of-fact voice, as if his universe had never been rocked, Jim asked, "Done your trig yet?"

Maris opened her eyes. If she spoke, she might break down. Finally, she risked saying, "I'd like to bump my head against Matthew's."

"Matthew?" Jim repeated, sounding jealous. "Who's he?"

This made Maris giggle. She felt better. "Don't worry! He's been dead centuries. When he built the Portico of Glory in Santiago Cathedral, he put a statue of himself inside the arch. Students go there before exams and bump their foreheads against his stone one to absorb intelligence. I read about it last night."

"Superstition! I bet you believe it, too. For Pete's sake, Maris, grow up. Do you realize that the number of nations now possessing nuclear power —"

"That's why the people of the Middle Ages brightened their world with heroes and saints!" Maris exclaimed. "Their security was so threatened, they had to take refuge in beauty." Jim looked bored, so she asked, "Heard about your summer job?"

"This morning." He was very pleased. "The National Park

Service. I'm going out to Wyoming, right after my last exam."

"Wyoming! Does that mean you won't come to Neville? Mother wrote —"

He shook his head. Maris felt grief-stricken. All summer without Jim!

He rolled over on his side and began stroking her leg. To her utter surprise, Maris started to cry.

This made Jim angry. He jumped to his feet, shaking the sand into Maris's eyes. "Okay," he muttered roughly. "Let's go back."

"No! Wait! I can't right now."

But he started for the rocks, where they'd hidden their clothes. Maris had never seen him look so angry. She tried to catch up.

Then she remembered the shell. She went back, hunting for the spot where Jim had thrown it. There were plenty of others, but Maris wanted that one. She found it, lying face down in the sand. Scooping it up, she ran after Jim.

He was already dressed, starting the Honda, swinging his legs impatiently.

Maris hurried. Sticking the shell in the pocket of her windbreaker, she climbed up behind Jim. Her nose pressed into his back. She smelled his essence, brought out by the sun. Jiggling along, she suddenly didn't care to be a separate person any more. That desire of her spirit to find its place and function was blacked out by the desire of her body. She shouted, "I'm going to your room. I want to." She thought he'd be overjoyed but he said nothing. Maybe he hadn't heard. She pinched his stomach.

"Quit it," he yelled. "You want us to have an accident?"

When they stopped at a red light, near College, she told him again.

He didn't answer. The light turned green. They sped off, down College Avenue, past Jim's Hall, and stopped, with the motor going, in front of Maris's.

Lonsie was hanging out of the window. It wasn't like her.
"Didn't you hear me?" Maris asked Jim, as she climbed
down unsteadily.

He looked at her angrily. "What do you take me for?" he
asked roughly.

Without a kiss, he was gone, leaving nothing but a cloud of
dust.

Maris was furious with him. Then she was furious with herself — whether for refusing or accepting, she didn't know.

4

THE MINUTE SHE OPENED THE DOOR OF THE ROOM AND SAW
Lonsie's face, Maris knew something dreadful had happened.
She glanced swiftly at the upright compass.

"The Dean wants to see you."

"*Me?*"

Lonsie nodded solemnly. "I thought, if you were going to
be hours kissing down there, I'd shout to you out the window.
The Secretary said, Come in before five." Lonsie glanced at
the clock. "It's too late. You'll have to go Monday."

Maris felt her heart drop. She was flunking out. Jim — she
had to tell him. She rushed to the telephone.

"Have you two broken up?"

With her finger in mid-air, Maris turned to Lonsie. "Broken
up? *Jim and me?*"

How impossible! *Broken up?* Until Lonsie asked that, it
hadn't dawned.

Maris put the receiver back slowly. The compass wasn't in
flower. Yet, something had died. She threw herself across the
bed and burst into tears.

"I could tell," Lonsie said. "Just seeing you arrive. The air
was crackling. And the way he nipped off, never looking

back —"

How Maris lived through the weekend, she never knew. Lonsie kept her from running away. That was all Maris thought of. Run away? She was too weak to walk.

Lonsie played her latest records over to cheer Maris, while they waited for Jim to call. He never did.

"If that's how he acts," Lonsie declared, "you're better off rid of him."

"But I love him."

Monday morning, as they crossed the Quad, Maris put her hand in her pocket.

"Look what I found at the beach," she cried, pulling out the shell. She stood still and gazed at it. "Lonsie! Remember that poem we had last term?

> Give me my scallop shell of quiet,
>   My staff of faith to walk upon,
> My scrip of joy, immortal diet,
>   My bottle of salvation,
> My gown of glory, hope's true gage;
> And thus I'll take my pilgrimage."

"Come on, Maris. This is no time for poetry. I'll be late to my lab."

Maris obeyed meekly, thinking of Sir Walter Raleigh writing this poem in the Tower of London, while he waited to have his head cut off. The meaning puzzled Maris. Their prof had only lectured on the meter and rhyme. Still, as she went to her own execution, the haunting beauty of the poem gave her courage.

At the door of the Dean's office, Lonsie squeezed Maris's arm and went on.

"He hasn't come in yet," the Dean's Secretary said. "Have a seat."

Maris didn't want one. She felt like pacing the floor.

Filing cabinets lined the walls of the office and jutted out into the room, looking as if they'd been added to and added to, as the College grew.

A feeling of rebellion came over Maris. She didn't want to be locked in one of those files, separated from four thousand, nine hundred and ninety-nine other students by a cardboard folder. She didn't want to be a paper person. Her soul wasn't in that file. But her soul — if she only knew where it was!

The rebellion evaporated the minute the Dean strode in. He was a big man with a bald head. Maris could tell he had a lot on his mind. Seeing her, he looked irritated, as if the last thing he should have to do, first thing Monday morning, was talk to a student.

The Secretary told him Maris's name.

His manner changed. "Come in," he said heartily, holding open the door of his office. "I waited for you Friday afternoon."

He'd found out that she'd cut her classes! With her grades —

"Please sit down," he said. "I have something important to tell you."

"I know I'm flunking," Maris blurted out, twisting her left hand with her right. Maybe, if she acknowledged it, he'd still let her take finals.

The Dean looked down at the folder on his desk. "No. You're not. I don't mean that you've done brilliantly, but it's impressive the way you've pulled up your math since Mid-years."

Jim! It was all because of Jim. She'd tell him the moment she saw him.

"A small college, like ours, can encourage the student with a special bent, even if she's lagging a little in her other subjects," the Dean was saying. Glancing down at the folder again, he frowned. "I see you've signed up to major in Nursery Training. Do small children fascinate you?"

"No. I have two younger brothers."

That made him laugh. "Then why —?"

"So I can get a job. My father has three of us to put through College."

"It's a very important field," the Dean said. "We want good people in it. But you ought to be looking toward an academic career, a doctorate. Wouldn't you like to major in Medieval History?"

Wouldn't she! If the Dean suggested it, surely her parents —

"Reason I sent for you," he was saying, "is —" He rummaged on his desk. "Where did I put it? Oh yes, Friday afternoon, when you didn't appear, I stuck it in the safe." He got up and left the room.

Maris took out the shell and cherished it. *Scallop shell of quiet.*

So she wasn't flunking! She could spend the next three years studying Medieval History! It was perverse, but now that she had her wish, she didn't want it anymore. Books were only shadows cast by life. A pilgrimage wasn't something to read about; it was an experience, the penetration of a mystery. For Sir Walter, walking to his death, it was the final reality.

Maris longed to ask the Dean what he thought *staff of faith, immortal diet* and *hope's true gage* meant today. They must still have significance or people wouldn't be learning the poem. Surely, a dean knew more than a prof, not just about which courses to take but why — the meaning of living and dying. No, with all he had on his mind, he wouldn't have time to go into such things.

He was back, carrying a large envelope. Sitting down again, he held it in the air, swinging around so he faced Maris, beaming as if he entertained the most boundless admiration for this Freshman.

She knew she was mistaken, confused, maybe fainting. She wanted to close her eyes, but she couldn't, when the Dean was looking at her this way.

"I called you in to tell you," he said slowly, waving the envelope and watching for his words to register, "that you've been awarded the Holmes Prize in Medieval History. This is the first time it's been won by a Freshman."

Maris was too stunned to register anything.

"Here are the conditions," the Dean went on, picking up a sheet of paper and reading. "The Holmes Prize, to be awarded annually for an essay which, in the opinion of the members of the Department of History, best describes the temper of the Middle Ages." He tried to hand Maris the envelope.

She didn't have the wit to take it. The room flipped over. That's why her term paper wasn't returned! The room went right side up.

"Our largest Prize, a very fine sum of money," the Dean was saying, sounding a bit envious. "Five hundred dollars. This ought to ease your financial worries."

Five hundred dollars! No, he said five dollars.

Dimly, Maris realized that she was supposed to reach out for the envelope. It didn't feel real. She dropped it in her lap and squeezed the shell.

Five dollars! Now she could order that *Pilgrim's Guide* from Paris.

"It's a great honor," the Dean was saying.

Not the honor but a flash of independence dazzled Maris. Five *hundred* dollars, that's what he said. She could do anything now, anything she wanted to!

"It's yours, of course," she heard the Dean say. "But if you take my advice," — his tone implied that Maris could hardly do otherwise — "you'll deposit the check with the Bursar against next year's tuition. So, you'll have nothing to worry about when you come back in the fall."

He stood up, indicating that Maris could go now.

Five hundred dollars! She was free!

Then Maris heard another voice, a strange one, though it was her own, saying the most unexpected words. She squeezed the shell with all her might.

"I'm not coming back."

5

Everyone tried to reason with Maris.

"You're crazy," Lonsie cried, when she returned to the room after her class and Maris told her the news. "Why throw the whole thing away?"

"I'm not. I have the money. For a minute," Maris added, giggling as she remembered how the Dean lost his temper, "I was afraid he was going to make me give it back. I couldn't wait to get out of his office. I ran across the Quad."

She held the check between her thumb and forefinger, gazing at it incredulously. *Pay to the order of Maris Miller, $500.*

She was dying to call Jim. Now that she'd, so to speak, made Medieval History pay — Should she call him? If he wouldn't call her —

Before she went to bed that night, she wrote to a bookshop in Paris and ordered the Twelfth Century *Pilgrim's Guide.* In her excitement, she splurged: she enclosed enough money to have it airmailed.

The Seniors gave Maris a terrific party. They were proud of their little Freshman. But they called her dropping-out intellectual suicide.

Even the reporter for *The College Daily*, who came to take

27

her picture — a shrimp of a Junior with a kinky beard that needed combing — put in his oar.

"This is a good school," he mumbled, while Maris sat blinking at his lights. "If students like you don't stick with it, what will happen to the joint?" He had insisted that Maris pose playing her recorder. "Just hold that whistle a little higher, will you?" Then he snapped.

The more people pleaded, the more stubborn Maris became. A tremendous exhilaration possessed her. One more hurdle — final exams — and she was free!

Her spirits nose-dived when she called her parents. First, they were pleased. It was a pity she had to spoil things by announcing her decision.

"We'll talk about that when you get home," her father said. "By then, you'll be calmer."

It was the last straw when Mrs. Key, the Housemother, invited Maris to her sitting room for coffee.

"So she can talk me into reconsidering," Maris told Lonsie. "I wish she wouldn't. I like her but I don't want to change my mind."

The sitting room was hung with Italian prints. A spray of dogwood stood in a tall blue jar on the coffee table. It gave Maris pleasure to enter this room.

Mrs. Key was a tall, impressive woman with very blue eyes and a lot of white hair wound high on her head. The girls said it was her sense of humor that took the sting out of their troubles. Now, Maris saw another quality.

Turning a couple of armchairs toward the fire, waiting till Maris was settled with her coffee, Mrs. Key did mention the advantages of College. But then she said, gazing into the flames, "Sometimes we have to do things that seem impractical to other people. If you feel a need to think your own thoughts for a time, you have the right to stay home."

"Oh, Mrs. Key," Maris cried gratefully, "do you really think so?"

"Yes. By fall, you may see things differently. This has been a hard year for you. Some Freshmen find it so. Later, they sail along. More coffee?"

She's what I want to be like when I'm old, Maris thought, holding out her little cup. But I'll never be that tall.

"Well," Mrs. Key said, "I just wanted to tell you how much I believe in your ability to decide your future. I hope you won't let anyone dissuade you. If you change your mind, you can always come back. You have as much right to do that as to stick to your present plan."

It was the nicest thing anyone said to Maris.

Her new freedom filled her with energy. Even the trig wasn't beyond her. All by herself, she reviewed the year's course and found she could do most of the problems. When she took her finals, she felt she'd done well. Wasn't it ironical? Now that it didn't matter anymore —

"A student of unusual promise," the Dean called Maris, announcing her Prize in the *College Daily*. He didn't mention the fact that she was ungratefully turning her back on her Alma Mater. In her picture, on the front page, Maris was holding her recorder at an angle which looked as if she didn't know how to play it.

Seeing her picture, Jim would surely call.

So many other people stopped Maris on the Quad to congratulate her — total strangers — that she was glad to be going home.

But Jim never called.

Lonsie was staying to see Stew graduate. She'd quit playing the field.

"I don't think I'll sleep here after you leave," she said. "Jane's roommate's going home. I'll move in there. It'd be creepy here alone."

It was a shock to Maris to discover how much she owned.

She slumped down on the window seat, exhausted from packing and depressed at the thought of leaving Lonsie.

"I might never see you again."

"It's your own fault! Why did you have to burn your bridges? What will you do, when you're a lady of leisure?"

"I thought I'd go to secretarial school, get a job in the fall."

It didn't sound very exciting. Was that what Maris really wanted?

"I may never see you again," she repeated the next morning.

They hadn't been to bed all night. Lonsie helped Maris pack her books in cartons. Around four, they made coffee.

"Who knows?" Lonsie murmured, running her hand along the side of the mug. "I may not be here myself. If Stew and I — He's got this fellowship."

When Maris drove off beside her mother, she could hardly bear to look back. Lonsie was standing on the steps of the Hall, waving.

At home, Maris discovered that her withdrawal from College cancelled out her glory. But why? Hadn't her parents always urged her to make her own decisions? Still, there was the money. They were impressed by that.

"Tomorrow morning, I'll take you downtown, so you can put it in the Savings Bank," her mother told her.

"Let's think it over, Lucy," Maris's father said. "If I bought a good stock with it, she'd have a better investment. Of course, Maris," he added sternly, "Mother and I would have been happier if you'd taken the Dean's advice and had applied this windfall toward your education."

Maris said nothing.

"What's that thing you keep fiddling with?" George asked.

"Yes," her mother put in, sounding anxious. "You seem to have developed a nervous habit at College."

Maris opened her hand and both George and Jack looked in it.

"Just a shell," George said, turning away without interest.

"Can I have it?" Jack asked.

"No."

All that first day at home, her parents tried to persuade Maris to return to College. She gripped the shell in her fist and kept silent.

"Very well," her father said, when they were all sitting out on the porch after supper. "If you won't listen to reason, we aren't going to force you."

"But, Maris," her mother added, also sounding resigned, "you'll have to get a job. You mustn't think, just because you suddenly have some money, that you can sit around the house all day."

"Oh," Maris cried, "That's the last thing I want to do."

And then, just as she'd heard herself saying something to the Dean which, up to that moment, had not been in her mind, Maris announced calmly, "I'm going on a pilgrimage."

6

UNTIL MARIS HEARD HERSELF SAYING THESE STARTLING WORDS, she didn't know her face was turned toward the Field of the Star.

To be a pilgrim! To walk through France and Spain with a knapsack on her back — now Maris saw that, from the moment the Dean handed her her freedom, this plan lay undisclosed in her mind. She'd meet other pilgrims. They'd walk along together, singing. When Maris got tired, she'd sit under a tree and play her recorder.

"A pilgrimage?" her father repeated, puzzled. "I'm not up on teen-age lingo."

"I'm going to Santiago. With my Prize money and baby sitting —"

"Santiago, Chile? Who's going with you?"

"Santiago de Compostela in Spain. I'm going by myself."

"Never heard of it," Maris's father declared. "Can't be much of a place."

"It's not. But it's important. Charlemagne went there and Saint Francis of Assisi. Then, thousands from all over Europe followed the Way of Saint James, stopping in monasteries. Knights and princes rode horseback. Most people walked."

32

"What for? Sounds awful."

"To meditate or do penance or to fulfill a vow. It was religious to them. Me — I'm interested in the art and architecture along the road, the churches and hospices built in the Twelfth Century for the pilgrims. There's something else," she added thoughtfully, "some mystery. I don't know what it is exactly."

"Have you friends at College who've been to this place?"

"Nobody I know ever went to Santiago, not even Professor Hammond."

Maris had never told her family about her world. Their interest surprised her. Even Jack was listening. "When the pilgrims reached Santiago," she explained, "they were given a shell, like this." She opened her hand.

"Seems a lot of trouble, just for that," Jack observed. "Easier to pick one up on the beach."

Maris felt deflated.

"You made that bicycle tour of France only last summer," her father reminded Maris. "Do you expect to go every year? It's George's turn next."

"Yeah," George put in, prepared to fight for his rights. "How about that?" Then he muttered, "All those churches. I'd rather go to Scout Camp."

"You don't speak Spanish, do you?" Maris's father asked her.

"A little. I have a phrase book. Some Spaniards understand French."

"Let's go inside," Maris's mother said. "It's getting cold out here."

Her father paced the living room floor. He couldn't settle down. "It's not the money," he told Maris. "If I thought it right, I'd send you. But not alone. If Mother wants to take you —" He glanced at her inquiringly. "We could batch it for a short time. What do you say, fellows?"

"We'd have a ball!"

"It's risky," Maris's father murmured. "Two helpless

women —"

Her mother looked indifferent to the danger. She had never
been abroad. "Let's go," she exclaimed eagerly. "We'll rent a
car. How far is it?"

"From Paris? That's where the Way starts. It must be a
thousand miles."

"I hope they drive on the right," her mother said anxiously.

This wasn't at all what Maris had in mind. If she couldn't go
on foot, be leisurely, stop to look at ancient country churches,
she'd rather stay home.

"I want to go by myself," she cried.

Her mother looked hurt. "Honey, wouldn't it be fun to
have a bat together, the two of us? I'd love to see Paris."

"I want to go by myself!" Maris was almost in tears. "I'm
confused."

"I'll say," Jack volunteered.

Their mother looked at him reprovingly, as if to convey that
she agreed, but he didn't have to rub it in. She smiled at Maris.
The idea of going abroad had intrigued her. Then, seeing how
Maris felt, she put her own wish aside.

Maris's father stopped his pacing and stood before her.
"Spain is no country for a young girl to hobo in," he cried.
"It's not the custom."

"I can take care of myself," Maris assured him.

He ignored that. "Maybe you could join some group. But
what will you do when you come back?"

Before her mother spoke about sitting around the house all
day, Maris hadn't even thought of making a pilgrimage. So
how could she say now what she'd do afterward? She had no
idea.

"It may take years. Who knows what I'll discover? I'm not
going to the end of the earth, Daddy, the way Charlemagne
thought he was."

"Try for a minute to live in the Twentieth Century, Maris.
Assuming you went, what will you do when you return? If I

ran my business this way, investing in some proposition without the faintest idea where it will lead, I'd be bankrupt."

"This isn't a business," Maris argued. "It's — well — spiritual."

"It's my business," her father retorted, "to prepare you for life. Without education —"

"George, you haven't finished your homework," his mother reminded him. "Go up now. And, Jack, I've told you three times to go to bed."

When the boys finally cleared out, Maris's mother turned to her and asked, looking embarrassed, "That young man you wrote us about — what's his name?"

"Jim Grant."

"Yes, Jim — he's not planning to meet you in Spain, is he?"

"No!" Maris cried so vehemently that her mother looked surprised.

"Have you quarreled?"

Maris nodded, avoiding her mother's eyes.

"I'm sorry," her mother murmured, but she didn't sound so.

What about? Suppose she asked that next. *What did you quarrel about?*

Maris's parents were so old-fashioned, they thought if a girl was brought up right and a boy was a gentleman, sex couldn't threaten them. They spoke about their own courtship gaily. It had been beautiful, innocent. Maris envied them. But how could people that old understand?

"These foreign men," her father was muttering. He cleared his throat.

Foreign men! Maris thought. She almost burst out laughing. What would her father think if he knew about the wolves at College?

"I can take care of myself," she repeated.

Could she? If it was a matter of using her fists when some stranger got fresh — yes. But Jim — he'd made her feel that she didn't want to be a distinct person anymore. If he had such power over her —

Her father was looking at her lovingly. "This is a romantic notion," he said. "But since you have your heart set on it, find someone to go with. How about your roommate?"

"Lonsie? She has a job. Besides," Maris said, giggling, "I can just see Lonsie making a pilgrimage, trudging along, her arms full of record albums!"

"Isn't there anybody else?"

Maris shook her head.

She wrote Lonsie and got an immediate reply. Lonsie understood how disappointed Maris was but, honestly, what a waste it would be of that Prize money to spend it on a pilgrimage! Lonsie was having a bad time herself. She and Stew wanted to get engaged. Her parents said she was too young.

Maris retreated into the Middle Ages. She sat in her room day after day, reading the *Golden Legend,* one of the first books to be printed in England. She'd discovered it in a modern edition at the Boston Public Library. It listed the miracles attributed to Saint James.

After the Saint was beheaded in Palestine, his disciples put the body in a ship and an angel blew the ship to Spain. There, before they could find a burial place, the disciples had many miraculous escapes — from Queen Lupa, the she-wolf, from wild bulls and "a dragon casting fire at them."

Maris read the miracles over so many times, she knew them by heart.

The *Pilgrim's Guide* arrived. It was marvelous. The Latin text was on one page, a modern French translation opposite. In quaint language, the *Guide* told the Twelfth Century pilgrims what they needed to know as they traveled to Santiago: which districts had the best food and wines, where the water was polluted, which ferrymen threw their passengers overboard to get their money, how to ward off wasps and horseflies. The medieval writer delighted in the misfortunes that had befallen those who failed to heed his advice.

One of the textbooks for that course Maris took in Romanesque and Gothic Art had photographs of the Cathedral at Santiago — early Twelfth Century sculpture, mostly the work of French artists, who followed the Way with the pilgrims.

Maris studied the South Portal until she was sure that, if she ever actually got to Santiago, she'd recognize the sculpture at once: God creating Adam by laying His hand over his heart; Jesus healing the blind; David playing his harp; a woman holding a skull in her lap, which was thought to be that of her husband or her lover — scholars were mystified by this. There were angels blowing trumpets, devils and strange beasts; a mother nursing her baby — all softly weathered, yet astonishingly clear and beautiful after eight hundred years.

The statue of Saint James, enthroned on the central pillar in the Portico of Glory, was by Master Matthew. Of heroic proportion, it was serene, other-worldly, gazing westward to eternity. Maris was in love with it.

One evening in July, as she sat in her hot room, mooning over these pictures, she heard George shouting to her. She ignored him. He called three times.

"What is it? I'm busy."

"Long distance call for you."

Long distance! Jim! Maris couldn't move. Jim was coming! She managed to get to the telephone. She strangled as she said, "Hello."

"Maris? Is that you? You sound funny."

"Lonsie!"

"Oh, Maris, something awful's happened. Daddy's put his foot down. He says I'm to give up my job and set the Atlantic Ocean between me and Stew. Nothing else is wide enough, he says. Can you imagine, Maris, the whole summer? Well, he did promise, if I feel the same way when I come back, we can get engaged. So I thought, if you're willing, I'd go with you to Santiago."

"You mean — When?"

"Soon as you can. Daddy wants me to leave right away. He has pull and he'll get us a flight. Could you be ready soon, before he changes his mind?"

"Could I ever! Oh, Lonsie!"

7

Getting ready for a pilgrimage took longer than Maris
foresaw. Foreign currency, packing —

Her parents insisted on an itinerary, so they'd never be out
of touch. This was also important to Lonsie, who counted on
finding a letter from Stew wherever she went. She wanted to
be home by September tenth to announce her engagement.
That gave them only seven weeks — two in Paris, four on the
road, one in Santiago — not time enough to walk. They'd have
to go by train.

Maris listed the towns the medieval pilgrims passed through.
Starting in Paris, she and Lonsie would visit Chartres, Orléans,
Tours, Poitiers, St.-Jean-d'Angely, Saintes, Pons, Blaye, Bor-
deaux, Belin, Bayonne, St.-Jean-Pied-de-Port. After crossing
the Pyrenees at Roncevaux, they'd travel westward through
Spain to Pampeluna, Eunate, Puenta la Reina, Logrono, Santo
Domingo, Burgos, Léon, Lugo and up Mount Joy, from
which, at last, they'd see Santiago.

"You're trying to do too much," Maris's father said. "Cut
out some places."

"I can't. They're all part of the Way of Saint James."

"You're not to hitchhike," he warned.

He took her to a tourist office in Boston. Maris asked the man there how to get from Bayonne to Pampeluna, via Roncevaux. He told her to take the Paris-Madrid Express and change in Burgos.

"That doesn't go through Roncevaux, does it?" Maris asked.

"Nobody goes there," the man said. "Skip it."

Maris thought, I'll wait till we're in Paris. There, everyone will know.

Her father got the names of reliable hotels in the towns where there were no Youth Hostels. That night, he wrote for reservations. He still insisted that Maris have a definite plan for the fall. "Why not spend the winter in Paris at that Student Residence you and Lonsie are going to stay in? Fly back there from Santiago. You could take some courses at the University."

It seemed important to Maris that she be free to follow her instinct, wherever it might lead. Still, as she packed her trunk, she began to like the idea of a year abroad.

On the pilgrimage, she and Lonsie would carry knapsacks. Until Maris started stuffing hers, she didn't realize how much she needed: books, writing pad, Scout knife, a sheet sleeping bag, required in Hostels, towels, a plastic dish and fork and spoon, to say nothing of clothes and toilet articles. What a lot!

The knapsack was getting terribly heavy. A blue over-the-shoulder flight bag took care of the odds and ends, purse and passport. Her *scrip*, Maris called it, after the bag the medieval pilgrims carried.

My shell, she thought suddenly. I mustn't forget my shell!

Now that she was getting her wish, she no longer fiddled with it constantly. But she stuck it in the corner of the scrip.

She went around the house, gaily singing the old French pilgrim's song:

> The things that are needed
> I have to prepare
> As the Fathers before me

Went well furnished there
With a staff and a scrip
With a hat, broad of brim,
And a cloak for protection
From gales that are grim.

Lonsie kept calling Maris up. "Are you taking your tweed coat?"

"No. It rains so much. Let's just take our trench coats."

Our cloaks, Maris would have liked to say.

She rushed, in order to have the last days free for visiting her grandfather. She had to say good-by to him.

It was a long way to Meddybemps. Whizzing along in the bus for hours, Maris got tired. She wasn't in trim for a pilgrimage — soft, from sitting over books all year. If traveling by bus was hard, how far would she be able to walk with the knapsack?

Her grandfather met the bus in Machias. Maris had forgotten what a tall, handsome man he was, even in his seventies. His courtliness had more in common with the Middle Ages than with the present.

While Maris stood in the aisle, waiting for the people ahead to get out of the bus, she saw him peering through the window, searching for her.

Maris jumped down. He caught her in his arms. His eyes overflowed with happiness.

They crossed the Machias River in his jeep, heading northeast. Maris loved the farms, the stretches of woodland, her grandfather's white house.

He had prepared a good meal. Maris wanted to help, but while she stood around, uncertain what to do, he brought it into the livingroom and placed it on a low table before the fire.

"I've brought you our itinerary," she told him. "Will you write to me?"

"Every week."

She was touched when she found that he'd gone all the way
to Orono to borrow books on medieval art from the University Library. He wanted, he said, to visualize what Maris was
going to see.

"Let me show you one of these books," he said, after the
dishes were done. "It's a collection of photographs of Léon.
The Cathedral has several statues of Saint James and pilgrims.
Their hats are different shapes but they're all decorated with
scallop shells."

He leafed through till he found the picture he wanted to
show her.

"That pilgrim's hat looks like my beret," Maris said, giggling.

Her grandfather turned to a statue of Saint James. "Do you
know what this hat reminds me of? The white cotton object
I wear when I go sailing!"

Maris burst out laughing. "That thing!" She loved it. She
couldn't picture him on his boat without it.

Her grandfather closed the book. He suddenly looked wistful.

"Your grandmother and I always planned to travel, when I
retired," he told Maris. "But by then, it was too late. I wish
you could remember her. You remind me of her so much —
your coloring and that golden down on your arms. It troubled
her, but I found it charming, something exclusively her own."

"I hate it," Maris cried.

Still, if her grandfather liked it, perhaps other people didn't
find it revolting. Maybe when you loved someone —

"How did you meet Grandmother?" Maris asked, gazing
into the fire.

"In Cambridge, at Professor Rowan's house. Her father
taught Harmony at Harvard, you know. I was in Law School.
I can still remember that evening, walking into Mrs. Rowan's
parlor. There was a crowd of girls. When I saw your grandmother, I knew she was the one for me. She wasn't the most
beautiful. But there was something so arresting in her face,

the same quality I love in yours — a hint of the rich life of imagination. I wanted to call on her. It wasn't easy, around Boston, fifty years ago."

"Like Spain today?"

"Not quite that bad! But very different from the way things are for you. Sometimes I think we were better off."

"How?"

"The way we're made," her grandfather observed, "we seem to put more store by things we have to work and wait for."

Maris had a sudden impulse to tell him about Jim. There was never a time when she was afraid of her grandfather. Couldn't she tell him?

No. He'd blame Jim.

Sunday morning, the service in her grandfather's church seemed intended for Maris. First, the New Testament Lesson from the Ninth Chapter of Luke:

And he said unto them, Take nothing for your journey, neither staves, nor scrip, neither bread, neither money; neither have two coats apiece.

The pilgrim could carry a staff on the rough road, a scrip for food and money. But the poor Disciples weren't allowed even that much.

Anyway, Maris and Lonsie didn't have two coats apiece, either!

The recessional hymn turned out to be John Bunyan's, *He Who Would Valiant Be*. Maris came out of the church, singing gaily:

There's no discouragement
Shall make him once relent
His first avowed intent
To be a pilgrim.

8

"You've never seen the Reservation," Maris's grandfather said at lunch. "I'd like you to meet the Passamaquoddies. Let's go over this afternoon."

As they drove past the Wild Life Refuge, he explained, "The Indians in the rest of the Nation are wards of the Federal Government. These are wards of the State of Maine. I think they're descended from those Red Paint People, who summered around here about the time your Romanesque churches were being built."

"Why are they called Red Paint?"

"Over near Blue Hill, graves have been found containing the red ochre with which they painted their dead. Centuries later, the Indians told Champlain about Norumbega, a city of fabulous splendor. He sailed up the Penobscot as far as Bangor, but he couldn't find it. Norumbega is probably legendary."

"Norumbega," Maris repeated dreamily. "I like these mythical places, like Atlantis. Who knows? They might have existed."

Her grandfather smiled. "You're a romantic," he said, "like your dear grandmother. The world needs them. They give sweetness to this terrifying age. We're coming to the Reser-

44

vation. I hope the Governor's home. He's not Governor of the State, you know; he's the head of the Tribe, a fine man."

They drove along a forest road to a lake. It was a beautiful spot, but the shacks which huddled on the shore needed repair.

"Last summer," Maris's grandfather told her, "some college students spent their vacation helping these folks to patch up their houses. They played with the children, tutored them. Friendship like that is what the Indians need."

"Look," Maris cried, pointing in horror to some broken bottles, which must have been hurled against the side of a shack.

"Don't be critical," her grandfather said sternly. "The liquor with which the white man subdued the Indian is still a curse."

Maris was disappointed in the Governor's house. She'd expected a mansion. He received them warmly, though. Her grandfather was clearly a cherished visitor.

"This is my granddaughter, Maris Miller."

She loved the pride with which her grandfather introduced her. But she began to feel sick when she heard the Governor telling of the hardships the Tribe endured over the winter. There was none of the picturesque grandeur here, which she'd always associated with the American Indian; only hopeless poverty. How could this have been allowed to happen?

When Maris and her grandfather left the Governor's house, they were surrounded by children, who were carrying pails to a faucet on the street. No water in those houses, she realized, shocked.

The children greeted their elderly friend affectionately, in English. Among themselves, they spoke a language Maris had never heard. This was totally unexpected. When she and her grandfather got back into the jeep, she asked him what it was.

"Abenaki," he told her, "their ancient tribal tongue. Don't you think it's remarkable, the way it has survived through all these centuries?"

"Yes. Did you notice? So many of the kids are blond — sort of smudgy."

He looked grave. "The girls have no jobs. White men come from town and get them for a night. Some of those children — nobody knows whose they are. The father's never heard from again. The mother has to go off to find work."

"How awful! Can't anything be done?" Maris asked her grandfather.

"If those white men had some sense of responsibility!" His anger surprised Maris. He was usually so mild. "People say what the Indian needs is vocational training. In my opinion, it's a better example from his white neighbor."

They visited several homes. In one, a newborn infant shared a crib with a toddler. Paper was pasted over cracks around the windows. The people were endearing. Maris meant to be friendly but she felt too shocked to speak.

Before they left the Reservation, her grandfather stopped the jeep again.

"Since the time of Champlain," he said, getting out and waiting for Maris to join him, "the Catholic Church has educated these Indians. Two nuns run the school. They're always cordial to this old Protestant." He knocked on a door.

A nun with a lovely face appeared. "Mr. Maris! I'm glad to see you."

"Sister, this is my granddaughter. Could we show her the church? She's more at home in Gothic cathedrals, but I want her to see the carvings."

The nun took them to a little church nearby. It was very simple. On either side of the chancel hung a bas-relief. Maris noticed the grain of the wood shining warmly through the high polish.

"This," the nun said, "is the Blessed Mother with the Christ child."

It was an Indian Madonna, a squaw with her papoose, delicate and appealing.

"That," the nun said, pointing to the other side, "is Saint Anne. Years ago, an old man living on the Reservation made these carvings. Many of the Indians did wonderful work in those days. But their art is dying out."

Maris's grandfather was watching her intently. "Aren't they beautiful?"

"Yes!"

When they were back in Meddybemps, sitting before the fire, he said, "I wanted you to see those carvings. They are to me what the statue of Saint James in the Portico of Glory at Santiago is to you."

"I'm looking forward to seeing that!" Maris exclaimed. "My prof says it's one of the finest Twelfth Century statues in existence."

"By the way, I've been meaning to ask: is he Saint James the Greater or Saint James the Less?"

Only someone familiar with the Bible knew enough to ask that.

"The Greater. Caxton calls him, 'The More.' "

All weekend, Maris had been dreading what her grandfather would say about her leaving College. She could stand up to everyone else, but if he was disappointed in her — He hadn't mentioned it. She waited till she didn't have to meet his eyes.

"You don't mind?" she asked, when he was putting a log on the fire.

"What?" He shifted the log on the andirons.

"My dropping out."

He hung up the tongs slowly. Then he turned. "You haven't dropped out," he said, sitting down on the couch beside Maris. "You're on leave. I don't believe for a minute that you won't go back, even if you need years to discover your purpose. You're simply putting first things first, seeking answers to questions that baffle us all. I admire you."

"*Really?* Everybody else —"

"Pay no attention. Most young people let chance push them into some slot and there they stay, either resigning themselves or chafing the rest of their lives." He took her hand and smiled at her lovingly. Then his expression became anxious. "You're going to find being alone almost unbearable," he warned.

"Oh," Maris cried. "I thought you knew. My roommate's going with me."

"So I understand. But from what you've told me, it would seem that, while the two of you get along well, at the deeper level you have little in common."

As her grandfather spoke of Lonsie, Maris saw herself with Jim, riding the Honda, kissing, arguing. Wasn't that exactly the trouble between them? At the deeper level —

"So," her grandfather was saying, "you'll be as good as alone, even with Lonsie along."

Maris managed to detach her thoughts from Jim.

"Wasn't it lucky," she exclaimed, "that Mr. Lonsdale put his foot down! Otherwise, I wouldn't have been able to go. Daddy worried so —"

Maris's grandfather went to his desk and took out a tiny box. "I found this at that little shop in Machias," he said, handing it to her. "From what I've read, Spanish people have an obligation to protect pilgrims. Fasten it to your beret and tell your father we have nothing to fear."

Maris undid the wrapping. Inside the box, lying on a strip of absorbent cotton, was a little silver pin, shaped like a scallop shell.

"Oh, Grandfather!"

Maris jumped up and threw her arms around his neck.

"*Au revoir*," he whispered. "Make a good pilgrimage. It's the hardest thing anyone can do."

I

HALF AWAKE, MARIS WAS CONSCIOUS OF A STEADY PING-PING. She sat up, not knowing where she was. Paris — she and Lonsie were in Paris! Rain was pelting on the skylight of their room in the Student Residence. She jumped out of bed.

"Lonsie! Wake up! We're here! Isn't it fantastic? Yesterday morning, we were still in the U.S.A."

Lonsie just scowled. "What time is it?"

"Almost twelve. No, it can't be. But I set my watch by Paris time last night." Maris held it to her ear. It ticked. "We've slept all morning."

"Only seven, back home," Lonsie mumbled, turning over and going to sleep.

Maris propped her elbows on the sill of the casement window. The mansard roofs of the Latin Quarter, glistening with rain, and the tall chimney pots cut off the view, but she could picture the Seine behind them. She could even imagine the medieval pilgrims in their cloaks and broad brimmed hats gathering to begin their journey together at the Church of Saint James. She had read that the ancient church was replaced in the Sixteenth Century by one whose tower still stood and she wanted to see that more than anything else. Right away!

51

I've never been so happy, she thought, looking forward to it.

But Lonsie — all the way over in the plane, Maris had this feeling that Lonsie was different, preoccupied, edgy, sometimes even silly. Was this love? She seemed both to have outgrown Maris and to depend on her.

Maris thought, She's never been to Europe. She doesn't speak much French. So she's scared. And the last thing she ever would have chosen was a pilgrimage.

"Get up," Maris begged, turning to her. "Don't you want to see Paris?"

The bathtub was in one room, the john in another. They must have been added after the old Residence was built, tacked on halfway down the winding staircase without any landing. One had to leap from the stair above.

It was Lonsie's first brush with foreign plumbing. "Quaint," she murmured. Then she said, "Let's have lunch on the Eiffel Tower and browse in the shops. I want to look at furniture, that beautiful French fruitwood."

Maris thought, The Eiffel Tower! Shopping! It's as bad as having Mother.

When they reached the street, though, she was ecstatic. "It even smells like Paris," she exclaimed.

She carried a guidebook, not the Twelfth Century one. This was up-to-date.

The rain had stopped. Bright sunshine made the pavement dazzle. But they'd only gone a few blocks along the Boulevard Saint-Michel when the rain started again, coming down so hard that Lonsie took out her sou-wester and Maris put on her beret with the shell pin perched over one eye. They had to find shelter.

Two doors away was a little restaurant. They ducked in and sat down at one of the tables on the sidewalk. It was protected by an awning and a trellis.

"I like this place," Maris said, looking around.

The waiter had a narrow skull and hollows under his cheekbones. He waited patiently while they studied the long menu.

Lonsie ordered frogs' legs — not, she explained to Maris, because she liked them. She didn't. This was simply *the* thing to do in Paris.

Maris chose *Coquille Saint-Jacques*, deep-sea scallops fried with parsley.

When they'd finished their lunch, Maris paid the bill.

Lonsie did some touching up with her lipstick. "Let's go over to the Right Bank," she said between her teeth. "This friend of Mother's bought the most beautiful diamond ring in the Rue de Rivoli. Cost about a third of what it would at home. Stew said if I saw one I liked, to go ahead and get it."

"An *engagement* ring?"

Lonsie nodded. "It'd be more fun," she admitted, "if Stew could pick it out. Wouldn't it be great," she went on dreamily, "to get one of those big, curlycue beds with a high canopy and red damask curtains? Do you think they'd send it?"

"To New Jersey? Are you crazy? Buy one at home. It'll cost less."

"That wouldn't be a French bed. Stew and I'd love a French bed."

They took a bus to the Place de la Concorde and began walking down the Rue de Rivoli, stopping to look in the shop windows. Lonsie fell for everything but she didn't buy anything. Maris was patient. She had studied the map. If they continued on this street, they'd come to the spot she most wanted to see.

It was hidden by surrounding buildings. Suddenly, they were almost under it. They stood still on the busy street and looked up.

"This is where the pilgrims started," Maris told Lonsie eagerly. "La Tour Saint-Jacques, it's called, The Tower of Saint James. From here, they crossed the Seine to the Ile de la Cité, passed Notre-Dame and, crossing the Seine again, left Paris by the Rue Saint-Jacques. Can't you just see them, trudg-

ing along with their staves and their scrips, singing? Isn't the
Tower graceful?"

"I like those gargoyles," Lonsie said. "Who's the guy inside
the arch?"

Maris consulted the guidebook to identify the statue.

"On this spot stood the Church of Saint James," she read
aloud. "In medieval times, it was surrounded by butcher shops,
tripe dealers, skinners and tanners. During the Revolution,
most of the Sixteenth Century church was destroyed. Only the
Tower remains. It is closed to visitors."

"Tough!"

Maris ignored Lonsie's candid lack of interest. She con-
tinued reading: "In the base of the Tower is a statue of Blaise
Pascal, the famous — Lonsie! It's the Tower Jim wanted to see.
He said, if he ever got to Paris —"

"So you're both in love with the same tower!" Lonsie exclaimed, amused. "If things equal to the same thing are equal
to each other, then people in love with the same tower are —"

"Here, Pascal performed his experiment on atmospheric
pressure," Maris read. She looked up at the Tower in wonder.

"Come on," Lonsie broke in. "Let's go. We have to see
Notre-Dame. Everyone at home'll ask me how I liked it."

As they walked toward the Seine, Maris kept marveling at
the fact that, for different reasons, she and Jim were drawn
to the same landmark.

"Wouldn't it have been funny," she asked Lonsie, "if we'd
met Jim there? You know, suppose he was in Paris, looking at
the Tower, just when we arrived."

"I thought he was out in Wyoming."

"He is."

"Then quit having these fantasies."

Near the bridge which led to Notre-Dame, there were
secondhand book stalls. Maris would have liked to linger over
them. Lonsie wasn't interested.

"Let's go," she urged, pulling Maris's arm.

"Wait! I've found a book about Abelard. Right around here's where he and Héloise — He was teaching at Notre-Dame. There was a school of theology there. She lived right around here, in one of these streets."

The Cathedral impressed Lonsie. "I like it," she said. "It has solidity, and still those tall towers look light."

Maris couldn't say anything. The simplicity, the serenity, the magnificent portals: Saint Anne's on the right, the Virgin's on the left, each with her child in her arms! Above Saint Anne, at the level of the Rose Window, stood Adam; above the Virgin stood Eve.

Homesickness unexpectedly struck Maris. In a tiny wooden church on the edge of the Maine forest, this same Saint held her child on one side of the altar, while the Virgin held hers on the other. For a moment, in place of the magnificent portals, Maris saw those primitive carvings, dear to her grandfather because they were in the likeness of the American Indian.

"I wish you knew my grandfather," she whispered.

Lonsie couldn't see the connection. "He's not a Catholic, is he?"

"No. He's a —" But Maris wouldn't state his denomination. None was wide enough to contain him. "He's a great human being."

Even that didn't describe his warmth and largeness of spirit.

They entered and stood under the Rose Window, looking up at the galleries and the vaulting. Maris studied the huge pillars that support the towers.

But Lonsie had only one thing on her mind.

"Were the Kings and Queens of France married here?"

"I don't know."

"Imagine walking up an aisle the length of this one! Daddy would start puffing."

Trailing after Maris, Lonsie hardly noticed the beautiful architecture.

"I never go to church any other time," she complained, in

the vast stillness. "Why, all of a sudden, because Stew and I want to live together, should I parade in one, wearing a fancy dress, a hand-me-down from Mother? A lot of old folks staring at me as I go by, blowing their noses —"

"Sh!" Maris whispered, embarrassed. People were kneeling on the pavement and at the confessionals. "Look at the Rose Window from here."

But Lonsie was still visualizing herself being married in Notre-Dame and recoiling from the thought. "Why," she asked defiantly, "should Dad give me away? He doesn't own me."

Maris shrugged. She was trying to study the stained glass.

"Stew doesn't want to rent a silly suit with striped pants. But Mother and Dad insist on a church wedding, champagne and all the trimmings. Come on, Maris. We've seen enough. Let's get out of here."

When they were in the sunlight again, crossing the bridge that led to the Latin Quarter, Maris asked, "What kind of a ceremony do you want?"

Lonsie looked thoughtful. "If there has to be some sort of public demonstration," she answered, "it'd be more genuine if we had it in the Student Union at College — you know what I mean: our own friends, sitting around in black turtle necks and levis, with their hair falling over their eyes, sucking cokes like bottle babies, strumming Lohengrin on their guitars, all of us being ourselves."

Maris burst out laughing. "That isn't what you want. Stop trying to act hip. You're not."

"Of course we're not hip," Lonsie agreed, laughing, too. "Stew and I never went around with that kind of a crowd. All I mean is: when we get married, I'd like it to be more what we're used to."

"How?"

"Stew and I should be looking at each other, instead of at some minister we don't even know. We should say what we really mean, when we promise to cherish and be faithful and stuff like that, not repeat antique words after the guy — words he reads out of some book, as if we didn't know enough to read them ourselves. If we stick together all our lives, it won't be because of that performance."

"You're sure your father's going to let you?"

"He'd better," Lonsie blurted out fiercely. "We're practically married now."

"You don't mean —?" Maris stood still in the street and stared at Lonsie.

So that's why she seemed changed! Lonsie had, as the kids at College said, proved herself a woman.

"Don't look at me that way, Maris. What's wrong with it? We're getting married. That makes it all right, doesn't it?"

"No."

"Why not? Have you forgotten how you almost — You weren't even secretly engaged."

Maris hadn't forgotten. She never would. What Lonsie said was quite true. The only reason she didn't do the same thing was: Jim left her. Lonsie hadn't criticized Maris. She'd been very understanding.

"I haven't forgotten," Maris said softly. "It's just that now — if he were to ask me now, I wouldn't go."

"Why not?"

"I don't know."

She suddenly felt years older than Lonsie. Sick in her heart, certain her feet wouldn't carry her farther, Maris stood there.

"Come on," Lonsie cried, striding ahead. "Quit making a mountain out of a molehill. Where do we go from here? My feet hurt."

A *molehill*, Maris thought, slowly dragging herself on.

2

ACCORDING TO THE GIRLS AT COLLEGE, HAVING A MAN GAVE one security.

The opposite seemed true of Lonsie. She was growing more and more edgy. If a day passed without a letter from Stew, she almost went out of her mind. When she got one, she was either silent for hours or so delirious with joy that Maris, who only heard from home, found it a trial to listen.

By the end of their second week in Paris, Maris wondered how they were going to survive when they got to the country. Mails were slower. Without the shops and theaters — At least, tomorrow, tomorrow they were going to Chartres! Lonsie would surely fall under the spell of that Cathedral.

Originally, they'd planned to spend tomorrow night at the Youth Hostel in Chartres and go on from there to Orléans, the next stage of their pilgrimage. But, in one of Lonsie's bad moments, Maris had agreed to come back to Paris, so that, if there should be still another letter from Stew, Lonsie wouldn't miss it.

Anyhow, the day after tomorrow, they'd set out with their knapsacks.

They were sitting in the Tuileries Gardens, enjoying the

58

sun, eating crescent rolls with cheese and cherries for lunch.
There was a feeling of repose and grandeur about the wide
vistas, the avenues of clipped trees, the carefully tended flower
beds. Beautifully turned out children walked by with their
mothers.

A chubby, dark-eyed little girl passed. "Isn't she cute?"
Maris exclaimed.

Lonsie turned away. "Will you be my maid of honor?" she
asked irrelevantly.

"I thought you didn't want a church wedding."

"Don't be stupid. Of course I do!"

"You're really getting married in May?"

"I guess so."

"I don't think the Sorbonne finishes in May."

Lonsie flared up. "Before making such a drastic decision,"
she cried, "you might have consulted me. To waste a whole
year, just because you got some money!"

"You talk like Mother," Maris told her.

"Shut up!" Lonsie screamed. "What you needed was to
have your head examined by one of those psychiatrists at
College Health."

"I don't need any psychiatrist! I know what I want."

"Your childish pilgrimage, do you mean?"

Now they were fighting. For almost a year, they'd roomed
together in harmony. Now they were out to murder each
other, here in the peaceful Gardens.

Why does she keep bugging me? Maris asked herself
bitterly.

Aloud she said, "Tell you what: let's go over to the Sorbonne after we've had lunch and find out when the courses
finish."

"Will they make you pay a registration fee? Suppose you
decide to go home?"

"Why would I go home?" Maris snapped. Then she calmed
down. "I'm sorry," she murmured. "I didn't mean to hurt

your feelings."

Lonsie nodded, as if she wanted to make up, too. But she still seemed unhappy. She glanced at Maris sideways from under her lashes — that trick she had when she was a little uneasy — and asked, "Is it to beg God to change His mind about — well, Jim — that you go to all those churches?"

"What do you think I am?"

"But isn't that why people pray, if they're faced with some ghastly destiny — aren't they begging God not to let it happen?"

"In the Middle Ages, people did ask for favors," Maris conceded, "victory in battle, protection from the Black Death. But me — it's the art and architecture that attract me."

As she spoke, Maris realized that, while the pilgrimage had barely begun, it was already a fizzle. She and Lonsie had seen a lot, yet the meaning she searched for with all this rushing around, her own relation to the world, her unique gift, never emerged.

She was nothing but a tourist, like last year, marching through museums and churches, viewing statues and buildings as one looks at one's fellow passengers in a bus, staring for a minute at their clothes, their figures, their faces, without ever encountering their souls.

"When we get to the country," she said to Lonsie, as they left the Gardens, "let's slow down some — sit by the wayside and think about things."

"I don't want to think," Lonsie cried. "It gives me the willies. On the way to the Sorbonne, we can stop at the Express. There might be a letter."

"You just got one."

"He wrote it at breakfast time. Maybe he wrote again after work."

At the Express, Lonsie stood in line at the mail window. Maris inquired about a bus or train for Pampeluna, going by way of Roncevaux. She'd already asked at a tourist office on the Champs-Élysées without getting the information.

"You must take the Paris-Madrid *Rapide* to Burgos," the woman had told Maris. "There you can catch a train for Pampeluna."

"But that doesn't go though Roncevaux."

Perhaps the woman didn't understand American French.

Here, a young Englishman waited on Maris. He looked through the timetable.

"There you are," he said, grinning triumphantly, "you take the Paris-Madrid *Rapide*, leaving at thirteen forty-five, arriving at Burgos —"

"But that doesn't go through Roncevaux," Maris exclaimed. "I want to —"

How were they going to see the place where Roland died?

No letter for Lonsie. As they left the Express, they both felt blue.

They took a bus to the Place de l'Hôtel de Ville. On the riverbank below Notre-Dame, couples were sitting in the sunshine, happily engrossed.

"Héloise and Abelard must have sat there, just like those kids," Maris told Lonsie, as they looked down from the bridge. "It's almost eight hundred years ago, but not really different. He sang her the songs of the troubadours the way they're singing rock and roll."

Thanks to the book Maris bought at the stall on the Quai, she knew quite a lot about Abelard.

"He was a brilliant fool, always scrapping with his teachers at the school of Notre-Dame, showing off, beating them in arguments. No wonder they threw him out! Then he came up this hill — Mont Saint-Geneviève — and started a school of his own. The students ran after him. That's how the University started."

"Didn't Héloise have that baby?" Lonsie asked.

"Yes. But they got married, only then Abelard became a monk and Héloise went into a convent. So they didn't have any home life."

Maris and Lonsie crossed the Seine again and walked up the Rue Saint-Jacques. Chinese restaurants and modern University buildings seemed incongruous in the street where the pilgrims once started for Santiago.

It was a steep climb. When Maris and Lonsie reached the Sorbonne and located the Registrar's office, it was closed. They found their way out of the building again, back to the Rue Saint-Jacques.

Maris looked at a map. "We're almost at the Panthéon," she said. "You must see that."

"I'm bushed," Lonsie muttered. But she trudged patiently up the hill.

Watching her, Maris asked herself, How can I not be in my roommate's wedding? Why did I say that to her? How self-centered can one be?

"I'll come home in May," she said aloud. "I'd love to be your maid of honor. After all, I'm not taking any courses for credit, so it doesn't matter."

Lonsie gave her a grateful glance, but it was wistful. Her feet must hurt.

They found a cafe from which they got a good view of the Panthéon, pushing their way through the crowd to a small, marble topped table. The noisy students spoke many languages and had many shades of skin.

Maris ordered two coffees.

Lonsie threw her arms across the marble top and rested one side of her head on them. Suddenly, Maris saw with horror that tears were rolling down the upturned cheek. She'd never seen Lonsie cry.

"What — what's the matter? Do your feet hurt that much?" Lonsie shook her head.

Putting her arm around her, Maris asked, "Are you sick or something? Do you want to go home? Maybe we can find a cab."

Sitting up, Lonsie blew her nose. She didn't look at Maris.
"We have — to — go — home," she sobbed, wiping her eyes
with her sleeve. "I don't mean to the Residence. I mean to the
U.S.A. That's why I didn't want you to pay the registration
fee. I've ruined your pilgrimage."

"What are you talking about? We've only been here two
weeks."

"I know," Lonsie wailed. "I know."

"Pull yourself together. Is it that you just can't live without
Stew?"

Lonsie made the effort. "I guess," she blubbered, "I'm like
Héloise."

Maris couldn't believe she'd understood. "You don't
mean —?"

"That's what made me so mad when you said I talked like
a mother. I'm afraid I'm — Oh, Maris, I don't want it. I don't
want it." She cried again.

Maris suddenly felt she was going to lose her lunch. Right
here, in the cafe, she was getting ready to upchuck. She looked
around desperately for the exit. But how could she leave Lonsie?

Sweat broke out on her forehead. Her beret was stifling.
She pulled it off and squeezed it. The shell pin dug into her
hand. Her stomach began to calm down but her own eyes
stung. The pilgrimage! To have to give it up now!

"Did you know before we left home?"

"Of course not! I wouldn't have come. I didn't want to. But
Dad was furious, the way I was with Stew every minute."

"Do you think he suspected?"

"I guess so. Maris, we'd better go to the Airline for reservations."

"Let's get out of here," Maris said. "I can't stand this place."

She paid the waitress. In the street, she took a deep breath
and felt better.

Lonsie had stopped crying but she looked ghastly.

As they approached the Panthéon, Maris asked, "Were you

on the pill?"

"No! We didn't *plan*," Lonsie cried indignantly. "It just happened. His job hadn't started yet and we spent the whole time together. We got to feeling closer and closer till we just had to be one. And we wanted it to be natural, beautiful — not spoiled with safeguards. We never dreamed ——"

Maris stared at the great dome of the Panthéon with the circle of columns around the cupola. She didn't know what to do.

"I don't want it," Lonsie wailed, chewing her knuckles. "I don't want it! Stew and I haven't even had our honeymoon."

"I bet the baby doesn't either," Maris murmured.

"The baby?"

"Doesn't want to be born."

"Oh, I never thought about the baby's angle," Lonsie confessed, wiping her eyes. "Gosh, yes! Stew and I'll have to be married right away. There won't be time to make much of a wedding. I may not even have attendants," she added, glancing apologetically at Maris. "Mother'll have to work that out."

Maris put her arm around Lonsie's shoulder. "Maybe you're just off schedule. Why not wait a week? We'll be in Bordeaux then. It won't take long to get back to Paris and we can fly home the same night."

"Don't you think we ought to make reservations?" Lonsie asked. "If we said it was an emergency — We wouldn't have to explain, would we?"

At that, they both laughed.

"You go in and look at the Panthéon," Maris said. "I saw it last summer. Anyway, it's Eighteenth Century. That little old church back there is what I want to see, Saint-Étienne-du-Mont. I'll meet you here in twenty minutes. Okay? Cheer up, Kid. I bet it's a false alarm."

Maris was about to go on by herself when Lonsie's next words froze her.

"A thing like this," she was saying, "puts an end to your whole life."

Maris grabbed Lonsie by the shoulder and shook her. "You're not thinking of doing something dangerous? Lonsie, listen to me —"

"Relax," Lonsie told her, smiling wanly. "I'm not contemplating suicide or abortion. We'll get married. But it puts an end to the life I planned, for now, anyway. Amble along, Maris, I'll be safe in here among the tombs."

Maris watched her go into the Panthéon. She herself was so distressed that, as she crossed the little square, she hardly remembered its history — the Tower of Clovis, the legends of Saint Geneviève and Saint Stephen.

Why did she have to give up her pilgrimage, just because of this baby nobody wanted? It wasn't fair!

She was drenched with perspiration and when she entered the cold church, she began to shake. Eager to get out into the sunshine again, she hurried through the nave, barely stopping to look at the famous rood screen with its wide arch and spiral staircases.

Women were praying in the Chapel of the Virgin. Tiptoeing by, Maris was suddenly stopped. A plaque on a pillar noted that Blaise Pascal was buried there.

Pascal! Jim's hero! All that remained of him lay under this pillar.

No, Maris thought, not all. Three hundred years later, three thousand miles away, a fellow named Jim Grant is using his ideas, carrying them forward in turn.

There was something awesome in this, glorious, too, a kind of immortality.

Then Maris had another thought, which made her so dizzy that she had to put one arm against the pillar to steady herself. Suppose what was happening to Lonsie had happened to her? If Jim hadn't been so angry that day —

She glanced down at the beret clutched in her other hand.

"Make a good pilgrimage," her grandfather had whispered, bidding her farewell, "it's the hardest thing anyone can do."

How hard, Maris hadn't dreamed, at the time. Now she knew. But, rough though it was, she had to make it.

This wasn't the "romantic notion" her father called it, or even something to satisfy her curiosity, which she kept claiming. Maybe it was childish, the way Lonsie said. But suddenly, it was an urgent necessity. Maris must have this chance to find out what she believed, to understand the cross currents in her nature, if she was ever going to control her destiny.

Staring at the shell pin, she could almost hear her grandfather saying, "Tell your father we have nothing to fear."

If Lonsie had to go back, with the shell for protection, why couldn't she make the pilgrimage alone?

She hurried out of the church, feeling surprisingly strong. For now she understood the nature of the protection. It wasn't only that people, seeing the pin on her beret, would feel duty bound to take care of a pilgrim. The protection was in her. She didn't need to *prove* herself a woman.

She was one.

3

THE NEXT MORNING, LONSIE STAGED A REBELLION. I'M NOT setting foot in another church," she declared. "This is my last chance to see Paris."

"But we're going to Chartres," Maris reminded her.

"You can. I'm staying here."

Neither of them had slept much. "I'm scared," Lonsie kept repeating, half the night. "I have to go home." She finally agreed to wait a week, on the chance that her fear was groundless. Now, in the morning, she looked haggard.

"You mean you're skipping Chartres?" Maris cried. "Any other cathedral, but Chartres!"

"I want to see the Grand Palais and the Trocadéro," Lonsie said. "Those science exhibits are supposed to be terrific. How can I go back and tell people the only museums I saw were the Louvre and the Cluny?"

Maris didn't know what to do. Was it right to go away for the whole day and leave Lonsie alone with all she had on her mind? Yet, to give up Chartres —

"Okay," she murmured finally, not nearly so resigned as she tried to sound, "I'll stay with you."

Lonsie wouldn't hear of it. She became so upset that Maris

promised to go.

"I'll see you off," Lonsie announced. "Where's the station?"

"Up the street. Gare du Montparnasse."

When they parted on the platform, Lonsie asked, "When does your train get back? Five-ten? I'll meet you here. We'll have dinner at our little bistro."

She was sounding more cheerful.

In the train, Maris recalled her grandfather's prediction, that she'd be lonely, even with Lonsie along. Maris had never been so lonely in her life.

But when the train pulled into the station at Chartres, her spirits suddenly soared. Slinging her scrip over her shoulder, she saw rising above the trees the spires of the Cathedral. They didn't match. She concentrated on the shorter, older one, majestic in its simplicity and perfect proportions, its almost human aspiration. It greeted her like an old friend.

As she climbed the hill to town, she passed the cinema. Gaudy posters advertised the current movie: *Goldfinger*.

Seems out of place here, somehow, Maris observed to herself.

At the side of the Cathedral Square, three women, dressed in the colorful, antique costumes of the region, sat in the sunshine behind a table on which their handiwork was exhibited: place mats, afghans, crocheted gloves.

Maris remembered these women, with their starched lace caps, grotesquely tall, perched on their old-fashioned hairdos, like white steeples. It was as if the women hadn't moved since she saw them sitting here in the rain a year ago. One of them held up a lace table-cloth.

A middle-aged American was considering buying it. He inquired in English whether it would launder. The Frenchwomen obviously didn't understand. So the man repeated his question in a louder voice.

The women weren't deaf. "Launder" simply wasn't in their English vocabulary.

"Will it launder?" the American repeated, raising his voice more and more.

He wasn't particularly attractive, but it was such a sudden joy to Maris, in this foreign land, to discover a fellow-countryman that she rushed over to the table and translated for him.

"*Ah, oui,*" the women assured the American, smiling in sudden comprehension, "*parfaitement, Monsieur.*"

The man didn't even glance at Maris. He took out his wallet and counted the paper francs in English. He never said, Thank you. It was as if Maris weren't a person, who'd done him a kindness, but merely a language gadget, which had served its purpose.

Hurt and embarrassed, wishing she'd left the old guy to shift for himself, Maris hurried to the Cathedral.

The Royal Portal, in its quiet dignity, quickly made her forget her irritation. There, on the right, was Our Lady of Chartres, serenely welcoming Maris to her house. The saints, the prophets, the kings and queens of France stood on their columns in elongated elegance around the three doorways.

Last year, when Maris came here on the bicycle trip, it was raining on and off, so the whole time was spent inside. Jerry, the leader of the group, was a good fellow, expert at patching a tire or putting on a tourniquet. But he didn't know beans about Gothic or any other art. With the help of the guide book, he had done his best.

Now, it was as if Maris were coming here for the first time. All winter long, she'd studied photographs of this Portal. Now she knew what she was seeing.

Christ in his majesty raised a hand to bless Maris as she approached the Cathedral. But as she entered, her old enemy, Euclid, looked down on her from the archivolt. In High School, she had the same trouble with geometry that she had with trigonometry in College. Never mind, she was through with math forever!

Just inside the door, a notice requested visitors to observe silence during their tour of the Cathedral.

As Maris walked in and looked down the long nave, she felt the impact of this silence as much as the strange effect of the glowing color, which plunged into shadowy spaces, making everything seem unreal.

Coming in from the bright sunshine, she was suddenly dizzy. She couldn't get her bearings. The incredibly beautiful color of the windows was clear, but the rest of the interior still appeared vague, so that she walked slowly, lest she trip.

People were moving through the luminous vastness, looking up, trying to decipher the stories written with those millions of bits of stained glass. Yet, there was no sound. The silence seemed to echo in the lofty clerestory and around the arches. It created an ambience, like the light and the spaciousness, but of a different element.

To Maris, the stirring stillness seemed more reverent than any spoken prayer or hymn. She felt suddenly cut off from the world, turned in to the very center of herself, that secret place from which her questing seemed to spring.

The color filtering down created an almost supernatural harmony, as though heaven were revealing its splendor to mortal eyes. The people of the Middle Ages believed this. To them, these windows were the poor man's Bible. He had but to look up to read what he was supposed to know. Earlier, the Bible had been illustrated in frescoes or mosaics on the dark walls of Romanesque churches. Here at Chartres, the same stories were told, not with paint or little pieces of stone, but with bits of glass through which the sun could enter. According to the monks of the Middle Ages, man best perceived God's glory in light, in shining gold and silver and brilliant jewels.

Gradually, Maris found her vision adapting. Somewhere, high above the nave, in the clerestory, there was a Saint James window. As things became less blurry, she located it.

Translucent blue circled the head of the Saint and glowed in his robe against a deep red background. The clerestory was so high that Maris had difficulty making out the detail, but she recognized the amber scallop shells sprinkled on the blue robe, like polka dots.

Turning back to look at the magnificent rose window and the three lancets above the Portal through which she came in, Maris found she could at last see normally.

But from this distance, it was impossible to distinguish separate figures in the rose. The colors flowed together and sparkled, like a huge cluster of jewels. The whole range of the spectrum glowed in the lancets: the marvelous blue of the Tree of Jesse; the Glorification of the Virgin: scenes in a round frame against a blue background, alternating with scenes in a square frame against a red background; the soft hues of the Passion.

One can bear only so much beauty. Maris turned away.

She continued up the nave, stopping to look at the antique maze laid in the pavement — the Road to Jerusalem, penitents called it, who were obliged to follow its course on their knees. No one was attempting this today.

As Maris approached the North transept, she moved reverently, for women were praying in the chapel of Our Lady of the Pillar.

If she were a *bona fide* pilgrim, Maris thought, she would have confessed her sins and received absolution before leaving Neville. When she reached here, she would pray, like those who were kneeling before the little pearwood statue mounted on a pillar. Others, coming in by the North Portal, approached the high candlestand and kindled a flame.

Maris felt like lighting a candle, too. For Lonsie.

Poor Lonsie was so clutched with fear that she couldn't be rational. It was too early to tell whether she was pregnant but she was convinced of the worst. Her helplessness shattered her. Like King Midas and the Sorcerer's Apprentice, she had set in motion forces she was powerless to stop.

For Maris to light a candle before Our Lady of the Pillar

seemed inappropriate. But she did sit down on one of the rush seated chairs in the chapel. She wanted to think.

Could what belonged essentially in marriage have a proper place outside it? Was it true what people at College were always saying, that if you were in love, it was the same as being married, even if you hadn't yet gone through some ceremony, which they called a holdover from the past? Love made everything right, these people said.

"Why not?" Jim asked, that day on the beach, when he tried to persuade Maris to come to his room. "Why not? You scared?"

And Maris had answered proudly, "No!"

But after what she'd lived through with Lonsie, if Jim were to ask her now, she'd answer, "Yes, I am."

That day on the beach, it was something else that made her hesitate — some feeling of fitness, like the symmetry of the arches in the Cathedral. Looking up at the lofty crossing, at the huge vaults suspended above the clustered columns, she longed to give her life the same beauty of design.

Maris shivered. She got up and crossed the transept, walking around the new altar, which looked raw in its Gothic setting. The sun was streaming in through the South Portal. She went out, grateful for the warmth.

Remembering the lectures at College, she felt sure she knew where to find Saint James among the Apostles of the South Porch. And there he was, half chiseled out of the stone, standing between John, his brother, and the other James, his cousin, called the Less.

Maris looked up in wonder. Her Saint was majestic yet human, lovable, with a wistful expression, as if he knew he was going to have his head cut off.

Jesus, walking by the Sea of Galilee, saw this young fisherman mending nets in a ship with his brother. When Jesus called, John and James left their father and followed him.

And he surnamed them Boanerges, which is, The sons of

thunder.

Maris understood that the sculpture wasn't supposed to represent a particular moment in the Saint's life. It was a composite of all the legends. He carried a sword, the instrument of his martyrdom. Over his shoulder was slung a scallop-covered scrip, as if he were making a pilgrimage to his own shrine, although this practice didn't begin until eight or ten centuries after his death.

His bare feet stood on the back of a tiny man, who squatted on a column.

Against the base of this column, a real-live fellow was sitting with his legs stretched out across the stone step, so that Maris, with her head in the air, almost tripped over his heavy boots. Beside him lay a knapsack. Like James overhead, he wore a beard.

That should have been a point in his favor, but Maris felt an instinctive revulsion. In Paris, she and Lonsie had run into a great many beards. Most of them belonged to boys who were spending their vacations, even a whole school year, bumming aimlessly from place to place, living on next to nothing, sleeping in doorways, on beaches, virtually begging, if they could evade the police, just so they didn't have to work.

To Maris and Lonsie, they appeared to be parasites, living off others.

But this fellow, Maris saw in the very next instant, wasn't like that. Observing him out of the corner of her eye, she decided he was what the girls at College called a "cute boy." "Comfortable" characterized him better. Even his beard was okay. On him it looked Old World, part of his culture, not a symbol of protest. His shirt, open at the throat, was clean. He must be about twenty. Weathered, relaxed, he'd be comfortable to have around. He was eating a crusty roll.

As Maris stood looking up at Saint James, studying details, she had a feeling that the fellow was looking at her, studying details, too. Meanwhile, he went **on eating.**

She pretended to be even more deeply engrossed in the sculpture.

But wouldn't he imagine that Maris was trying to catch his attention?

With thousands of saints springing from the walls of the Cathedral, like a heavenly population, the fellow would naturally wonder why she had to pick for intensive study just the one at whose feet he happened to be sitting. How was he to know of her special interest in James? He probably didn't have the faintest idea which saint he'd decided to camp beneath, when he got hungry.

He was taking a swallow from a canteen, but even with his head tipped back, he kept his eyes on Maris.

She must run away. No! She must walk slowly, as if each Apostle fascinated her — Paul, John, James the Greater, James the Less, Bartholomew —

But before Maris had a chance to move, the fellow spoke to her in the easy tone of one student speaking to another.

"*N'est-ce pas que c'est beau?*"

There was such eagerness and enthusiasm in the fellow's expression, as he spoke of the beauty overhead, that Maris felt her own face light up in response.

It was too late to run away.

4

The fellow reached up and offered Maris a piece of his crusty bread.

She thanked him in French, explaining that she'd brought her lunch. To prove this, she opened her scrip and extracted a *croissant*, some cheese and a tomato, standing around uncertainly, embarrassed.

With that same eagerness, the fellow patted the pavement beside him, looking up at Maris in invitation.

She hesitated. But then she settled down next to him at the feet of James the Less, extending her legs along the wide, stone step.

The fellow looked pleased. "Are you French?" he asked, moving his knapsack, though it wasn't in Maris's way.

She laughed. He must be a foreigner himself, not to know!

"My accent's not that good," she cried, flattered. "I'm American."

He was Swiss. He came from Brienz in the German speaking canton of Berne. But he was an engineering student at the University of Lausanne, so French was his second language.

"Mine, too," Maris told him. "I'm a medieval scholar."

Was that honest? She had quit school. She didn't have to

75

tell him, though. It was impossible, anyway, because he looked so impressed.

"This is nice," she said, leaning back against the base of the column. "The reason I hesitated was, it didn't seem quite reverent to sit here and eat. But why shouldn't one? After all, the Cathedral's for living, not a museum or a mausoleum. In the Middle Ages, pilgrims camped inside, when there was no other place for them to sleep. Fairs and markets were held there, too. Must have been quite a mess with all those people and their animals. That's why the pavement's lower at the west end than on the other three sides. Have you noticed? It's so they could slosh water around and it would run out the front door."

"You should have come here in May," the fellow exclaimed, in an interval when his mouth wasn't full. "I was a pilgrim myself, then. There were eight thousand of us — university students from many parts of Europe. We walked fifty miles with our bedrolls and provisions, meeting right here, in the South Porch, to attend a special evening Mass. But we didn't camp in the Cathedral," he added, amused at the thought, "and we didn't bring our animals."

"Eight thousand!" Maris exclaimed in astonishment. She didn't know a single student who would want to make a pilgrimage, except herself.

"They come every May," the fellow explained. "It was the most moving experience of my life. So now, on my vacation, I decided to return. But it's different, when you're alone. In May, we walked in groups of five, the width of the road, you know. We had a rule — either we discussed some matter of great seriousness or we remained silent. At the end of each hour we stopped to rest and regroup, so we had an opportunity to hear many opinions."

"What did you talk about?"

"Conditions for world peace, changes in the Church, the new liturgy. Many people cannot adjust to the slightest innovation. They want everything to remain just the way it was when they were children." He turned to Maris, looking slightly troubled. "Because you are a medieval scholar, has your thinking stopped at the Middle Ages?"

Maris giggled. "I hope not! But, you see, I'm not a Catholic," she explained, earnest again. "Go on, tell me more about the pilgrimage."

"It was late afternoon, when we got here. Our clothes were soaked. We'd been walking for two days in the rain, sleeping in barns or fields, wherever we happened to be, living on the sandwiches we'd brought with us. Toward the end, they began to taste stale. There were so many of us, it took hours before we could all file into the Cathedral. The chairs had been taken out, to make room."

"You stood all through the service?"

"No. We spread our bedrolls on the pavement and sat on them, wedged in like upright sardines. When we arrived, that marvelous colored light was streaming through the windows, especially the West Rose. As dusk gathered, it drained the color out of the glass, little by little, first the reds, then the yellows. Finally there was just pale blue and at last, that went, too. Only candles illuminated the choir."

While the fellow spoke, Maris watched his face intently. There was something open and uncomplicated about it, as though he looked out on a world he found good. Maris envied him.

It must be because he has faith, she thought. But doesn't he realize what's happening — the bomb?

An engineering student could hardly be oblivious to that.

"For two whole days, while we were walking to Chartres, we had had these heated discussions, about the position of the altar, the language of the Mass. Some people held such strong opinions, they could have murdered those who didn't agree."

"In the Middle Ages, they actually did," Maris observed. "They burned them at the stake."

"But, you know," the fellow said and his voice became

exultant, "when we stood in the Cathedral and sang the re-
sponses, squeezed together so tightly that our elbows dug into
our neighbors' ribs, we were suddenly unified."

Maris turned to him in excitement. "Did it change you?"
she asked. "When you got home, did you see things in a new
way?"

The fellow was silent, apparently thinking this over.

"I cannot believe," he answered finally, "that those who
made the pilgrimage together could ever take up arms against
each other. Don't misunderstand. We Swiss are ardent patriots.
But there is something higher."

"Yes!"

"Something above all religions, too. If they have any meaning — any meaning at all — it is that they make men brothers.
Isn't that so? What else is Christ, whichever name He goes
by?"

"I wish I could have been there," Maris murmured.

"Next May," the fellow told her. "You must come next
May. One does not have to be a Catholic. Any student may
join the pilgrimage."

For a moment, Maris saw herself happily walking from Paris
to Chartres with those students. But then she remembered.

"I'm afraid not," she said. "Next May, I'm going to be in
a wedding, back home. That is, if everything's all right. A
friend of mine. She's sort of making a pilgrimage with me to
Santiago — I hope."

"Santiago de Compostela? I've never known anyone who
did *that*." He looked at Maris with respect. "The Way of
Saint James is long. You're walking?"

"No. Trains and buses. It's not a *bona fide* pilgrimage, you
know. If it were, we'd carry certificates, which would be
stamped by somebody official, every place we stopped. When
we presented the certificates in Santiago, we'd each be given
a scallop shell."

"You won't get one? After going all that distance?"

"It doesn't matter," Maris assured the fellow, because he seemed to be distressed. Then she realized that it mattered a lot. "If I were a *bona fide* pilgrim," she added, "I'd be entitled to join a confraternity, a society of pilgrims. They flourished in the Middle Ages. Don't you think it would be interesting to belong to something like that, a group with experiences like one's own?"

The fellow shrugged. "Doesn't seem very important," he said. "What would they do? Get together once a year, have a feast, talk about the good old days when they walked the roads; the blisters on their feet."

Maris laughed.

"You and your friend can form a confraternity of your own."

"No! She doesn't go for that sort of thing. Besides, she may have to rush home next week. Something unexpected — we don't know yet. If she should, do you think I could go to Santiago alone? I'm eighteen."

"One needs a companion," the fellow answered, "but only to share the experience. If she isn't in tune —"

"I wanted to go by myself in the first place," Maris explained. "You see, for me it is a *bona fide* pilgrimage, even if no one else thinks so. I'm trying to find out —"

She hesitated. Never had she spoken so openly about her feelings. But why shouldn't she? After lunch, they'd part. She'd never see this fellow again. Why not say what she really felt, for once?

"I want to taste the things that are here — you know: infinity, grandeur, light, color, spiritual beauty, everything I wish for in myself. Do you understand?"

He nodded gravely.

"What I'm going to do with my life," Maris blurted out. "That's mostly what I'm trying to discover."

"And your studies are a handicap," he murmured sympathetically.

Maris felt puzzled and hurt. "How?"

"So much has happened since the Middle Ages. With the world in its present agony, what have you to contribute? When you told me you're a medieval scholar, I thought, How wonderful! In America, a girl like you has already attained this eminence. In Switzerland, it would take years longer. You would be in your twenties. But now, I see your studies are a disadvantage."

"You're mistaken! My studies have been of great benefit," she declared angrily.

To prove it, she told him about her Prize. It did sound a bit braggy. But this wasn't something that happened every day, especially to a Freshman.

"I'd like to read your essay," he said. "Do you have it with you?"

"No."

He looked disappointed. "What have you to contribute?" he asked again.

"I could always teach," Maris murmured vaguely. "I mean — I could have, if I hadn't left College. But, well, I'm not a candidate for a degree anymore."

There — she no longer claimed to be a scholar! It would have been awful to continue misleading him.

"I got confused," she added in a much smaller voice. "I'm counting on the pilgrimage to help me see things from a new angle."

"I hope it may," he told her fervently, smiling with such gentleness that it was clear he cared deeply about what was going to happen to Maris.

But he was standing up, bending over the knapsack, strapping on his canteen. He was returning home. His father needed him to help with the haying.

Maris felt more than disappointment as she watched him preparing to leave. She felt actual grief. This was the first pilgrim she'd ever met.

As he wiggled his knapsack onto his shoulders, he looked at Maris anxiously. "Are you afraid?" he asked softly.

"You mean of traveling alone, being robbed?"

"No! We Europeans aren't such barbarians as you think. I don't mean that. Are you afraid of coming face to face with the person you will discover in yourself? For it will not be the one you are used to. Seeing things in a new way — you seem eager to make this leap."

"Yes!"

"But how do you know what it may mean? It may demand doing things you will find very difficult."

"I know," she murmured. She hadn't realized it until he said it, yet she repeated gravely, "I know."

"Are you afraid?" he asked again.

"A little. But I have to go."

"And you will have to go on."

"Where to?" Maris asked in alarm.

The fellow shrugged. "Who knows where the pilgrimage may lead you?"

He started down the steps.

"Wait," she cried, opening her scrip and taking out her recorder. "I want to play you the song the French pilgrims sang in the Middle Ages, as they walked to Santiago."

Standing at the feet of James the Greater, Maris played the haunting chant.

The fellow stood on the step, listening, looking both reverent and joyful. When Maris finished, he lingered another minute in silence. It was plain that he didn't want to leave.

Since he was about to depart from France — even though he was going home to his parents and not to Saint James — Maris sang the words for him, too:

> When we departed from France
>   In great desire
> We left behind our father and mother

Sad and forlorn;
Our hearts had such a great desire
To go to Saint James,
We left behind all pleasures
To go on this journey.

When Maris finished singing, the fellow smiled his thanks.
"*Adieu et bonne chance*," he said.

Then he hurried down the steps.

Maris watched him until he reached the corner. Before rounding it, to pass before the Royal Portal, he looked back and waved.

Sadly, Maris returned the recorder to her scrip. As she tucked it in, her hand brushed against the scallop shell she'd tried to give Jim weeks ago.

5

When Maris went back into the cool Cathedral, it seemed empty. Actually, tourists were everywhere, practically standing on their heads as they tried to read the stories shining through the colored glass.

The Cathedral seemed empty, Maris realized, because she half expected to find herself wedged in among those eight thousand students. She had an overwhelming desire to be part of such a multitude, joining in their singing with all her might, letting her voice ascend to the high vaults and reverberate amongst the arches.

There was only the haunting silence, which intensified Maris's loneliness until it became almost unbearable. The Swiss fellow had stirred all kinds of feelings in her.

But before she had gone more than a few steps around the chevet, she was stopped by the window in which the Chartres blue glows with supreme intensity. Here, surrounded by angels, the Twelfth Century Virgin sits enthroned against a red background, holding the golden Child on her lap. All-encompassing pity and love, shining through this window, stilled the tumult in Maris, leaving her quieter as she walked on.

Then she saw a sign at the back of the choir requesting

visitors not to deface the walls and she was shocked. What kind of people, she asked herself, outraged, would impose their own so-called art work on these treasures?

Now, at last, she stood before the Roland Window.

The scenes, depicted against translucent blue, were all exactly the way Maris had described them in her essay, only more beautiful than she had remembered.

Starting at the bottom and continuing upward, going from right to left, as one has to read these windows, she identified Charlemagne gazing at the heavens, inquiring where the great road, the Milky Way, might lead. In the next scene, he was commanded by Saint James to follow it westward. Directly above, Charlemagne conquered Pampeluna.

And there were the flowering lances, which had so upset Maris in her dream before her last date with Jim! A portent of death.

In the medallion opposite, Roland ran his sword through the stomach of the giant Fierabras.

Above these scenes, Roland, left alone with the dead of the rear guard, struck the rock and blew his horn, knowing that he too must die.

That part of the *Chronicle of Turpin*, Maris had learned by heart.

> He lifted his sword and wept upon it. Then, wishing to break it, he struck a rock, but split it from one end to the other and drew forth his sword intact. Then, he blew his horn with such force that it cracked in twain, so they say, and the veins of his neck started. And, carried by an angel, the sound of his horn reached Charlemagne.

In the very top circle, Charlemagne sat in an imperial chair, resting his head on his hand, brooding over a sin he had committed, a sin so bad that he didn't dare confess it. So God sent an angel, bearing a scroll on which the name of the sin was written. Then Charlemagne repented and was pardoned.

Glancing at her watch, Maris discovered that it was much later than she thought — three o'clock. A couple of hours had gone by, out there on the South Porch.

There was barely time to go into the center of town and get something for Lonsie. At College, neither of them ever went away for a day without bringing back a tiny gift to the one who stayed behind. But if Maris missed that train, Lonsie would be furious.

Maris sighed as she passed the Saint James window because she couldn't linger there. She only glanced hastily at the bottom corners, where the donors of the window, the Merchant Tailors' Guild, were showing cloth to a customer and measuring it off with an ell.

As Maris passed the next chapel, she read the sign beside it:

> Believers, stop and pray. And you, who come here solely to view the art — we should thank you for passing in silence, with respect.

She passed in silence, with respect, and hurried on to the Chapel of Our Lady of the Pillar, where, this morning, she sat on the rush seated chair.

A couple of little girls, running in through the North door, giggling, almost collided with Maris. They had brought their dolls to hold up before the pearwood statue, as they had seen other mothers hold up their infants for the Virgin's blessing.

Although the Chapel was crowded with worshippers, no one shushed the little girls. This wasn't just a Sunday place for them; it was their home.

Most of the worshippers were women. Many had troubled faces. Kneeling before this Virgin, did they find strength?

Looking down the huge nave, Maris thought about the people who'd rebuilt the Cathedral after the fire, at the end of the Twelfth Century: the men, women and children who hitched themselves to the oxcarts and pulled the stone blocks in from the quarry; the farmers, who brought the substance from their lands; the glaziers and masons, who labored to create all this beauty. The Cathedral had been rebuilt by love.

Now Maris wished she could understand the mathematical proportions of the architecture, the use of Euclid's golden section and the notion of musical consonance.

Why wasn't she starting College this fall? She'd know so much better what she wanted to get out of it. Last year she'd been too young, too poorly prepared, just as she'd been too immature to appreciate the Cathedral when she came here the first time.

Now, looking up at the clustered columns, clear to the vaulting, she felt something spring from the depth of her being. It was elusive. Her mind couldn't take hold of it. Instead, it took hold of her, held her fast in that ambience of silence and light and love and pity and purity. All her troubledness fell away for an instant. She was secure and serene. For she felt close to the heartbeat of the universe.

But what its nature was, how you communicated with it, where to find it, she couldn't understand.

For a brief moment, she felt this wasn't necessary. It was no less present and real because it remained a mystery.

If Lonsie could have this experience, she thought, she'd feel differently about being married in church. It would mean something to her. But Lonsie wants to know through her mind — she only trusts the evidence of her senses, not "the evidence of things unseen."

"I don't go for this mystery bit," she would surely say, if Maris tried to describe her experience — or words to that effect.

Maris herself felt a certain dissatisfaction with the fuzziness of her thinking. She was caught between the need to understand in rational terms and this deep inner insistence on something that defied logic.

She went out by the North door because she had to see Saint Anne. This was her Portal. Very handsome, too. But Maris only had time for a passing glance. Into it she compressed her own admiration for the Gothic sculpture and her grandfather's concern for the Indians — all mixed up.

By now, it was so late that Maris couldn't go into the center of the town. She decided to buy Lonsie a pair of those hand-crocheted shortie gloves she'd seen displayed, when she translated "launder" for the American.

The women behind the table greeted her like an old friend.

"The English," they said, "we can understand them. But the Americans — *oh là là!*"

Maris felt warmed by their friendliness. Then, as she tried a white spider web on one hand, letting the attached mate dangle from her wrist, she had a sobering thought.

That American was no more of a person to me, she said to herself, than I was to him, though I hope my manners were better. It wasn't because he was a human being in need of help that I rushed up, but because he happened to speak my native language. I must be homesick.

They had simply used each other. Maris hadn't liked the man. Now, she didn't like herself.

She paid for the gloves, put them in her scrip and said, *Au revoir* to the ladies. There was no time for wandering through the narrow cobbled streets of the old town, as Maris had expected to do, no time for going down to the River and crossing the ancient bridge, to look back at the Cathedral rising above the steep roofs.

On the way to the railroad station, she passed a bus marked Orléans. If Lonsie's edginess hadn't upset their itinerary, they'd both be boarding it this very minute.

They would look back through the rear window across the wheat fields, to see the Cathedral rising above them as if floating on air, the way Maris had seen it in photographs.

What's the difference? she asked herself. I fuss too much.

The way she'd dragged Lonsie around Paris, in and out of all those churches — there was something a little fanatical about it, wasn't there? If Maris hadn't been so wrapped up in her own exploration and had been more sensitive to Lonsie's needs, perhaps Lonsie would have confided sooner and Maris would have been more sympathetic. Lonsie had lived through a dreadful time by herself. At night, in that other bed, she must have suffered, unable to communicate her fear, even to her best friend.

As the train pulled out and the spires of Chartres disappeared, Maris grew impatient to get back to Lonsie. The Swiss fellow was right, every pilgrim needed a companion.

Suddenly, she was glad he couldn't read her essay. From being secretly proud — terribly proud — she suddenly felt ashamed. It was unworthy, juvenile.

Who was Roland but a warrior? At Chartres, they put a nimbus on him, but that didn't make him saintly. He was a symbol of violence. It was said that at the Battle of Hastings, when William the Norman invaded Britain, his minstrel, Taillefer, rode at the head of the army, chanting the *Chanson*, as he threw his sword in the air and caught it again. Taillefer's singing so inspired William that he pressed on to victory.

That wasn't what Maris wanted to glorify — war! She had, without realizing, fallen under the spell of these legends, like those medieval people, who knew no better.

No wonder she'd been so confused about her major! Her face was turned in the wrong direction.

At dinner, she'd try to explain to Lonsie how she felt about her essay now. In English, to someone who was so close, it would be possible.

Lonsie would take advantage of this new mood to exert pressure. Why not come back to College? Maris would have no trouble resisting.

Nearly a whole year in Paris — that chance would never come again.

Besides, if she were to go back to College now, she wouldn't know any better than she did last spring what she wanted to concentrate on. All she was sure of was: it must have meaning, it must be helpful.

"With the world in its present agony, what have you to contribute?" the Swiss fellow had asked.

What?

She yearned to do great things, to make the world a better place because she lived in it.

But while she saw now that Roland was only a child's hero, that she had played with him and Oliver and Anselm the way a little boy plays with toy soldiers, unaware of the real meaning of war, of death and destruction, she still wanted to go to Roncevaux. It had been the first stop for the Jacobean pilgrims coming from the Basque country, their first night on Spanish soil.

And also, Maris said to herself, even if Roland is nothing but a warrior, I don't want to break up with him completely.

That was a funny expression to use about someone who'd died in the year 778 — *break up!*

The train was entering ugly suburbs, nearing Paris. Long before it came to a halt, Maris was looking out of the window, although she knew it was too early. She hoped Lonsie'd like the gloves.

When the train finally stopped and Maris got out, she couldn't find Lonsie. Hurrying through the gate, she scanned the station, end to end. Right here was where they parted this morning and where Lonsie had promised to be. She was usually prompt.

I never should have left her alone, Maris reproached herself, as she paced up and down. Her heart was beating violently. With all Lonsie has on her mind —

Maybe it wasn't that bad. Maybe Lonsie was only sick. Or she hadn't got her letter from Stew and she was acting up. But, deep down, Maris had an awful feeling that it was neither of these relatively minor disasters. Something dreadful had happened.

For the hundredth time, she glanced at the large clock.

Telephone — that was the thing to do! No sense waiting around here, if Lonsie was back at the Residence.

But Maris didn't have the token one needs to call from a Paris booth. Finding the newsstand, where she might perhaps be able to buy the token, then looking up the number and fooling with the strange mechanism, maybe pushing the wrong button — in the end, the complicated process would take longer than walking down the Boulevard.

She practically ran. By the time she arrived at the Residence, Maris was in such a fever of anxiety that she took the steps two at a time. She opened the door of the room and stopped on the threshold, aghast.

Lonsie was standing in the midst of incredible confusion, holding an armful of clothes.

What struck Maris instantly was the change in Lonsie's expression. She looked positively radiant. But then, seeing Maris, she became woebegone and contrite.

"Didn't you get your letter?" Maris asked, out of breath.

Lonsie nodded. "I got it." She seemed to be bracing herself to say something. She looked at Maris and swallowed visibly. "We're going home."

6

Maris shut the door. Her heart was pounding.

"I've spoiled your pilgrimage," Lonsie wailed, but her expression was so happy that the regret sounded comical.

Maris threw herself across the bed.

"Sorry I couldn't meet your train," Lonsie rattled on nervously, as she continued packing. "I was afraid to leave here on account of the Airline. The man's going to call me back, soon as he gets a cancellation."

So she was serious about going home!

"Can't you wait a few days?" Maris cried. "Wait and see. Maybe — You said last night you'd wait till we got to Bordeaux."

Lonsie pressed a pair of shoes into her suitcase. Then she turned to Maris.

"I called up Mother and she told me to come right home."

"You — what? *Called her up?*"

"I had to, Maris. It was worth every franc, believe me. After I left you at the station, I went to the Express and suddenly, while I was standing on line at the mail window, I simply *had* to talk to Mother. So I asked that nice English boy at the counter how to call New Jersey and he told me where to go."

91

I never should have left her alone, Maris reproached herself. I might have known she wouldn't be able to take loneliness, not for one day!

"It was amazing, how fast I got the connection," Lonsie was saying. "Mother and Dad didn't mind me waking them up. They were so relieved to hear my voice because, when the operator told them it was a trans-Atlantic call, they thought I'd had an accident."

What else would you call it? Maris wondered bitterly.

"Mother told me Dad had been feeling awful because he'd practically put me out of the house against my wishes. That's why they want me to come home."

Maris was stunned. Mr. Lonsdale had reversed himself! *Her* father never would. Once he decided something —

"Did you tell your mother — you know — what you're worried about?" she asked.

"Not over the phone, Maris. I couldn't, with the whole Atlantic Ocean listening in. Matter of fact," Lonsie added a little sheepishly, "soon as I heard her voice, I got this feeling that everything was going to be okay. Probably, I'll never have to tell her. It was just knowing that something so horrible could happen, that's what made me panic."

It looked to Maris as if Lonsie had wanted to go home so badly that, unconsciously, no doubt, she had grasped at the least desirable excuse. How unlike the old sensible Lonsie! What a strange person love had made of her!

"Don't think it's just because I want to see Stew," she was saying. "My parents, this is my last chance to spend a summer with them. Why waste it over here? But I'm terribly sorry — doing this to you, after you spent your Prize money and all. Not that I wasn't ruining your pilgrimage, anyway."

This was certainly true.

"The man at the Airline was so nice," Lonsie hurried on, trying to zip up her overstuffed suitcase. "He said he'd do his best to get us on some flight, maybe changing in London. Is that okay?"

Us, Maris repeated to herself, bewildered.

She got up and went over to the window.

It was almost seven o'clock, yet there was still a lot of light in the sky. The leaden roofs were a dull, dull gray.

What was the right thing to do? Maris didn't know. But she knew what she was going to do.

"Is that okay?" Lonsie repeated.

"I'm staying," Maris told her, trying to sound calm.

"By yourself? Oh, Maris! You'd better come home. It wouldn't be right for me to leave you by yourself. Your father —"

"He isn't going to like it," Maris admitted.

If there was ever an understatement, this was it!

"When will he begin to realize that you're grown-up?" Lonsie cried. "Someone ought to tell him. Do you want me to ring him, when I get home? I'll explain how well you're getting along in French and how you can take care of yourself. He'll believe me, won't he?"

Maris felt doubtful. "My grandfather, he's the only person who could possibly make Daddy understand. I don't think even he —"

"Shall I ring your grandfather? I'll ring them both."

"Yes. Do that. And I'll write tonight. If Daddy still wants me to come home, after we've both explained, I'll go. He can write to the Youth Hostel in Bordeaux or Bayonne. Let me check the itinerary."

Maris went to the chair on which she'd thrown her scrip when she came in. The itinerary was folded inside her passport.

"I'd better go down to the *Bureau* and ask Mademoiselle Berthe to ring the Airline," Lonsie said, "have her explain that I just need one seat. It'll be easier to pick up than two. You're sure now? Think about it a few minutes before I go and phone."

Maris was sure. Only, in the pit of her stomach —

She'd forgotten about the gloves. When she opened the scrip, she found them, lying on top.

"I brought you something from Chartres," she told Lonsie, handing her the present. "With all this excitement, I don't suppose you're in the mood."

But Lonsie loved the gloves.

"They're cool," she exclaimed, cutting the thread that held them together and trying them on. "If people at home ask whether I've been to Chartres, I'll say, 'No, but my shorties come from there.'"

Maris watched her turn her hands palms up, palms down. "I met a cute Swiss boy at the Cathedral," she murmured dreamily, recalling the way he looked, reverent and joyful, as he stood on the step, listening to her play the pilgrim's song. "We ate lunch together."

Lonsie, pulling off the gloves and smoothing them into a pair, stopped suddenly and looked anxiously at Maris.

"It was fun," Maris went on. "We just — you know — clicked."

"*Oh?*"

"He has a beard, but, Lonsie, he isn't at all hip, honestly. Probably it's just when he's walking for days that he doesn't try to shave. He's clean and there's something terribly nice about him — comfortable."

"What's his name?"

Maris stared at Lonsie. "I don't know," she said, surprised.

They had talked about so many things! She'd spoken to him of feelings she'd never shared with anyone. Yet, she didn't even know his name!

"You mean, he didn't introduce himself?"

"No."

"Did he ask you your name?"

"No. He just patted the pavement for me to sit down beside him, at the feet of the Apostles. He was sitting under James

the Greater so I went and sat under James the Less. He offered
me his bread but I had my lunch."

"Maris, I don't think you ought to go wandering around
Europe by yourself. Your father's right, really. It isn't safe.
You're too much of a pushover. These men are very polished.
You ate lunch and then what did you do?"

"We talked about our pilgrimages."

"At the feet of the Apostles?"

"Yes."

"*Oh*! You just talked about pilgrimages." Lonsie giggled.
"I'm not worried."

"He made one to Chartres last May with eight thousand
students. Imagine! But he doesn't seem to think studying the
Middle Ages is good for much."

"You'll get over it some day," Lonsie predicted, "like those
little girls who're crazy about Greek gods or horses. They get
over it, sooner or later."

"I love the Middle Ages!"

"Did you ever stop to think what would have happened to
you and me, if we'd lived then? People with our ideas, who
don't believe in everything the Church teaches would have
been boiled in oil, or something equally ingenious."

"Yes," Maris was obliged to admit. "When Charlemagne
went to Santiago, he had all the Moors baptized. According to
the Chronicle of Turpin, 'those who would not be baptized
he put to the sword, or into the power of those who were.'
You can imagine what that last part means."

Lonsie listened patiently, but with an absent-minded look.

"The past two weeks, I've been in dozens of your old
churches, seems like," she said. "Yet, when I was so worried,
there wasn't any place for me to turn. When the chips were
down —"

Maris thought, If only there were some way I could communicate what I felt at Chartres! Not in words — she has to
sense it in me, somehow.

Then Lonsie said the most astonishing thing. "You're the only person I've ever really known who seems to believe there's some power that makes sense. You're looking for it, for truth. If you didn't have faith in its being there, you wouldn't keep looking. While I was so scared, that's what gave me comfort."

She came over and, for the first time in the year they'd spent together, Lonsie hugged Maris.

"You're sure you want to stay?" she asked solemnly.

"I'm sure."

A second later, Lonsie was rushing happily down the stairs.

7

Events moved so fast that Maris didn't fully realize what was happening until she got back from the Airport, long after midnight. Then, walking into the empty room, which was strewn with the remains of Lonsie's possessions, she was overcome.

"Sorry to leave things in such a mess," Lonsie had said, when the Airline called to say there was a cancellation.

"That's okay," Maris answered magnanimously, then.

But now, facing the prospect of straightening the room alone, she felt had.

She pushed a mountain of crumpled wrapping paper, guide books, and streamers of worn nylons off her bed and threw herself across it, just for a couple of minutes. She couldn't undress or brush her teeth — let alone write home — before she'd relaxed a bit.

The next thing Maris knew, it was ten o'clock in the morning. The bedside lamp was burning; she was lying in the same clothes she'd worn to Chartres.

The other bed was empty. But a great part of Lonsie still rested there. On the pillow lay a clutch of hangers, a squeezed-out tube of shampoo, a single loafer, tweezers, and admission tickets to all the museums Lonsie had visited in Paris.

Lonsie herself must be still in the air, high above the Atlantic. Maris's eyes wouldn't stay open. Her head was splitting. She hadn't had a thing to eat since she sat beside the Swiss boy, almost twenty-four hours before. It was too late for breakfast.

And this, Maris realized with a start, was the day she was leaving for Orléans. She'd planned to take the eight o'clock train, so she'd have the day for sightseeing. Not only did she have to straighten up after Lonsie, she had to pack her own things — the suitcase she was leaving here and her scrip and knapsack.

She closed her eyes again, unable to bear the bright light.

Why hadn't she gone home? What ever made her think she wanted to stay in Europe all by herself? Her father was going to be furious.

At noon, Madeleine, the chambermaid, unlocked the door. Her black hair was newly teased. When she saw Maris lying in bed, dressed, she jumped.

They were around the same age.

"I'll check out in an hour," Maris promised, making no move to get up.

"Don't hurry yourself," Madeleine implored her. "I can clean here later."

Maris staggered down to the bathroom, almost forgetting about the missing landing in her sleepiness. By the time she'd bathed and put on fresh clothes, she felt better. She went out to the little cafe on the Boulevard, where she and Lonsie had had their lunch that first day, when they were driven to take shelter from the rain. They liked the place so much that they went back several times.

"You'll have to learn to drink wine, Maris," Lonsie had said that first day. "Just the way we learned to drink coffee. Remember?"

"I don't like it."

"But in France, everyone drinks wine. You have to." -

She had ordered a bottle with every meal and she had always insisted that Maris take "just a few sips."

Now Maris was on her own. She didn't have to drink anything but water.

The waiter with the narrow skull and hollows under his cheekbones remembered her. Where was the other *demoiselle*?

Maris explained that she'd gone home.

"So you are alone," the waiter murmured, as he set the soup before Maris. "That is sad — to be alone."

While she ate the good cream soup with a ponderous spoon, Maris did some planning. The first thing she'd bought in Paris was a condensed timetable of the French Railway. Consulting it, she saw that there were several afternoon trains leaving from the Gare d'Austerlitz for a junction called Les Aubrais. There she'd catch a local that would take her to Orléans. It wasn't far.

By the time Maris returned to the Residence, she had more courage.

She made a pile of Lonsie's things. Some had intentionally been left behind — discarded. Some, like the comb and brush, had obviously been forgotten. Maris would have to send them to New Jersey.

"Keep in touch," Lonsie had called, as she passed through the gate at the Airport. She was wearing her new gloves. Waving, she disappeared from sight.

Right now, Maris felt decidedly in touch! How was she going to pack all this stuff? She had no wrapping paper heavy enough and it took hours at the post office on the Boulevard just to buy a stamp. Surely, Lonsie could get along without these things until Maris returned from Spain. They barely fitted into the suitcase. Maris had to put all her weight on the lid to get it closed.

It was now three o'clock.

While Maris washed her hair, she made a firm resolve: to carry less on her back than she'd originally planned. Yesterday, just the scrip seemed heavy. She wasn't in condition yet.

But what could she eliminate? She needed a change of clothes and various housekeeping articles, which weren't supplied by the Hostels. Then, her recorder, notebook, the timetable, road maps and the Twelfth Century *Pilgrim's Guide* — that was the most important of all. Just these things added up to considerable weight.

There wasn't room in the knapsack for the trench coat. Maris would have to wear that and stick the beret in her pocket.

Her hair was still damp, but she was in such a hurry to get off that she put on the white blouse and blue cotton skirt she was going to live in on the pilgrimage.

She left the room regretfully. Paris was in her blood.

Mlle. Berthe, the *Directrice* of the Residence, was sitting in the *Bureau* when Maris came down.

"Do you know where I could stay in Orléans?" Maris asked her. "I find there's no Youth Hostel."

"Something suitable for a young girl traveling alone," Mlle. Berthe murmured to herself, as she took out a thick hotel book. She ran her finger down a list of names. "*Le Rossignol,*" she said finally. "*Oui, c'est ça.*"

A small, reasonable hotel, quite near the station, not at all pretentious. She had not herself descended there, Mlle. Berthe admitted *franchement,* nor did she know anyone who had, but there was no reason to suppose that *Le Rossignol* was not as it should be.

The name pleased Maris — The Nightingale.

"I'll see you in five weeks," she told Mlle. Berthe, shaking hands with her. "I'm looking forward to returning already."

As she shut the heavy iron door of the Residence behind her and stood on the bright Paris street, ready to take off, with the pilgrim scrip over her shoulder and only the barest necessities on her back, Maris felt a sudden elation, a sense of freedom she had never experienced.

Now she could do whatever she wished, wander where her feet would take her, as long as she stuck to the itinerary, so her parents would know where to reach her. Tomorrow night, she'd be at the Hostel in Tours, where she stayed last year, with the kids on the bicycle trip. It would be like going home. The following nights she'd be in the Hostels at Poitiers, Saintes, Bordeaux, Bayonne. Tonight was the only time she'd have to stay in a hotel until she got to Spain. There were no Hostels there.

Now she could act like a proper pilgrim. At lunchtime, she'd sit by the roadside in the shade of a tree and eat. Then she'd play her recorder. She'd pass the time of day with people walking by. She'd have leisure to meditate on the meaning of all that she saw and what she wanted to do in the future.

Before her lay the Way of Saint James.

Now, Maris thought exultantly, as she took a bus to the Tower, now, at last, my face is turned toward Santiago, the Field of the Star.

part 3

I

At the tower of Saint James, Maris found no pilgrims waiting to accompany her to Santiago, singing the ancient song,

> When we departed from France
> In great desire . . .
> To go to Saint James.

There were only a few worn out old people, sitting on iron chairs in the park, where the rest of the church once stood.

Pascal was in his usual place, at the base of the Tower. But Maris didn't stop to moon over him. She was afraid of missing her train.

The station was huge and ugly, crowded with people. After Maris bought her ticket for Orléans, she still had time to go to the window marked, Information for Travel to Spain.

Here, she thought, as she stood on line, she'd surely find out how to get to Roncevaux. This was headquarters. She wouldn't be crossing the border for another week. But it might be hard to get this information once she left Paris.

She had studied her timetable. She knew there was a train from Bayonne to Saint-Jean-Pied-de-Port. How could she continue to Roncevaux? Was there, she asked the man at the window, a bus going over the Valcarlos Pass to Roncevaux and on to Pampeluna?

He leafed through a huge timetable. It took a long time. He was not familiar with these places, he explained. No one ever crossed the Pyrenees by that route, except in a car. "You must take the Paris-Madrid *Rapide*," he told Maris, shaking his head. "Change in Burgos."

"But that goes through the valley, not over the Pass," she argued, exasperated. "How can I get to Roncevaux?"

"Why go there? The *Rapide* will take you to Spain faster."

Don't you remember? Maris wanted to cry out. That's where Roland blew his horn for Charlemagne, blew till the veins in his neck burst. Don't you remember?

Alas, whatever it was this modern Frenchman listened to in the cafe of an evening, it wasn't the *Chanson*, which every wandering minstrel would have sung for him in the Middle Ages.

He shook his head with finality. "Impossible," he said severely. Then he looked over Maris's head to the person next on line.

Defeated, Maris turned from the window. A whole flock of people were waiting behind her, glowering because she'd taken so long. She wiggled her shoulders, trying to make the knapsack less uncomfortable.

Crossing the Pyrenees at Roncevaux was going to be a problem, she realized, as she got in the train. She'd wait now until she reached Bayonne. Surely there, she'd be able to find out.

It was a commuters' train. People were going home from their day in Town, tired and grumpy. Nobody spoke to anybody else.

The knapsack was too bulky to go overhead. Maris set it at her feet. It was in everybody's way.

You, she said silently to a large man, who kept kicking it, you, with your wardrobe full of clothes at home, your kitchen full of dishes, your bed all made, ready to receive you, with a down puff just big enough to cover your stomach — why are you so nasty about a poor pilgrim's few belongings?

She pulled her beret out of the pocket of her trenchcoat and put it on, there inside the train, hoping the man would see by the shell pin that she wasn't an ordinary camper but a pilgrim. He didn't even notice the pin; he was too busy kicking the knapsack.

When she reached Les Aubrais, Maris felt relieved. The local was waiting and in only a few minutes, she was in Orléans.

She had never stayed in a hotel alone. Mlle. Berthe's guarded recommendation did nothing to allay her anxiety. Still, the place had a nice name.

It was near the station. By the time Maris got there, she was thankful that she didn't have to lug the knapsack and scrip any farther.

In the small vestibule of the Hotel, a sharp-nosed woman sat behind a desk marked, *Reception.*

She made it immediately clear that she believed tourists should carry distinguished luggage and that, moreover, she didn't approve of young girls who went about by themselves. One never knew what might come to pass. One was liable to fall ill, or lose one's money, or have a bad encounter. In such cases, she said sternly, where it was a question of one night only, it was prudent to demand payment in advance.

Maris wanted to say, Madam, in Orléans, of all places on this earth, a young girl should be treated with respect. Have you forgotten how Joan of Arc saved your city?

But she kept cool and gave the woman the francs.

Up three flights of stairs after an aged porter, who carried the knapsack, along a dark corridor, around a corner, down two steps. Finally, the porter stood aside to let Maris enter a small, carpety room, almost filled by a double bed. Not only the worn floor covering but the table cloth and bedspread had a high pile and geometric designs, like carpeting. The window looked out on the blank wall of the next house.

After the porter had set the knapsack on the table and Maris had given him a franc, he departed, looking happily surprised.

Maris tried to lock the door. The large key fitted, but it wouldn't turn. She went out into the corridor to compare the number of the room with the number dangling from the key. It was the right key; it simply didn't work. Anyone could walk in.

I don't dare ask that sharp-nosed woman for another room, Maris thought. And I can't leave, because she has my money.

The armchair, that would make a good barricade. It was almost too heavy to tug over the worn carpet, but Maris persisted. As soon as the chair stood against the door, she wanted to go to the john. She had to push the chair away again to get out.

Lonsie'd call this "quaint," Maris thought, when she reached the narrow cell at the other end of the corridor.

Nothing happened when she pulled the old-fashioned chain. After the third pull, she decided to give up. Suddenly, a thunderous torrent so shook the cell that Maris jumped. When she was back in her room, at the end of the corridor, around the corner and down two steps, she could still hear the roar.

Maris couldn't wait to get out of the place. She stood on the sidewalk in front of the Hotel, not knowing which way to turn. She had to find a restaurant. How she wished she were back in Paris, heading for the little bistro in the Boulevard Saint-Michel!

There was a Square in the distance. Walking in that direction, Maris saw that the statue in the center of the Square was of Joan of Arc, sitting astride her horse, when she was at the height of her glory.

This was how the people of Orléans chose to remember her — proud, victorious, not burning at the stake.

The restaurant facing the Square looked nice.

I hope it isn't expensive, Maris thought, as she went in.

There was a wonderful aroma. She suddenly felt famished.

"Mademoiselle est seule?" the waiter asked, as he showed her to a table.

"Oui."

He raised his eyebrows.

At least, he wasn't making her pay for the food before she swallowed it. All he did was hand her a menu and the wine list.

Maris pushed the wine list aside. How would the waiter take it when she asked for a carafe of water? That didn't cost anything and waiters wanted their customers to run up a big bill.

She studied the long menu, handwritten in violet ink. What did she like? Lonsie had always done the ordering for both of them. Foods interested Lonsie, especially foreign ones. To Maris, it was all the same whether she got a Chateaubriand or a hamburger. So she had always let Lonsie choose for them both. Now she was obliged to say something quickly.

The waiter stood before the table, fiddling with his serving napkin. His eyebrows, Maris observed, as she glanced nervously over the top of the menu, were going up.

What did she want? She wasn't hungry, suddenly. When she came in — But now —

The eyebrows were higher.

Then Maris did an unforgivable thing. She didn't intend to; it just happened. She laughed at the waiter.

In a huff, he walked off and attended to someone else. By the time duty forced him to return, Maris had made her choice.

"Culotte de boeuf," she ordered, in the authoritative tone of a lady who has dined out alone since she was weaned. That, she knew, was some kind of beef. *"Pommes dauphin,"* — potatoes to recall Joan's Dauphin Charles — *"chou farci."* She'd often eaten stuffed cabbage in Paris. For dessert she ordered *"prunes au vinaigre,"* — plums cooked in vinegar. This didn't sound very good, but it was billed on the menu as the specialty

of the region, so Maris had to try it.

The waiter brought the food. It was wonderful.

Saint Joan, Maris thought, while she ate.

Shaw's play was on the reading list of that English course she and Lonsie took together. Maris had suffered with Joan. How well she knew what it meant to be pushed around by feelings which other people couldn't understand! While nothing very dreadful had happened to Maris yet because she had these feelings, they certainly made her an outsider, as vulnerable as Joan.

But even more terrifying than this defenselessness was the challenge it presented to her courage and integrity. If she, Maris, were obliged to face some awful test, would she be able to stand up to it bravely? Would she hold fast to her convictions?

Joan had the authority of saints behind her. Maris had only herself.

When she finished dinner, she paid the bill and tipped the waiter.

He became positively respectful. His eyebrows were down on his lids.

Maris left the restaurant and crossed the Square to walk around the statue. On the pedestal were scenes from Joan's life, showing her hearing the "voices" in Domrémy, appearing before Charles VII, entering Orléans, assaulting the Fort des Tourelles, wounded at Paris, in prison at Rouen, and finally, burned at the stake.

It was getting dark.

Depressed, Maris returned to the carpety room. She switched on the one dim bulb and pushed the armchair against the door.

As she climbed into the double bed, she resolved to stay awake all night. Her mother always said, when her father complained of his insomnia, that one didn't need to sleep, as long as one relaxed.

Maris thought it was going to feel strange and lonely, being in a double bed. But this one was so full of bolsters and pillows and so smothered by the lumpy puff that there was hardly room for her. She lay on her left side so that she could keep an eye on the door.

I was burned all the same, Joan said, in the Epilogue, when she was told centuries later that she'd been declared a saint. *Can they unburn me?*

Remembering these lines, Maris shivered.

Why did everyone here treat her like a child? She was older than Joan was, when she saved Orléans. Joan was only seventeen.

In Paris, people had been kinder. After two short weeks, Maris and Lonsie were part of a little neighborhood, like a village in the very heart of the vast City. They had made friends: Madeleine, Mlle. Berthe, the waiter with the narrow skull. No one acted as if Maris and Lonsie were too young to be let out.

But Maris felt like a scared child, lying here, amidst the lumps, watching the door. Just for a few seconds, she let her eyes close.

They flew open when she heard footsteps outside. She sat up, clutching her passport and Express checks and her plane ticket, which she'd hidden under the bolster. Anyone who robbed her would get very little money. Her father had told Maris not to carry much but to cash the checks as she went along. Still, if her passport and plane ticket were taken, how would she get home?

The footsteps had long since continued down the corridor, but Maris's heart was still pounding. She stuck her valuables back under the bolster and lay down.

Suddenly she remembered that she hadn't written to her father to ask if she might continue the pilgrimage alone. She ought to get up. If she sat directly under the dim bulb, she'd probably be able to see enough to write by. In the morning, she'd take the letter to the post office. Even then, her father would hardly have it in time to answer her before she reached Bordeaux or Bayonne. Why hadn't she written from Paris? She must get up and do it at once.

But if she wrote now, Maris thought, lying there, keeping an eye on the door, if she wrote now, she wouldn't ask her father to let her continue the pilgrimage. All she wanted now was to go home.

Early in the morning, she'd rush back to Paris and hop on the first plane.

She didn't care if she never saw Santiago.

2

MARIS SHUT HER EYES AGAIN, JUST FOR A SECOND. WHEN SHE opened them, she was turned toward the window. Daylight showed through a gap in the heavy curtains. She must have fallen asleep.

It was eight o'clock!

No one had stolen her money or her return ticket or her passport. They were right there, under the bolster.

Jumping out of bed, she said to herself gleefully, I can leave here now! Goodbye forever!

She got out the timetable and looked up the trains for Paris while she dressed. She wasn't going to spend another night like this. She could catch a train out of here in an hour. There were others at ten twenty-eight, twelve twenty, sixteen thirty-one —

The best thing was to put her knapsack in the *consigne* now, and eat breakfast. Then she'd go back to Paris and get a flight home. Mlle. Berthe and Madeleine would be so surprised! Even if the Residence was full, they'd find a corner to put her in. The waiter with the narrow skull would welcome her, too.

Tonight, Maris said to herself joyfully, as she walked out of

113

the Hotel, tonight I'll be in Paris!

Mlle. Berthe would telephone to the Airline for her.

When she hopped off the plane in Boston, her parents and brothers would be waiting with the Valiant to drive her to Neville.

Yes, she had made a ghastly mistake, not going back with Lonsie. In fact, the whole idea of a pilgrimage was absurd. Just restlessness. She'd fly home, enroll in secretarial school and settle down.

No.

After a couple of days at home, she'd go down to Maine and spend the rest of the summer with her grandfather.

By this time, Lonsie must have telephoned to him and to Maris's father. Maris did hope her father wouldn't have a fit. No need for him to get worked up now. If he only knew!

Maybe she ought to go to the post office right away and send him a cable. That would calm him. But how could she, until she found out her flight number and arrival time? She'd cable from Paris, right after she got in touch with the Airline, if they had space.

She found a cafe and ordered breakfast. It was crowded with men, stopping off on their way to their jobs. They stared at her.

This hour of the morning, they seemed to say, a kid like you belongs at home.

Sitting there, chewing a stony roll, Maris suddenly saw exactly what was going to happen. The only strange thing was that she hadn't seen it sooner. She really was dense. *Her mother would join her — fly over and meet her.* Of course! Her mother was dying to see Europe. As soon as Lonsie called and announced that Maris was alone, her mother would hop a plane.

It was the obvious solution. Maris's parents would never leave her over here alone.

Excited, she tried to figure out how long it would take before her mother could arrive. Perhaps three days. Probably, when Maris walked into the Hostel in Bayonne, there she would be sitting, beautifully dressed as always, her hair freshly set, looking out of place, with her heels and her "distinguished" luggage.

The idea of Maris's mother staying in a Youth Hostel was hysterical. Not that old people weren't admitted. Last year, Maris had run into quite a few. But they were a different type.

Ridiculous! How could her mother ever get to Bayonne on her own? That was out of the question. She'd naturally want Maris to meet her plane, help her through customs and all. In that case, Maris mustn't go to Paris yet. She'd be out of touch. The thing to do was: stick to the itinerary; go on to Tours tonight. A cable with her mother's arrival time might be waiting for Maris at the Youth Hostel even now.

She'd stayed there last summer, on the bicycle trip. Her group had filled the dormitory. Tonight, she'd be with girls she didn't know. But she wouldn't have to keep an eye on the door.

If she found the cable in Tours, she'd return to Paris tomorrow.

As Maris left the cafe and walked toward the Cathedral, it suddenly came over her how lucky she'd been to think of this, instead of rushing home! If she had done that, she'd have become her mother's little girl again, who would be considered incapable of taking care of herself. Now, she was going to be taking care of her mother, making the arrangements, in command of the language, translating francs into dollars.

The first thing she'd do was cancel the reservations in the Hostels. They'd have to stay in places where the plumbing — Her mother would insist on a private bathroom.

Orléans was a town of blue slate roofs with red chimneys. It had been so badly bombed during World War Two that it was still rebuilding.

What Maris had come here for, in obedience to the Twelfth

Century *Pilgrim's Guide* — a miraculous chalice — she couldn't see. It had been destroyed in one of those wars, centuries ago.

I've lost the magic — whatever it was that made this pilgrimage seem so important, only yesterday — she said to herself, as she stood before the Cathedral.

Little of the original building remained above ground. Although the facade reminded Maris of Notre-Dame de Paris, she didn't like it because on each tower perched a magnificent Eighteenth Century wedding cake.

She felt the way she had when she lost Jim. This time, what she'd lost was herself. That mysterious urge to walk the roads, meditating — which everyone except her grandfather considered crazy — had suddenly left her. She was on the other side of the world now, wondering why she was here. If she could just get home!

The town was filled with tourists. Before the Cathedral, hundreds of cars and buses were parked in the Place Saint-Croix. There was even an ambulance with English license plates. Some bedridden person was so eager to see Orléans and so wealthy that he or she had been brought all the way by ambulance. Was such a thing possible?

Inside the Cathedral, she searched for a person in a wheel-chair or on a stretcher, but there was no one.

The chapels in the apse were Thirteenth Century, so Joan must have given thanks here for her victory over the English. At the height of her triumph, could she have had any intimation of the agony to come?

She had a chapel of her own these days, with a life-sized Twentieth Century marble bishop kneeling at her feet. Quite an upgrading!

Can they unburn me?

When Maris left the Cathedral and crossed the Place Saint-Croix she looked for the English ambulance. It was gone.

She thought she'd go to the market and get some food for her lunch.

As she walked through the busy town, it suddenly dawned on her that she hadn't looked up the trains to Tours, only to Paris. Then she wondered whether she couldn't go by bus. There had been a number of them parked in front of the Cathedral.

The trouble with me is, I don't have my mind on the pilgrimage now. I'm just thinking about Mother.

To be the one in charge would be a new experience. Maris looked forward to it.

The market was interesting. The vegetables looked so fresh that she would have liked to buy some for her supper, but she couldn't carry any more.

Back in the Place Saint-Croix, she found a bus marked, Blois. She went over and spoke to the driver. She wished to go to Tours, she explained. Could she make a connection in Blois?

Yes, he told Maris, but there wouldn't be time for sightseeing. A bus for Amboise left Blois directly and in Amboise she'd catch another bus for Tours.

"You won't be able to visit the chateaux," the driver said, "but it's a pretty ride along the Loire. Hop in. I leave in twenty minutes."

"Oh," Maris cried, "My knapsack's at the station. I'll have to get that. Is there time?"

The driver grinned. "Hurry! For you, I'll hold the bus."

Maris almost burst into tears. Someone was being kind! Everyone else had been so hostile.

It was, as the driver had foretold, a beautiful ride along the Loire and both chateaux were imposing. But as they were Renaissance, Maris wouldn't have been interested in the interiors, even if she could have visited them.

She changed buses in Blois and again in Amboise.

When she got out in Tours and shouldered her knapsack for the long walk to the Hostel, it was hot and Maris felt very tired. She had had to take off her trench coat. Where she carried it over her arm was damp. The straps of the knapsack were chafing her shoulders.

This was far from the dream she'd had of sitting under a tree, playing the recorder.

Mother will want to rent a car, she thought happily.

Then, she stood stock-still in the road, for the truth hit her. Her mother didn't own a passport. To get one would take a couple of weeks. Vaccination, packing, securing a flight — Whatever made Maris think her mother could take off on a moment's notice?

As she stood there, so overwhelmed with disappointment that she could have cried, a car rushed up from behind and Maris had to jump into the grass on the left side of the road.

The car passed, leaving a cloud of dust. Maris couldn't see. Then she heard the brakes go on and a man leaned out from the right side of the car.

"*Voulez-vous aller a l'Auberge de la Jeunesse?*" he asked. The accent was very British.

Maris couldn't see the man's face, but, as the dust settled, she saw children's heads popping out of the windows.

"*Oui.*"

Shouting a grateful answer, Maris stared up the road in amazement. This, she was practically certain, was the car she'd mistaken for an ambulance, back in Orléans.

3

THE CAR BACKED UNTIL THE FRONT SEAT CAME ALONGSIDE. The left door was opened for Maris by a woman with short, reddish gold hair and a crinkly smile.

Nice, Maris thought, as she smiled back gratefully. She slipped off her knapsack, heaved it onto the seat, and climbed up. Not pretty, but the nicest woman she'd ever seen.

She was wearing plain country clothes — a white, square-necked blouse with a green print skirt.

Maris couldn't help sitting on a little of the skirt as she squeezed into the narrow space. Her right arm, deeply tanned and covered with golden down, touched the woman's left one, which was burned pink by the sun and covered with freckles. The two arms — so different — looked funny, side by side.

The man leaned forward, smiling in welcome, as if Maris were a friend of the family who'd dropped in to visit. Then he drove on. He seemed both very gentle and decided, which made Maris think of her grandfather.

When he asked Maris, in bad school French, how far she had come, she realized that these people didn't know her nationality.

"From Orléans," she answered in English. "I took three

119

buses."

"Oh, you're American!" the man exclaimed, laughing. "How fortunate for us! Our French isn't very good."

His statement brought a snicker from the back of the car. Maris turned and found herself being inspected by the children.

"What a pity we didn't pick you up in Orléans," the woman cried. "We were there ourselves this morning."

"I know," Maris told her. "I saw your car. Matter of fact, I thought it was an ambulance."

"It was," the children shouted.

A small girl added plaintively, "Elsie has to go into hospital."

Maris, hampered by the knapsack, only managed to turn halfway around. She tried to appear sympathetic, even if she didn't know which of the two girls was the ailing Elsie. All four of the children looked blooming. They seemed to be sitting on bunks.

The car came to a standstill within sight of the Hostel. Maris jumped out and slammed the door, thinking the people were going on.

"Thanks for the ride."

"We're stopping here the night, too, if there's room," the woman explained. "So many of us — And we don't know whether they'll let us in, because of Periwinkle. She's too young."

They were all getting out.

"Oh, I hope you can stay," Maris said, with all her heart.

Maybe, she thought eagerly, we'll be in the same dormitory. Arriving together —

They stood on the drive, assembling the family, seeing to the luggage, a unit of their own. There was no excuse for Maris to hang around.

"Thanks," she said again, reluctantly entering the building. In the vestibule, she opened her scrip and took out her

Youth Hostel pass. The identifying photograph was the one that had been taken for her High School Year Book, not much over a year ago. How childish her face was then, all closed up, like a cocoon!

When the Housefather took the pass and read her name, he said in French, "There's a cable for you."

"A cable!"

Her mother was coming! She really was!

The man rummaged in a set of pigeonholes, while Maris thought she'd collapse from suspense. "And a letter," he added, handing them both to her.

The letter was from her grandfather. Maris tore open the cable.

My permission to finish pilgrimage alone take care write oftener, it said. It was signed, *Father*.

Tears sprang to Maris's eyes. She couldn't run away because the Housefather was writing down the numbers of her bunk and dormitory. She tried to hold the tears back but —

The family that had given her the ride was trailing into the vestibule. Maris felt something on her shoulder.

"Have you had bad news?"

The woman's arm was around Maris's shoulder and her nice face was peering at Maris with concern.

"No. It's all right. I was sort of hoping my mother'd come over." Maris glanced down at the cable, as if she had perhaps overlooked this part of the message, but it wasn't there. "Going alone isn't as much fun as I thought," she admitted.

"*Voici*," the Housefather said, holding out a slip of paper with the bunk and dormitory numbers. He sounded a little impatient, as if he couldn't be expected to hold it forever, while Maris and the woman gabbed.

Maris wiped her eyes and reached for the slip. The children surrounded her. The woman joined her husband, who was speaking to the Housefather.

"Which one of you is Elsie?" Maris asked, trying to act as

if nothing were wrong.

They giggled.

"You were riding in her," the older boy explained. He looked about ten or twelve. "She was a retired London County Council ambulance when we bought her — L.C.C. D'you get it? We fitted her out for camping."

"But she has to go into hospital," the tiny girl said. "She puffs on hills."

The child was very cute, with dark ringlets and light blue eyes.

The older boy translated into adult language for Maris's benefit. "There's trouble under the bonnet. She has to go into the *gar*age. That's why we have to stop the night somewhere."

"You mean the whole family *sleeps* in her?"

"Yes," they cried, all four.

The mother returned to tell the children happily that they might stay. The Housefather had seen their predicament, she said, and had kindly made an exception for one night.

"Perhaps the girls and I will be in your dormitory," she said to Maris. "What's your number?"

They compared the slips they'd been given and found they were different.

What a letdown! Maris was dying to be with them.

"By the way," the woman said, "our name is Addison."

"I'm Maris Miller."

"Maris, this is Selwyn, our eldest. This is Cressida. That's Ian and the little girl's named Sarah, only we call her Periwinkle, not because she moves like a snail, which she does when she's called, but because of the color of her eyes."

As their mother laughingly made these introductions, the children, who'd been at ease and outgoing, drained the expression from their faces. They took on a defensive blankness, as if they thought they were expected to be polite.

"This is Peter," Mrs. Addison continued, when the father joined them. "Peter, this is Maris Miller. I'm Valerie," she added.

No sooner had they made friends than they left. Their dormitories were in another wing of the building.

Maris found hers — a large, sunny room, crowded with double decker beds. This early in the afternoon, it was empty, except for one girl.

Maris had been assigned bunk number twenty-nine. As she looked at the numbers, she saw that the odds were the lowers and she felt glad. Her shoulder ached. She didn't feel like climbing into an upper.

But when she found twenty-nine, it was occupied by that one girl. She was taking rollers out of her hair.

"Do you speak English?" the girl asked. "There was a mix-up. I was assigned the upper, but when I got here, I found someone had taken it. She couldn't understand me, so as this was empty, I took it." She gave no sign of moving.

Maris saw through this. The girl didn't want to climb into an upper bunk, either. Arriving first, she had simply swiped Maris's lower.

Maris wasn't going to start an argument. She took off her knapsack and pulled out her sheet sleeping bag.

Then she took the Hostel pillow and blanket off the upper bunk. Standing on the edge of the lower, keeping out of the girl's way, Maris spread her sheet sleeping bag over the top mattress and stuck the pillow into the pocket at the head, which served as a case. When she tucked the blanket under the thin mattress, her shoulder ached terribly.

"You traveling with a group?" the girl asked, while Maris was making the bed up over her head.

"No, I'm alone."

"It must be grim, unless you're an oddball. I'm touring Europe with this fellow. We have a Mini. It's neat. We've been everywhere."

"Just you two?"

"Sure. What's the matter? You square or something?"

"No."

As a matter of fact, Maris was jealous.

"Why don't you latch on to one of the boys you meet touring around? Plenty of them available."

Without answering, Maris climbed into the upper and stretched out, exhausted. Not for long, she told herself. She had to go out before the stores closed and buy food for her supper.

But first she wanted to read her grandfather's letter. It was, she saw by the postmark, a week old, written before he heard from Lonsie.

Life in Meddybemps, he wrote, was very pleasurable. He rose early in order to see the birds and smell the pines when they were still covered with dew. He spent half his mornings on the Lake, tacking around without need to get anywhere. Some days, he went to one of the beaches in Machias Bay and roamed the rocks, looking for jasper. He had found a beautiful gold and cinnamon piece that he was polishing up. Mounted, he thought, it would make a handsome brooch for Maris's mother.

Last Sunday, he'd gone as usual to visit his Indian friends on the Reservation. They felt encouraged because the State had a new plan for better housing. That Sister at the School never failed to ask after Maris. She had always wished to make the pilgrimage to Santiago. Maris, she said, was standing in for her.

But I explained, Maris's grandfather added, *that yours is not a religious pilgrimage in the sense that hers would be, not only because she'd make it according to the customs of her church, but because she'd go with a clear objective, while you are open to whatever inspiration you may receive.*

I hope, my dear, he concluded, in his old-fashioned style, which suited him so well, *that you are finding your heart's desire. I miss your annual visit. The cottage seems quite desolate without you. But I am proud of your spiritual sturdiness and self-reliance.*

Those last words threw Maris. If he only knew how little sturdiness she had, how her shoulders ached, how desperately she wanted to go home!

She turned over on her stomach and let her tears flow into the Hostel pillow.

How could she go home now? After the fuss she'd put up about making the pilgrimage alone, telling her mother she didn't want her, to admit she couldn't take it —

What made her father change his mind? Lonsie must have done some fast talking. Or was it her grandfather, who was always on Maris's side? If they only knew how she really felt!

It wasn't like her father to give in, unless he was convinced. He must have decided that she was old enough now to take care of herself.

Lying still like this, her shoulder felt better. The girl below must have left. The room was very quiet.

Maris let herself dream. It was silly, but comforting.

She was traveling through Touraine, looking up at the Milky Way. The Addisons were there. She was playing her recorder for them. Through Poitou, through Aquitaine —

4

SUDDENLY, THE BUNK SHOOK. THAT GIRL WAS BELOW, AFTER all.

No, one of the little Addisons was standing on the lower. Her eyes were just level with Maris and she was looking at her with a roguish grin.

"Wake up," she said, "it's teatime."

"Oh, hi! I'm not asleep."

"Yes you are. Wake up. Mummy says, will you come to tea?"

Maris rubbed her eyes. "Gosh! I'd love a cup of tea."

"Not a cuppa. High tea."

Maris didn't know what that was, but just to be seeing the Addisons again — She sat up.

"I have to get washed first," she told the child. "You're Cressida, aren't you?"

The little girl nodded, looking Maris over appraisingly. "Are you grown-up?" she asked uncertainly, cocking her head. "Or only half?"

"My father thinks I'm grown-up," Maris answered proudly. "So I guess I am. How old are you?"

"Six."

126

Maris jumped down from her bunk. The lower was empty. She took fresh clothes out of the knapsack.

"You run along," she said to Cressida. "I'll be down, soon as I'm ready."

Maris remembered the way to the dining room from last year.

There were so many Addisons that they filled a whole table. A place had been set for Maris next to Mr. Addison. When she appeared, he gave her that same smile that had welcomed her into the car.

They had brought their dishes in from Elsie. A large china teapot stood beside Mrs. Addison. It was covered with one of those English cosies. There were square plates of bread and butter, lettuce, cucumbers, jam and cake. In front of each person stood a little egg cup.

The Addisons were camping, but they were having the same meal, served with the same graciousness, as they would have had at home. As soon as Maris sat down, they made a ring of hands around the table. Periwinkle started it, reaching out her short arms to a brother on either side. Mr. Addison held out his hand to Maris. Selwyn stretched his across the table.

Maris didn't know what was going on. Was this some game? She took both hands.

For a moment, there was silence. The Addisons bowed their heads. Then everyone let go and started talking and eating at a great rate.

"This is neat!" Maris exclaimed, looking at all the food. "I expected to go to the store."

"What's that?" Cressida wanted to know.

"The shop," her mother translated.

"To buy food for my supper," Maris explained to her. "And I was too tired — you know. Was I really asleep?"

The little girl nodded. She looked very pleased because she had this special tie with Maris.

"Tell us about yourself," Mrs. Addison begged. "Where is your home?"

"Neville, Massachusetts."

Mr. Addison told Maris that he was a schoolmaster in Southampton. "Val's a social worker," he added, looking at his wife as if she were too modest to speak for herself.

"Only mornings," she put in, "whilst the children are at school."

Maris explained about the pilgrimage, how her parents had been unwilling to have her make it alone; how they had relented when Lonsie came along and that Lonsie had suddenly gone home.

"So, I kind of thought Mother would come," Maris murmured.

"This pilgrimage — ?" Mr. Addison asked, looking puzzled.

"Ever since the time of Charlemagne, Mr. Addison, people have —"

"Peter," he broke in. "Please don't call me Mr. Addison. I'm on holiday!"

"And Val," his wife added, smiling.

Maris nodded gratefully. She explained about the medieval pilgrims going to the shrine of Saint James.

"If they started from Paris, the way I did, they came to Tours because of Saint Martin. You know about him, of course."

"No," Peter said, "I don't. I knew, of course, that Tours was a source of revenue for Mary Queen of Scots. But I'm afraid I'm ignorant about Saint Martin. Tell us."

"He met a beggar, one cold winter's day, and gave him half his cloak."

"That was kind of him," Periwinkle declared solemnly.

Maris smiled at her. Then she turned to Peter. "English pilgrims went to Santiago in boatloads," she told him. "Have you read *Purchas His Pilgrims?*"

"Yes, when I was up at Oxford. I'm afraid I've forgotten."

"In it," Maris explained, "there's a poem by an Englishman who went to Compostela in the Fifteenth Century:

> Which way I went, I shall you tell.
> And how be the way I did dwell.
> First to Plymouth to sea went I,
> And landed in the Trade of Brittany.
> There we rested days two,
> And through the Race then did we go.
> To Bordeaux, to that fair City;
> And there was I days three."

Selwyn leaned across the table, waiting politely for Maris to finish. When she stopped for breath, he asked, "What's that Race?"

"The cockling sea around Brittany," his father put in. "It's very rough."

"Many of the pilgrims speak of seasickness," Maris told them. "This one seems to have had a strong stomach. He went over the Pass I hope to cross, if I can find the way. He describes places I'm going to. Burgos he calls 'Borkcz' and Léon, 'Lyones.' Of Léon he says:

> Bedding there is nothing fair,
> Many pilgrims it doth impair.
> Tables use they none of to eat
> But on the bare floor they make their seat.

"At last, he reaches Mount Joy, the hill just outside Santiago, from which the pilgrims got their first glimpse of the Cathedral spires.

> On this side the town, miles two,
> By a chapel shalt thou go
> Upon a hill it stands on high
> Where Saint James first shalt thou see,
> A Mount Joy . . ."

Maris loved the way the children responded to the doggerel. Even the little girls had a faraway look in their eyes. She tried to think of something that would particularly appeal to the boys.

"After the defeat of the Spanish Armada," she told them, "Drake set sail for Spain, intending to capture Santiago. The Archbishop was so frightened that he started to dig up the remains of the Saint to hide them. But then he said, 'Let us leave our holy Apostle, who will protect himself and all of us.' And Drake sailed away."

"What I find difficult to understand," Peter said, "is why this shrine should be in Spain. That seems an odd place."

"It is. The legend claims that after Saint James was beheaded in Palestine, two disciples carried the body to a boat by night. They had neither sail nor rudder, but 'by the conduct of an angel' the boat arrived on the Atlantic coast at a place near Santiago."

Ian turned to Maris and asked gravely, "Did they take his head along, too?"

She laughed. "Yes. I've seen a picture of a Spanish painting that shows his head — halo and all — resting on his feet in the boat."

Val leaned across the table toward Maris. "Are you a Roman Catholic?"

"No. I haven't been brought up with any religion. My parents are very liberal. I don't know what they think. I wish I did."

"How do you come to be making this pilgrimage?"

"Everybody asks me that! It seems to puzzle people. I'm interested in art history and — well, I'm sort of hunting for something. I don't exactly know what it is. Is that so queer?" Maris asked shyly.

"Not at all," Val answered. "You're a Seeker."

"What's that?"

"During the War, I lived with a family of Quakers. They

were constantly doing just that, searching for the meaning of life. They referred to themselves as Seekers. I was ten at the time. Now, twenty-five years later, I still remember them with special affection and regard. That's where I learned our grace, that you just shared with us. They always held hands around the table for a moment of silent thanks before a meal. When Peter and I were married, it was the one practice we decided to establish in our family."

Cressida was trying to recapture Maris's attention. "How many brothers and sisters do you have?"

"Two brothers, George and Jack."

"Do they like fishing?" Selwyn inquired.

"I don't know."

"Do they collect stamps?"

"I don't know. I guess I don't pay attention to them."

"Don't you like them?"

"Not much."

The moment she said this, Maris felt sorry. It was the truth, but she shouldn't have admitted it to the children. As a matter of fact, now that she thought about George and Jack, it wasn't the truth — not anymore.

"I didn't mean that!" she exclaimed. "Of course I like them. When I was younger, they got on my nerves. Now that I'm grown-up, I'm quite proud of them, actually. George is going to be a naturalist, I think. And Jack's a terrific ball player."

Selwyn and Ian looked tremendously interested.

"After we've done the washing up, let's go for a walk," Peter suggested.

"I wonder what made Daddy — I mean, Father — change his mind," Maris said, as she dried a square plate. "He was dead set against my making the pilgrimage alone. Why would he cable now —"

Peter chuckled. "Fathers grow up, too, you know," he told Maris, turning to her from the dishpan with dripping hands. "I happen to be intimately acquainted with one! He's constantly forced to realize that his children are ready for more scope. It would have been a pity if you had abandoned your quest. Don't you think your father looked at it that way?"

"I guess so," Maris murmured.

Her father growing up — what a strange idea!

She had assumed that her parents were always just the same, finished, static, like a snapshot taken long ago. To think of them as still capable of revising their opinions! It made her wonder whether she really understood them.

Some hostelers were playing their guitars and singing in the common room. It sounded like fun, but Maris wasn't attracted. She preferred to go out for a walk with the Addisons.

5

They strolled about the grounds of the Hostel. The boys stayed close to Peter. Val held Periwinkle by the hand. Cressida clung to Maris.

"Maybe later," Maris told the child, "we'll see the Milky Way."

It was a lovely evening, surprisingly mild for this part of France. Twilight lingered with a silvery luminosity that reminded Maris of the interior of Chartres Cathedral.

She felt overwhelmed by the beauty of the evening and the delight of being included, for the moment, in what was clearly a circle of great love.

Since Val and Peter didn't seem to know any of the Charlemagne legends, she told them how the Emperor had followed the Milky Way westward across Spain to Santiago de Compostela and on to Finisterre, where he flung his lance into the sea, proclaiming, "Farther no man can go."

Suspended between dusk and dark, enchanted by the legend, no one spoke for a moment.

Then Val surprised Maris.

"I taste a liquor never brewed —
From Tankards scooped in Pearl —"

133

she quoted. "Do you know that? It's one of my favorites."

"Oh!" Maris exclaimed. "How do *you* know it? Emily Dickinson's from my part of the world. My grandfather's always quoting her."

> "Till Seraphs swing their snowy Hats —
> And Saints — to windows run —

"I know something about your part of the world, Maris," Val told her. "I've been there. It was during the War. My home was in London. When the Blitz began, my brothers and sisters and I got an invitation from a family named Whittier to visit them for the Duration. They're the people I told you about before, who called themselves Seekers. They'd heard of us through friends. Our parents felt the older children ought to stay in England and endure the War with everyone else, so they sent only me. I was homesick, but it was one of the happiest periods of my life."

"I almost didn't get her," Peter told Maris, his eyes twinkling. "She liked it over there so much, she might have married an American."

"What about us?" Ian asked. "Would we have been American?"

"It never could have happened," Val assured him. "I love England and I never would have married anyone but Daddy."

"I wouldn't want to be anything but British," Selwyn declared.

And Maris thought, I wouldn't want to be anything but American.

She tried to see herself through the Addisons' eyes. To them, Americans were people with such compassion for children that they offered to take unknown ones into their home.

To the French people, she was never Maris Miller. She was "*la petite Américaine.*"

What a responsibility — being even a small embodiment of one's country! The whole United States of America rested on

Maris's shoulders.

And — as if that weren't bad enough — the Swiss fellow had spoken of something he called even "higher," which he'd experienced as a pilgrim.

It was overwhelming, all one had to be.

Maris turned to Val. "Whereabouts did you live in the States?"

"Kendal. That's a small town in Rhode Island, near the Connecticut border. You've been there?"

Maris shook her head. She'd never even heard of it.

"Do go some time and tell the Whittiers I sent you. They live on the riverbank, about a mile from town, as you go toward Little Narragansett Bay. They're wonderful people to know."

Maris explained that she wasn't going home for a long time.

"Have you taken your degree?"

"No. I left College."

Val gave Maris such a worried, questioning glance that Maris asked, "Do you mean, did I flunk out? No, if I wanted to go back, I could."

They returned to the Hostel. It was time, Val announced, to put the children to bed. Tomorrow they must make an early start. Assuming Elsie was restored —

"How do you all fit," Maris inquired curiously, "at night?"

Val explained. "Peter and I have the bunks. There are two pipe berths that let down over them, where we put the little girls. Selwyn sleeps on the floor between us and Ian on the front seat. It's a bit of a squash. Still, we've been on the Continent a fortnight. We get along very well."

"Are you going back to England?"

"Not yet. We're visiting friends in Bordeaux, but not for another three days. We're going to linger in the country, stopping to savor and enjoy."

This was the way Maris had dreamed her pilgrimage would be.

"Bordeaux was one of the pilgrims' shrines," she said. "Between here and there, they stopped at Poitiers, Saintes, St.-Jean-d'Angely —"

"How do you know where to find these pilgrim places?" Peter broke in. "We're going to Poitiers. I didn't know it had that significance."

"Aymery Picaud, a Twelfth Century monk, who came from around Poitiers wrote a *Pilgrim's Guide*. It's quite amusing. I have a modern edition of it in my knapsack. Would you like to see it?"

"Very much. Bring it down to breakfast."

"Yes," Val said. "We're expecting you for breakfast. Shall we say eight?"

"Great!" Maris exclaimed. "And thanks again for supper, I mean, tea." "Oh," she said, turning to Peter, "will you be able to read the *Pilgrim's Guide?* You said your French isn't very — It's Latin on one side and French on the other."

"I can read the Latin," Peter assured her, smiling. "That's what I teach." He turned to Val. "Let's take Maris with us."

"To Poitiers? Let's!"

"All the way to Bordeaux."

"We could manage the days, but where would she sleep?"

"We men can sleep out of doors."

"And when it rains?"

"We each have a mac."

"Oh, no," Maris protested. She was dying to go with them. It was the most wonderful thing that had ever happened to her, meeting them. But she didn't want to give them any trouble.

"We don't mind rain," Selwyn said. "Let's take Maris with us."

"Let's!" It was unanimous.

Maris struggled with her sense of duty. "I'm afraid I can't," she wailed. "I haven't seen Tours yet and I have to stick to the pilgrimage route."

"We'll go your way," Peter said. "It can't be much longer. Besides, we have plenty of time — three days. We'll get the maps out at breakfast and you can show me the road."

Val put her arm around Maris's shoulder, the way she had done when Maris opened the cable. "We'd love to have you with us," she said. "We'll manage somehow. Do come."

"There's nothing I'd rather do," Maris cried. "I'm going to write my parents about it right away."

They said goodnight for at least the third time and went off to their dormitories.

Maris sat up in her bunk a long while, writing. She thanked her parents for permission to finish the pilgrimage. She didn't mention how she had longed for her mother. She wrote mostly about the Addisons, what a wonderful family they were and about their exciting invitation.

Before she had time to sign off, the lights went out.

Maris snuggled down inside the sheet sleeping bag, "happy as a clam," as her grandfather would say. She realized suddenly that he would have been disappointed, if she had run home. He missed her, but he had his heart set on her making a good pilgrimage.

6

Maris overslept. The Addisons had almost finished eating when she appeared in the Hostel dining room, bringing the *Pilgrim's Guide*. She was warmly greeted, but she felt too worried to smile.

"You're going to sleep on my side of Elsie," Cressida told her joyfully. "Mummy said so."

"Sorry I'm late," Maris muttered. As Val handed her a mug of coffee, she blurted out, "I don't know if I should go with you. I just remembered — my father told me not to hitchhike."

"Oh!" Val exclaimed. "I never thought our invitation could be called that."

"It's not as if you stood in the road wagging your thumb," Selwyn argued. "You didn't ask us to take you."

"But you're strangers. I mean, this time yesterday, I hadn't even heard of you." Then she added, afraid she might break down, "I *feel* like I'd known you ages."

"Perhaps you should trust your feelings," Val said quietly.

Cressida started to cry. "I want Maris to come with us!"

"Listen to this," Peter said, looking up from the *Guide*. "Blow your nose, Cressida, and listen.

138

Pilgrims to Saint James, whether rich or poor, should
be welcomed by all men with charity and consideration.

Maris, that is authority enough for your coming with us!"

He was joking, but he was obviously trying to reassure her.
He read on, freely translating the Latin.

"Many have incurred God's wrath because they would
not take in a poor pilgrim.

You must come, Maris, for our sake!"

"I suppose it is a little unusual," Val said thoughtfully, "but
my parents sent me all the way to America for four years to a
family they'd never heard of. To be sure, it was wartime.
Do you think, if I wrote to your mother and explained who
we are — ?"

Maris grabbed the offer. "Would you do that? Would it be
enough?"

"If it were one of my children, I'd consider that enough,"
Val answered. "I'll write at once, before we leave the Hostel,
air post. I have another thought: I'll give your mother the
Whittiers' address in Rhode Island. She can communicate with
them. They'll vouch for our character!"

Peter and Maris went to the Housefather's desk to collect
their Youth Hostel passes.

"This is the nearest I'll come to having a pilgrim's certificate," Maris told Peter wistfully, as she looked at the date and
the name of the Hostel, which had been stamped on the pass.

When Elsie was retrieved from the *gar*age — "in radiant
health," Peter told Periwinkle — the Addisons carried all their
dishes and gear out of the Hostel and stowed Maris's knapsack
and scrip under one of the bunks.

"Jump in," Peter told her, holding the left front door open.

"If I were a medieval pilgrim," Maris said happily, settling
in beside Val, "I'd thank Saint James for this miracle."

They drove to the center of Tours and mailed two letters to Neville, Massachusetts, *États-Unis.* Then they parked
Elsie and walked toward the Tower of Charlemagne.

Standing beside the Basilica, Cressida and Periwinkle recognized Saint Martin.

"There he is! There he is!" they cried. "He's cutting his
cloak in half to keep the beggar warm."

In the Cathedral, Maris found the Saint James window. She
recited for Selwyn and Ian the story from the *Golden Legend,*
which it illustrates.

> There was a man of Almaine, and he went with his
> son to Saint James about the year one thousand four
> score and three, and came to Toulouse for to be
> lodged, and their host made them drunk. Then the
> host took a cup of silver and put it in their malle.
> And on the morn, when they were gone, he followed
> them as thieves, and found the cup in the malle and
> anon they were brought to judgment. The son was
> hanged, and the father went forth weeping to Saint
> James, and came again thirty-six days after and then
> went to see his son, who said: Right sweet father,
> weep no more, for the blessed Saint James hath al-
> ways held me up. And when the father heard him
> speak, he ran anon to the city and people came and
> his son was taken down all whole and the host was
> hanged which had put the cup in the malle.

The two boys listened with relish.

"Maris," Peter exclaimed, "I've just read that story in your
Guide."

She pointed out the scallop shells on the Saint's robe.

"Why shells?" Ian asked.

"Maybe because he was a fisherman. Nobody really knows.
In Spain, there's a second part to the story. After the boy was
hanged, his parents continued their pilgrimage. When they

returned, a month or so later, they found he was still alive. They ran to the judge and asked him to cut down their son. The judge was just about to carve a chicken dinner. When he heard about the miracle, he said, 'It's no more true than that this hen should stand up and the cock should crow.' Whereupon, the hen stood up on the platter and the cock began to crow! So, the boy's life was saved."

Selwyn and Ian loved that one.

"What's even more curious," Maris added, "is that in the little town where the miracle is supposed to have happened — Santo Domingo de la Calzada — they still keep a live cock and hen in the Cathedral."

"Do you mean," Peter asked, "that same legend was told here and in Spain?"

"Legends and art were carried back and forth by the pilgrims. Minstrels, who went with them, sang the same *chansons* everywhere."

They didn't stay very long in Tours.

"We're country people," Peter explained to Maris, "so you mustn't mind if we skip over the towns."

They traveled slowly, stopping often to let the children run around, to swim in a brook, and again to spread a cloth by the roadside for elevenses, lunch and tea. They looked for wild flowers. Maris leaned up against a tree and played her recorder.

Peter translated bits of the *Guide* as they went along. When they were coming into Poitiers, he made everyone sit on the grass while he read.

> After Tours, you will come to Poitou. It is fertile land, full of good things. The people are vigorous, good fighters, used to handling bows, arrows and spears.
>
> Two brave French pilgrims once asked for lodging at Poitiers but no one would take them in. At the last house, they were welcomed by a poor man. That

night, a violent fire broke out. It spread rapidly from
the house where the men first asked for shelter to
the one where they were taken in. About a thousand
houses burned, but that one was spared. This is why
the pilgrims of Saint James should receive a warm
welcome.

Peter turned to Maris, enjoying the childish vengefulness
of the *Guide*. "You see what an evil fate you've saved us from
by coming with us! If we hadn't invited you, Elsie might
have burned. Seriously, you've made our journey much more
interesting. One tends to rush through a foreign countryside
without any realization of what went on in it before one's own
time."

"We knew about the Battle of Poitiers and the Black Prince
and Eleanor of Aquitaine, Father," Selwyn reminded him.

Before camping for the night on the outskirts of Poitiers,
they stopped at the Youth Hostel so Maris could inquire for
mail. There was none.

It took a little maneuvering to get everyone ready for bed.
Peter and the boys made a lean-to against the side of Elsie
with a poncho. They seemed to think it was a great lark.

Maris was so happy, lying in her narrow bunk surrounded
by she-Addisons of various sizes, that she wanted to stay
awake. She had a lot to think about. But before she had a
chance to reflect on the wonderful day that was ending,
Cressida was leaning over from her pipe berth, whispering,
"Good morning."

In Poitiers they visited the Church of Saint Hilaire, Saint
Martin's teacher.

Maris told the children about the miracle of Saint Hilaire
— how, being locked out of a council by hostile monks, he
shattered the bolt of the door by the mere force of his voice!

They went on to Saint-Jean-d'Angely, where only the
facade remained of the ancient Abbey.

That evening, Maris offered to prepare the high tea. Val seemed pleased to let her do everything except the actual brewing.

"That's a wife's job," she declared. "No one else can make tea just the way Peter likes it."

There was less fuss getting ready for bed. The boys had the hang of fixing up the lean-to.

When they stopped at the Youth Hostel in Saintes the next afternoon, Maris found a letter from Lonsie.

EVERYTHING'S OKAY! she began in exultant capitals. *Just a false alarm. You were right. But I'm glad I'm here. I told everyone I was too homesick, which was true. Only Stew — he knows.*

You'll laugh, Maris, but even that short bit of pilgrimage meant a lot to me. All the way back in the plane, I kept thinking about things. Stew did some thinking, too. We're a very staid couple! The idea of us making a pilgrimage on our honeymoon sort of got under his skin. Wouldn't that be something?

She had called up Maris's parents and grandfather. They were very sweet and understanding.

Don't worry, I think I convinced your father that you can take care of yourself. He has more respect for you than you think.

Respect! Maris repeated to herself, unable to believe it.

It must be as Peter implied — her father had "grown up."

On an impulse, she told Val all about Lonsie after tea, while they knelt by a brook, washing clothes. She described the anxious time in Paris.

"You poor ducks! All by yourselves, with no older person to turn to. That was too much to bear alone."

Maris pushed the hair out of her eyes with a wet wrist. "Why," she said, surprised, turning to Val, "we wouldn't have told anybody, even if we'd been home. We don't know anybody old who'd have understood. You — I guess, if I was in trouble, I'd tell you. But how many people are like that — people one can talk to without getting criticized?"

"That's unfair," Val retorted. "Just because they don't agree with you doesn't mean they're critical. Besides, why should they endorse what they consider wrong? Don't you believe in sincerity? If you worked on my cases with me, you'd understand why I have such strong feelings. Every day, I see the results of Lonsie's type of reasoning, not just illegitimate children and disease but the emotional suffering of women who've discovered that a relationship they entered into held less commitment than they'd assumed."

Maris stood up and looked down at the clear water trickling over her toes. "Last spring," she said slowly, "I might have done the same thing. But when this happened to Lonsie, I had a feeling that I don't need to prove myself a woman. Do you think a girl does?"

"What do you call me?" Val cried, turning to Maris. "I have a happy husband and I've borne four children. Wouldn't you say I'm a woman? But I didn't have to prove it in advance!" She was half angry, half amused. "Besides," she added, wringing out a shirt of Peter's, "there's a lot more to being a woman than just that aspect."

They collected their washing and started across the field toward the place where Elsie was parked. From the distance, they could see Peter and the children doing handstands.

Maris felt uncommonly lighthearted. All the way back from the brook, she threw her wet garments into the air and caught them again, just for the heck of it.

7

At bedtime, there was a thunderstorm. It rained so heavily that Peter and the boys couldn't go out. Maris felt embarrassed. If it weren't for her — But the Addisons were unconcerned. They put both little girls to sleep on the front seat. The rest of them settled down to an evening of card games by the light of a lantern. Around ten o'clock Val made cocoa in the narrow galley.

It was snug, sitting there, squashed together, eating and drinking, with the rain pattering overhead. They talked about the gypsy caravan, which had passed them at dusk.

"Picturesque lot, aren't they?" Peter observed. "Marvelous, the way they've kept their identity against brutal opposition."

"Do you know how they made their way into Spain?" Maris asked.

Peter shook his head.

"In the Fifteenth Century, they posed as pilgrims bound for Santiago. Everyone offered them hospitality."

"Nowadays, people are less charitable," Val said. "Some towns won't let them stay more than three days."

"I almost wish we were accompanying you," Peter said dreamily. "There's a poetic magnetism about those words in the *Guide*,

Inter duos fluvios quorum unus vocatur Sar et alter
Sarela, urbs Compostella sita est . . .

Between two rivers, one of which is called the Sar and the
other Sarela, lies the town of Compostela."

"I wish you were coming," Maris exclaimed, "oh, I do wish
it!"

"Another time, perhaps," Val told her, "we'll meet your
plane from America and we'll all go there together in Elsie."

"They'll take us for gypsies," Peter said.

"Are there Indians in your part of America?" Ian asked
Maris, as he spread a Rye Vita wafer with Marmite.

Selwyn laughed at him. "You blooming idiot! She doesn't
live in the wild West. We drove the Indians out when we
colonized the country. America isn't what you see on the
telly."

"As a matter of fact, there are Indians in my part of America," Maris told them. "There are two tribes in Maine, where
my grandfather spends his summers: Penobscots and Passamaquoddies. But they're not at all like those who live in the
Southwest. You've seen pictures of big, handsome men with
feathered bonnets. Some of these people scarcely have enough
to eat."

"How shocking!" Peter exclaimed. "Doesn't the Great
White Father look after them?"

"The State of Maine gives them some help, but there are
few jobs where they live, on the edge of the forest. Miserable
though the Reservation is in some ways, they cling to it. They
even speak an ancient tribal language, Abenaki."

"It surprises me that such conditions exist," Val said, shaking her head. "What they need is a social worker!" She
laughed. "Can they use a schoolmaster, too?" She turned to
Peter. "François would be interested in hearing about those
Indians, wouldn't he?"

"Very much."

"He's the anthropologist we're visiting in Bordeaux," Val explained to Maris. "He was up at Oxford with Peter. They've been friends ever since."

The boys couldn't keep their eyes open. They spread their sleeping bags on the floor and stretched out on them, very much in each other's way, but they fell asleep instantly.

Peter took his last look at the *Pilgrim's Guide*. "Listen to this," he commanded. "It's about the country we're in now and where we'll be tomorrow."

> Then you will come to the Saintonge country. Crossing an arm of the sea, you arrive in the Bordelais, where wine is good, fish abundant but the language is rough. It takes three days for tired men to cross the Landes, where there is neither bread nor wine, fish or water. Take care to protect your face from the enormous gadflies which swarm there in summer. If you do not step carefully, you will sink up to your knees in sand.

> Having crossed this country, you come to Gascogne, rich in white bread and red wine, well wooded with meadows and pure springs. The Gascons are hospitable to the poor. Sitting around the fire, they eat without a table and drink from the same goblet. They sleep all together on a thin layer of rotten straw.

"Just like us!" Peter exclaimed, throwing back his head to laugh, "only we have no rotten straw." He read on:

> Leaving this land, the Santiago road crosses two rivers. You have to take a boat. Cursed be the boatmen! They extract from everyone, rich or poor, a piece of money. For a horse they extort four pieces. As the boat is small, made from a single tree trunk, it can hardly hold the horses. Take care when you

climb in. Do not fall in the water.

Only embark with a few passengers because if the boat is overloaded, it sinks at once. Many boatmen, having received their money, take such a large group of pilgrims that the boat turns over and all are drowned. Then the boatmen rejoice over the spoils of the dead.

"Maris," Peter said, looking up from the book, "You've enriched our whole stay in France."

No one had ever made Maris feel so important.

"Yes," Val put in, "the children are going to miss you, especially the boys. You've made the countryside meaningful to Selwyn and Ian. They were beginning to get restless."

"Tomorrow," Maris promised them, "We're going through some wonderful towns — Saintes, where I must visit the Church of Saint Eutrope. It has marvelous Romanesque capitals. Daniel in the Lion's Den is famous. Then we'll pass through Pons. The pilgrims' hospice stands outside the old city wall, so *jacquots* returning from Santiago after the gates were locked had a place to spend the night. Best of all, we'll pass through Blaye, where Roland was buried beside Aude, his girl. She was Oliver's sister. Wouldn't you think, if Roland really cared, that he would have married her and settled down, instead of warring all the time?"

Val and Peter laughed.

"Tomorrow," Peter said, with a hint of the schoolmaster in his voice, "you will have to turn your attention to the classical period, Maris. Here in Saintes, there's a Roman triumphal arch and an arena where, it is said, twenty thousand spectators watched the gladiators perform."

"What are you going to study in Paris?" Val asked.

"Gothic Architecture and Medieval Geography. I'm looking forward to it."

Peter was suddenly fast asleep, sitting up in a corner of the

opposite bunk with the *Pilgrim's Guide* open on his lap. No
wonder! It was midnight. He had done a lot of driving.

Val looked at him. Tenderness shone in her eyes.

Maris thought, she's the kind of wife I want to be and he's
the kind of man I want to marry.

The tenderness was still shining in Val's eyes when she
turned back to Maris and asked, "Won't you have to take
your degree at home eventually?" Before Maris could answer,
Val put a second question to her: "Was there someone you
were running away from?"

"Oh, no!" But even as Maris made this flat denial, she knew
she was denying the truth. "I guess I was," she admitted in a
whisper. "I was running away. He wanted me to do something I didn't want to do. Well, I didn't and I did."

Quietly, so as not to wake Peter, Maris fished under the
bunk and pulled out her scrip. Way at the bottom was the
shell she'd given Jim. She held it tightly in her palm for a
moment. Feeling it again gave her a thrill of pleasure.

"Look," she said then, holding it out to Val, "I found this
on the beach one day, when we were goofing off instead of
studying for exams. It's the badge of Saint James, you know.
His name happens to be James. I made him a present of it, but
he was so mad, he chucked it way across the sand. Later, I
picked it up."

Val took the scallop shell and studied it by the light of the
lantern.

"When I was a child in Rhode Island," she murmured wistfully, "we used to go down to Little Narragansett Bay and
hunt for shells behind the dunes on Napatree Point. Terns
nested in the tall grasses and the beach pea grew out of the
sand. This brings it all back."

"Jim wanted to be committed," Maris explained. "But I
think now he didn't know what that means — to be *totally*
committed. Is that possible?"

"Quite. This shell — what are you going to do with it?"

"Oh, I just carry it in my scrip. It's my talisman, like the pin in my beret. I showed you that."

"Yes, only the one in your beret was a gift, wasn't it? Didn't you say your grandfather gave it to you?"

Maris nodded.

"This one signifies something else."

"Anyway," Maris said, "I'll have it when I finish my pilgrimage. If I were a *bona fide* pilgrim, I'd be given a scallop shell. Since I'm not, well, I'll have this one."

Val put the shell back in Maris's palm with a little pat, a loving gesture, which gave emphasis to what she said: "There must be others, like you, going to Santiago, who aren't *bona fide* pilgrims, yet who are seeking the meaning of life."

"I doubt it," Maris cried. Then she remembered that she must keep her voice down.

"How can you tell, till you get there? If I were you," Val said gently, "I'd hunt for someone like that and present it to him or her."

Maris looked at Val swiftly. "Oh, not this shell! I wouldn't want to part with it."

"Not now. But when you reach the end of your pilgrimage, you may wish to," Val whispered. She turned to the window. "Look, the rain's stopped."

Maris didn't understand what Val meant. It wasn't the moment to inquire because Val stood up. She stepped carefully over the sleeping boys, opened the back door and jumped down.

Maris followed her. They were both barefoot. The grass felt deliciously cool and wet.

"Come and spend your Christmas holidays with us," Val begged. "The children would consider that a superb present. We'll show you a bit of England."

"I'd love to!" Maris exclaimed. Then she said shyly, "When you gave me the ride the other day, I was sort of at an end. I guess you could tell. That's why you were nice to me."

Without answering, Val put her arm around Maris.

"I'd lost the — well — vision, which had been drawing me to Santiago," Maris admitted softly. "Now I have hold of it again. How can these things come and go? I mean, how could I have been so crazy to make the pilgrimage and then, the minute I was scared and lonely, I wanted to run home? Sometimes, I think I'm just living in a legend."

"There's nothing wrong with living in a legend," Val said thoughtfully, "so long as one penetrates beneath the story to that special quality which makes legends immortal. That ageless vitality — isn't it what we crave for ourselves? Even Emily Dickinson — shrinking from the people around her, practically unpublished during her lifetime — that was her legend. Yet, all the while, she was actually communing with a much larger world than the circle of her neighbors — with us, who live a hundred years later and who sense the ecstasy of her creation.

> 'A word that breathes distinctly
> Has not the power to die'

That's what I aspire to. I want to breathe distinctly, not in poetry. I can't do that. But in my actions."

Maris listened, awed. Val was describing her own dreams. Looking up, she saw that the clouds had broken. The stars were beginning to appear.

With her arm still resting on Maris's shoulder, Val began to sing. The sweetness of her voice turned Ophelia's plaintive song into something joyous, a kind of promise.

> How should I your true Love know
> From another one?
> By his cockle hat, and staff,
> And his sandal shoon.

part 4

I

NOT SINCE THOSE EVENINGS AT COLLEGE, WHEN MARIS SAT ON
the window seat in the room she shared with Lonsie, dreaming that the students on the Quad below were actually minstrels and paladins, pilgrims and monks; that Founders Hall
was a crenellated tower from which a portcullis was lowered
against invaders and wolves — not since those evenings had
Maris been so under the spell of the medieval legends as when
she reached Bordeaux, where the Addisons left her.

Coming there that morning from Saintes, Peter had made a
detour westward to the Estuary of the Garonne so that the
children could see Blaye. It was important, he told them in his
schoolmaster's voice, because it had been a Roman camp.

But to Maris, Blaye was the place where Roland was buried
beside Aude. Charlemagne, hearing the blast of Roland's horn
way off in Saint-Jean-Pied-de-Port, rushed back to Roncevaux, only to find that the knights of his rear guard were dead.
Oliver and the others he buried at Belin in the Landes of
Gascony. But Roland he took as far as Blaye. There, in the
Basilica, on a rock near the River, he placed the white marble
sarcophagus.

Nine hundred years later, at the end of the Seventeenth

155

Century, the Basilica was taken down to make room for the Citadel. What became of the white marble sarcophagus or of Aude, nobody seemed to know.

Peter parked Elsie and they all got out. It was exciting, walking around the ancient town.

Maris felt awed. Blaye! She'd read about it as long as she could remember. She was in Blaye!

Those two towers, she learned from the Addisons' guidebook, belonged to the Castle of Rudel, where the troubadour Jaufré was born. Maris had read about his infatuation with Melissinde of Tripoli, the faraway princess he'd never seen.

> Beloved of a distant land,
> My heart is anguished for your hand . . .

Embarking for North Africa in his search of Melissinde, Jaufré fell sick on board the boat. He reached port just in time to locate his princess and die in her arms.

"A typical Twelfth Century romance," Maris commented, when she told the Addisons the story. "The troubadours were fascinated by unattainable love."

As she said this, she wondered, is that my trouble? Am I looking for a kind of love that doesn't exist?

Parting from the Addisons was almost more than Maris could bear. At the gate of the Youth Hostel in Bordeaux, they all kissed her goodby — except Selwyn and Ian — even Peter, who insisted that she come to Southampton for Christmas.

"Send us a postcard," Val called out of Elsie's window, as they drove off. "We'll be home on the eighteenth. Tell us how you crossed the Pass."

The Youth Hostel was attractive. It served as a recreation center for the neighborhood. There was music. People were singing and playing Ping Pong.

But for Maris, it was as if they didn't exist. Being lonely, she should have tried to make friends. Instead, she felt withdrawn. Music didn't suit her mood. Her thoughts were melancholy and centuries away. Only by retreating into her dream world was it possible to survive the sudden solitariness.

There was no going back now. She knew that. She'd have to push on, over the Valcarlos Pass to Roncevaux and across the North of Spain. Even when she reached Santiago, she'd be alone. When she got back to Paris, there wouldn't be anybody she cared about.

She'd have to wait till Christmas to go to Southampton. Christmas! That was so far off.

Peter had suggested that Maris rent a bicycle in Bordeaux. She had told him that she wanted to go to Belin because the medieval pilgrims passed through there so they could see where Oliver and the rest of Charlemagne's knights were buried.

The Housefather gave Maris the address of a bicycle shop. The bike she got felt strange. It had no coaster brake and the handlebars seemed wider than the ones at home.

Setting out through the streets of Bordeaux, she wobbled a little. Then she got used to it.

She visited the Church of Saint Seurnin, as the *Pilgrim's Guide* instructed her to do. In the crypt, she couldn't help wishing she were one of those small children whose mothers bring them to the tomb of the Saint, believing this visit will make them grow up strong.

It was gloomy. Maris quickly returned to the sunlit street.

Lunch cheered her. She had stumbled upon a restaurant that would have delighted tourists by its charm, but it seemed to be patronized entirely by local people. She ordered chicken *à la Bordelaise* and *aubergines* — eggplant, spiced with shallots and garlic.

That night, Maris washed her hair and wrote home.

Early the next morning, she set out on the bicycle for Belin, passing through the Landes. Winds, blowing westward from the Atlantic into the Bay of Biscay, had brought quantities of sand inland. Pine trees were planted on these dunes. For long stretches, there were few houses, only endless pines, each with a little bucket, which made Maris think of sugar maples in Vermont. These buckets collected resin.

Halfway to Belin, Maris passed a crowd of men and boys gathered by the roadside. They semed to think her appearance very amusing. She pretended not to notice and biked on as fast as she could. Some miles farther on, another little crowd was waiting. As Maris came along, everyone hooted. This time, she got off her bike.

"What's so funny?" she demanded to know.

The boys were silent but the men explained. Today, there was a bicycle race from Bordeaux to Dax. They'd been standing here hours, waiting to see it, expecting a team of men to streak by. Instead, who should come puffing along, with blond hair streaming after her, but a solitary girl!

Maris laughed with them. She could see the joke.

Belin was hardly more than a village. Maris found no trace of the knights. But there was a little restaurant on the main road, where she ordered duck liver with raisins because the proprietor told her it was the specialty of the Landes. She didn't expect to like this. It turned out to be great.

While she was eating, the bicycle racers passed, hunched over their handlebars. Yes, she must have come as a surprise to the men waiting by the roadside!

She went back to Bordeaux and returned the bicycle.

The following day, she left by train for Bayonne.

Although she was only just coming into the Basque country and she didn't yet know how she'd get across the Pyrenees, Maris already heard, with her inner ear, the blasts of Roland's horn.

> The mountains round about are lofty, but high above them rises the sound of his horn. At the third blast, it is split in twain.

Thus sang Taillefer at the Battle of Hastings.

Saint James was waiting for Maris at Bayonne, standing in the porch of the Cathedral, dressed like a pilgrim.

If Peter were here, Maris thought, he'd be sure to tell the children that when Eleanor of Aquitaine married Henry Plantagenet, Bayonne became English and remained so for three hundred years. It was hard to imagine now.

She bought two bars of chocolate. One she ate, the other she stowed in her scrip. Bayonne was a chocolate town. Jews, driven out of Spain by Ferdinand and Isabella, brought cocoa with them and started the industry.

Maris wandered along the river, looking at the ships. She found a *bistro* where she ate truffles and *paté de foie gras* and pimentos. She was becoming quite a connoisseur of French cooking! The waiter persuaded her to have some *touron* for dessert. That turned out to be a fruit and nut cake, very rich but delicious.

While she ate, Maris read letters she'd found waiting for her at the Hostel — one from her mother, repeating in four pages what her father had cabled in ten words, urging her to take care, especially in speaking to strangers.

That seemed unrealistic, since Maris didn't know a soul here. Everyone she spoke to was a stranger. Her mother's next words came as a surprise.

We felt it was very mature of you, not to come rushing home with Lonsie. Your father and I were impressed by your judgment.

Impressed! This wasn't the reaction Maris had expected.

What a change! Maris had proved something to her parents — what, she couldn't understand, since she felt no different. All along, she had known she could take care of herself.

But that her father could "grow up," as Peter put it, had seemed quite impossible. This letter gave her the feeling that she had become almost her parents' peer. When she went home, they would all three be on a different footing. It was a strange idea, but it was nice.

Her grandfather was jubilant over her decision. It would have been a defeat to come back, he wrote, just because Lonsie was homesick. Hadn't Maris wanted to make the pilgrimage alone, all along?

He was reading about the *Conquistadores*, the subjugation of Mexico by Cortes and his men, for the sake of gold and good-looking women, whom they branded.

They had no use for those female prisoners who were not good looking. My stomach isn't strong enough for the account of their butchery. Did you know that Saint James was in the thick of this slaughter, riding on his white charger? It's a side of his character I wasn't prepared for.

Yes, Maris knew the Spaniards had invoked Santiago in the midst of their bloodiest campaigns. They claimed he was miraculously present at the battles, riding his charger, brandishing his spear, trampling on the enemy. But Maris had chosen to ignore this side of his character.

I have been studying your route, her grandfather went on, *and I wonder whether you happened to pass through Cadillac. I see it is not far from Bordeaux. That is where the Seventeenth Century adventurer came from who carried the name of the town to our Mount Desert.*

No, Maris hadn't been to Cadillac. It wasn't on the Way of Saint James and Maine was far from her thoughts.

She was worrying about how she would get to Roncevaux tomorrow. There was an 8 A.M. train from Bayonne to Saint-Jean-Pied-de-Port. She could get that far. But how would she cross the Valcarlos Pass and go on from Roncevaux to Pampeluna?

Tomorrow night was supposed to be her first in Spain. She was supposed to sleep at the hotel in Pampeluna, where her father had made a reservation. And nobody could tell her how to get there.

2

When Maris woke up the next morning, she didn't want to get out of bed. Her muscles were sore from all that biking and she hadn't had much sleep.

The girls in her dormitory had talked till after midnight. They were a mixed lot — French, Italian, Japanese, German, Austrian, Danish, Norwegian. Speaking a sort of French, they stated their differing views, mostly on political issues, laughing as they realized how impossible it is to discuss ideas with a tourist's vocabulary. Yet, they were earnestly trying to communicate the truth as they saw it.

Where you come from determines what you believe, Maris discovered.

She felt like an outsider. Not that the girls weren't friendly. But somehow they made her feel that she was set apart, more affluent and privileged and powerful — not quite with it in the hard business of survival.

"You can't understand," one of them murmured. "You don't know how it is to have foreign troops in your country."

"No," Maris admitted.

Last year, when she was hosteling, she traveled in a group of Americans. She seldom exchanged more than a few words

161

with people of another nationality. Those kids had argued and quarreled, but they had the same background. Now, finding herself among strangers, Maris realized that the Americans had thought very much alike.

Suddenly, she was sleeping in a room with girls who not only looked different, but *were* different. In spite of their obvious determination to get along with each other for one night, there was an immeasurable space between them, which they could never bridge. Maris didn't want to believe this, but it was all too apparent.

This morning, the girls were sleepy and silent, standing in line at the basins in the washroom, hardly noticing each other, preoccupied, like Maris, with the mechanics of travel and getting to the day's destination. It was pouring.

Maris left after breakfast. In the station square, there was a small church with a belfry in the facade that looked like a California mission. Spain wasn't far away!

The man at the window sold Maris a ticket for Saint-Jean-Pied-de-Port, but he couldn't tell her how to go on from there.

"When you arrive, you may find some conveyance," he said. "If not, you can always come back."

"Come back! But I'm going to Spain. I have a reservation in Pampeluna tonight. There must be a bus or something."

The man shrugged in the French manner and said pleasantly, "It's a pretty ride. If you can't get over the Pass and you have to return, you'll have had a nice look at the scenery."

Maris felt furious. She couldn't believe he didn't know. St.-Jean was only an hour and a half away.

"In this rain," she exclaimed, "the scenery!"

Maybe she ought to give up — go on to Burgos via the Paris-Madrid *rapide*, which she could pick up here, as all the tourist people had told her to do, forget Roncevaux — *Forget Roncevaux?* She couldn't do that.

In the train, sitting on a hard wooden bench, surrounded by Basque men eating breakfast on their way to work, Maris took off her sopping trench coat and her beret.

Rain, zigzagging down the glass, made it impossible to see any of the beautiful countryside the man at the ticket window had mentioned.

The Basques ate silently, thick bread and sausage. They drank from wine bottles. They stared at Maris. All of them wore berets like hers, but weathered. Had she pulled a boner, wearing a beret in the Basque country? It was masculine headgear here.

Embarrassed, Maris took out the *Pilgrim's Guide* and began to read, so she wouldn't have to meet the stares.

> In the Basque country, the Santiago road goes over a lofty mountain. It is the gateway into Spain. You have to travel eight miles up and eight miles down again. Those who climb this mountain believe they have touched the sky with their hands.

Eight miles up and eight miles down! Maris repeated to herself. Suppose she had to walk? Her muscles — She ached all over.

> On the summit is a place called the Cross of Charles, where Charlemagne prayed to God and Saint James. Toward the north is a valley called Val Carlos. There Charlemagne took refuge after the battle of Roncevaux. Here the Basques used not only to rob pilgrims going to Santiago, but to stride them like donkeys and ride them to death.

Maris peeked up over the top of her book. The Basques were still staring at her. They didn't look like robbers. They seemed good-natured.

She wanted to speak to them, inquire if they knew the way over the Pass, but she felt strange.

Then she had a marvelous inspiration.

The Basques love music, she thought, putting the *Guide*

back in her scrip and taking out the recorder.

Keeping her eyes down, she began to play the first tune that came into her head — Ophelia's song, which Val had transformed into a joyous promise. Was anything more fitting, than Shakespeare's air about a Jacobean pilgrim with his cockle hat and staff?

While she held the last note, applause broke out around her. Looking up, she found the men were grinning.

"*Encore!*"

This time, it must be something gay. She played, "Turkey in the Straw."

"That's American," she told them shyly in French, when she'd finished.

"Are you American?"

The way they asked it, with their Pyrenean accent, the way they looked at her, Maris felt sure these men had never seen an American before — not a young female, anyhow. She must seem like a creature from some mythical world.

One of the men offered her his wine bottle. Maris knew this was an act of international friendship and that she was letting her country down by declining. But she simply couldn't face taking a swig from that bottle. The man kept insisting, while the others watched intently. When Maris refused for the third time, they all looked disappointed.

"Do you know how I can get from Saint-Jean to Pampeluna?" she asked, turning from one to the other.

They shook their heads. "*Ah, ça!*" they muttered darkly. "One needs papers. They cost money."

They began to kid each other about contraband. Clearly, they weren't above a little smuggling, if only in fantasy. Were they to travel to Pampeluna, their tone implied, their route would not be past the custom house.

She remembered what Peter had said about the thousands of refugees from the Spanish Civil War, who lived here, near the border, and the bad feeling that still existed. By telling these people that she wished to go to Spain, she had perhaps touched on a sore nerve. She sensed something sinister, the helpless resentment of freedom-loving patriots who have had to come to terms with defeat. She knew that, in the Middle Ages, the Basques had themselves been driven northward by the Spaniards.

Maris looked out of the window. Beneath the raindrops, she could make out soggy fields, newly ploughed, red earth, orchards, clipped poplars. If the sun had been shining, it might have been a cheerful countryside. As it was, to Maris, turning away from the imprint of sullen history on those dark faces around her, it was sinister. The men were good-natured; their heritage was cruel.

She recalled what Aymery Picaud had said of these people in the Twelfth Century: that wherever they went, they took a horn around their necks and two or three javelins in their hands; that when they were hiding, they communicated with their companions by imitating the to-whit-tu-who of an owl or the howl of a wolf.

It was they who, five centuries before that, pursued Charlemagne after his conquest of Pampeluna and overtook Roland at Roncevaux.

A shiver went through Maris.

At Saint-Jean-Pied-de-Port, it was teeming. She scurried into the little station and asked the man who was moving baggage how to get to Pampeluna. He shrugged and walked away.

She found the stationmaster and asked him. He told her there was no conveyance across the border.

Maris was afraid she might break down and cry. These people, who lived so close to Spain, never went there. They obviously didn't want Maris to go, either. She was caught by political quarrels that didn't concern her.

To turn back now, so near — not fifty miles from Roncevaux —

3

MARIS LOOKED FOR SOMEONE IN AUTHORITY TO APPEAL TO — A *gendarme* — but there was none. Shouldn't she take the next train back to Bayonne — if there was a train?

Maybe, the stationmaster conceded, softening a little, if Maris walked up to the town and inquired at the tourist office, maybe there she'd get some information.

"In this rain!"

The stationmaster shrugged and walked off.

A moment later, a bus drove up before the door.

The young man who was moving the baggage came over to Maris and whispered, as though he had no business telling her what his boss refused to say, "That bus will take you to the frontier."

She showered him with thanks, shouldered her knapsack, and went out to ask the bus driver how she could get from the frontier to Pampeluna. That, she figured, was another forty or fifty miles.

"Tomorrow, there might be some way," he answered vaguely.

"Tomorrow! I have a reservation in Pampeluna tonight."

But Maris couldn't afford to hesitate. The bus was about to

166

leave. She could go along or she could stay here.

Feeling that she was burning her last bridge behind her, she jumped in and found a seat among a lot of Spanish-looking women and children and crates of live chickens.

Suppose there was no connection at the frontier? Where would she sleep?

The bus drove through the town of St.-Jean, named Pied-de-Port because it lies at the foot of the Pass. Here, at a Hospice near the Citadel, the medieval pilgrims spent their last night on French soil. By the gate in the old town wall, Maris saw a signpost pointing, even now, to the Way of Saint James.

She tried to imagine the place on those long-ago mornings, when church bells rang, priests said prayers, women stood in their doorways handing out food, and children tagged after the *Jacquots*. With their long gray cloaks and cockle hats and staves, the pilgrims walked through this very gate and started the long climb over the Pass, forced to cover the twenty miles between here and the Hospice at Roncevaux by nightfall.

Today, no one but Maris Miller had this ambition. And even she didn't care to attempt it on foot, by herself.

It took a long time to get through the little town because the driver was shopping for all the housewives on his route. He went into the butchershop and came out presently with a naked quarter of lamb, which he set down on the seat beside him. Then he went into the bakery and returned with his arms full of long French loaves. These he laid, unwrapped, on top of the meat. There were several shopping baskets to be filled.

At last, the bus took off, through a gorge beside the river, up a winding road, past whitewashed houses with exposed beams and gray tile roofs.

The rain had lessened and the newly washed green hills were beautiful. It was only a short ride, but it took ages because the driver had to deliver the things he had bought, first at one house, then at another, all the way up.

Finally the bus reached a bridge and stopped. The women and children got out and disappeared. Maris didn't bother to check on what became of the chickens.

"You walk across the bridge," the driver was saying, "and you're in Spain."

Maris was the only person going over.

Midway, she stood still, wondering whether she hadn't better turn back. Looking down at the rushing water, she reminded herself that it was all very well to be persistent, but discretion was the better part of valor, as her mother was always saying.

I've had it, she said to herself flatly.

In France, she could talk to people. They might not always be helpful, but she could find her way around. Once she entered Spain, no one would understand her. She'd be completely isolated. If she didn't find a way over the Pass, what would she do?

But even while she was deciding to return, her feet carried Maris relentlessly over the bridge and she arrived at the tiny custom house. The coat-of-arms on the door told her she was on Spanish soil.

When the customs officer saw Maris's American passport, he expressed no desire to peek into her knapsack. He explained that the passport check point was five kilometers up the mountainside. He listened courteously to Maris's question, in French, about a bus for Pampeluna. It was clear that he understood, because he shook his head.

Desperate, Maris had a sudden inspiration.

"You see," she said, pointing to the shell on her beret, "I'm making a pilgrimage to Santiago."

The officer nodded gravely. Maris felt sure she'd got through to him. He told her in Spanish to be patient. She understood enough of the language to conclude that he was

telling her to wait. But whether he meant there'd be a bus
some time today or only tomorrow, maybe never —

She took off her knapsack and laid it down beside her feet,
in the road.

"Spanish people spend their whole lives waiting," someone
had told Maris, when she was about to leave Neville.

That hadn't mattered particularly, then. Now, when she
was the one who was doing the waiting —

She shifted from one foot to the other. Would she have to
wait all day? What was she waiting for? When it grew dark,
what would she do?

It was the first time in her life that she was homeless, not
sure where she might be, when night closed in. Her father
had so carefully made that reservation at the hotel in Pampeluna. What good was it? A shiver of fear passed through her,
as she looked up at the steep hills all around. There was a
sharp freshness in the air, coming from the mountains beyond.

Making an effort to be rational, Maris told herself that it
was unlikely she'd have to spend the night out here. But she
couldn't put down the terror, which was beyond anything
she'd ever experienced. A young girl, a foreigner, unable to
speak the language, at anyone's mercy — She couldn't get
away, there was no one but that officer to turn to and she had
no idea what was in his mind.

Those men in the train had given her the sense of something
sinister in these mountains, the defilement of blood wilfully
spilled, indelibly staining the centuries.

If her father knew what a fix she was in! He was absolutely
right. She had to admit it. This was a dangerous thing to do,
to travel alone. Just now, Maris would give anything to be
back home.

Thirty men of Lorraine —

It was no comfort to recall the pilgrim in the *Golden
Legend*, caught alone here in the Pyrenees at night. Maris

wished the words didn't keep going through her head.

Thirty men of Lorraine went together on pilgrimage to Saint James about the year of our Lord a thousand and sixty-three. It happened that one of them was sick and his fellows abode and waited on him fifteen days, and at last they all left him, save one, which abode by him and kept him. And when it drew to night, the sick man died.

When it was night, the man that was alive was sore afraid for the place which was solitary, and for the presence of the dead body, and for the cruelty of the strange people, and for the darkness of the night that came on.

4

A CAR WITH FRENCH LICENSE PLATES CAME OVER THE BRIDGE and stopped at the custom house. The back seat was piled high with luggage. The officer asked the man and the girl in the car where they were going.

"Pampeluna."

The officer beckoned to Maris. As she picked up her knapsack and drew closer, she thought he was explaining to the driver that she was a pilgrim. He was asking him to give her a lift. So that was what the officer had in mind!

Where would I sit? Maris wondered. All that luggage —

"This is a honeymoon," the man said indignantly. "We don't have room for a third party."

When he drove on, Maris felt relieved. She hadn't liked his looks.

Almost immediately, another car came. It was Belgian. There was an old couple in it. The man drove; the woman did the talking. In reply to the officer's question, she said they were probably going to Pampeluna.

The officer explained about Maris.

"If we can render a pilgrim a service," the woman said, looking Maris over, "we'll be glad to. But we may not go all the way. We're just out for a drive. We'll be glad to take her as far as we're going."

The customs officer opened the rear door for Maris, smiling in farewell. She thanked him and jumped in. She felt nervous about this. As the car started up the mountainside, the couple on the front seat were guarded.

We don't trust strangers, they seemed to say. But a pilgrim — how can one refuse?

When they discovered she spoke French, they seemed more at ease, but Maris was still tense. She wasn't afraid of the people; she was afraid of being dumped part way over the Pass, where there wouldn't be a living soul and maybe no other cars coming along.

Already, the houses had thinned out. There were only a few deserted cowsheds. The road was very narrow, zigzagging in hairpin turns, higher and higher.

Am I hitchhiking now? Maris asked herself. I didn't stand in the road, wagging my thumb, as Selwyn put it. I didn't even know this was what I was waiting for. Will I really get to Pampeluna tonight?

At the passport check point, the man stayed in the car. The woman got out and so did Maris.

This officer spoke French. He was a handsome Spaniard and he treated Maris gallantly. She asked whether she might stay here and pick up another ride, as the people who had been kind enough to bring her this far weren't sure whether they were going all the way to Pampeluna.

The officer looked a little troubled.

"You're welcome to stay," he said, "but there may not be another car going in that direction today."

Maris felt a rush of terror, such as she'd experienced on the bridge. "I-I'd better stay here," she said to the woman. "Thank you very much for bringing me this far. I'll get my knapsack."

"Let's see what my husband has decided," the woman answered.

Back at the car, husband and wife exchanged meaningful glances. Then they announced that they were going all the way to Pampeluna. They must have been planning to go there from the outset. They had simply protected themselves, in case they didn't like Maris.

From then on, they were friendly.

When Maris was back in the car, she looked at the little violet rectangle the officer had stamped in her passport.

Policia Valcarlos, Entrada, it said, with the date of her entrance into Spain.

The day and month leaped out at Maris, August fifteenth. This was the anniversary of the Battle of Roncevaux! The discovery excited her so that she told her host and hostess. "That was in 778," she added.

"Imagine!" the woman exclaimed, shaking her head incredulously. "Almost twelve hundred years ago!"

Now that I'm in Spain, Maris said to herself, I must learn to call the place, Roncevalles — pronounce the *c* like *th* and the double *l* like *y*.

The man was an expert driver. He took the hairpin turns so skillfully that if another car had come in the opposite direction, they wouldn't have collided.

Maris had never seen such mountains. The peaks were steep, conical granite thrusts, lost in mist. Below, the valleys were magnificently green, yet uninhabited. She felt alone in the world, with only these two strangers.

"I can't tell you how grateful I am," she said, "I don't know what I'd have done, if you hadn't been willing to take me." Then she felt forced to acknowledge, since she had wangled the ride under slightly false pretenses, "I don't have a pilgrim's certificate. When I reach Santiago, they won't give me a shell."

Maris told them how difficult it had been to get information and she described the sense she had had in the train of bloodshed staining the memories of those good-natured Basques.

"I'm American," she explained. "These political quarrels have nothing to do with me. And still, I felt drawn in, through those men, though they hardly said anything."

"No one can escape," her host observed. It was the first time he had said more than a word or two. "When you come here, you become part of the country, for the time being, kin to the inhabitants. If you don't, you might as well stay home and look at transparencies in your *salon.*"

"I've never felt so involved," Maris admitted, confiding, "it's terrifying."

"Yes. But those tourists who rush through a countryside happily oblivious to the marks of violence on it learn nothing. That kind of indifference to other people's misfortune breeds further warfare. I don't know much about Charlemagne, but Napoleon — his troops crossed up there, on the retreat from Pampeluna." He pointed to the somber mountains in the East. "Even today, the wanton killing, the burning of villages during the Peninsular War — these terrors still linger in the consciousness of people who no longer remember or never knew of the events."

The road was so narrow and winding that the man couldn't take his eyes off it, yet, for an instant, he gave Maris an admiring glance in the rearview mirror.

"You may not have a certificate," he said, sounding as if he didn't care, "but you possess something of much greater value, sensitivity and sympathy."

That was a nice thing to say. Maris was getting fond of these people. She wished she had something to give them. But there were only essentials in her knapsack. Yes, she did have a gift.

Opening the scrip, she drew out the bar of Bayonne chocolate and handed it to the lady. "Please accept this," she said, with all the French elegance she could command. "Thank you for your kindness."

Both the man and the woman were voluble in their appreciation. It was as if they had never known gratitude.

"There's the Cross of Charlemagne," Maris told them, as the car reached the top of the Pass. "And the Chapel. Look! Over there!"

She knew the words from the *Pilgrim's Guide* by heart:

> Roland's strength, they say, was such that he split a
> rock from top to bottom with his sword. Upon that
> rock there stands a chapel.

The man stopped the car. "Would you like to get out for a moment?"

"Oh, thank you!"

How understanding! It would have been agony to rush past the place where Roland died.

The Cross, Maris read, as she came close to it, marked the spot where the skeletons of two unusually tall men had been unearthed — such big skeletons that it was assumed they must be the remains of Roland and Oliver.

But Charlemagne buried Roland in the citadel at Blaye, beside Aude, his lady! Maris said to herself. And Oliver was buried at Belin!

Like many of the medieval legends, this one had various versions. Several localities laid claim to the same bones. Actually, Maris supposed, the truth was neither here nor there but in the hearts of people, whose own bondage and misery invested these remains with glory.

When Maris entered the diminutive chapel, she realized it was new. It would hardly hold more than half a dozen people. A window was broken and rain, blowing in, had flooded the floor. Neglected, without a soul in it, the place seemed to have little meaning.

The moment Maris stepped outside again, she felt she was indeed "touching the sky," as it said in the *Guide*. Not only touching — she was in it. A cloud enveloped her, sprinkling her face with fine rain, cutting her off from the people in the car, who were only a few yards away. She couldn't even see the stony road at her feet.

> Then to the Dale of Rouncevale it is the way,
> A dark passage, I dare well say . . .

Centuries ago, that English pilgrim also experienced terror here.

> In that passage my mouth was dry . . .

So's mine, Maris thought, swallowing nervously.

She knew she was somewhere between the Chapel and the Cross of Charlemagne, but she couldn't see either one. She might trip or get lost, wander so far that she'd be separated from these people, who were her lifeline. Without them, she'd never get back to civilization.

They would wait for her a while and then, becoming impatient, they'd drive off, leaving her to wander in these mountains all day, all night.

Suddenly, the cloud rolled away, showing scraps of sky the color of Periwinkle's eyes.

There was the Chapel; there was the Cross! Maris could see the people in the car quite distinctly. They were eating the chocolate.

How silly to think they might give up on her if she didn't return! They never would have driven off. If she had lost her way, they would have come searching as faithfully as if she'd been their child. They were joined to Maris by their humanity, as strong a bond as any blood relationship.

It wouldn't sound right, put into words, but Maris wished she could tell them how much all this meant to her — not just getting the lift she needed, but the knowledge that people cared about someone of no importance to them, for whom they had no responsibility.

In a countryside which was forever stained with ancient

cruelties, Maris had been shown the most uncommon kindness. Those Spanish officers and these Belgian strangers made her feel they'd do anything to help her reach her goal. Beginning with the Addisons, she was being passed from unknown hands to unknown hands and gently carried over the rough places.

The cloud, which had so isolated Maris a minute ago, left her cheeks cool and damp. She smelled the life-giving force rising out of the sodden earth. Somewhere in the distance, there must be a mountain torrent. Maris stared in wonder at the fanciful, wild shapes of the earth's crust, thrown up around her in a ring of gigantic peaks. It was as if her eyes and ears were only just opening, as if her senses had never fully functioned before.

She felt terribly small, surrounded by those towering masses, which stretched from the Bay of Biscay to the Mediterranean Sea. She had no means of imagining the time span between today and that distant age, when the Pyrenees rose out of the sea, sank below the waves again and were hurled up once more by the earth's movement. It was simply inconceivable that such mountains could ever have budged, that they had not endured and might not continue to endure forever.

Yet, for all their immensity and jagged roughness, there was something companionable about these peaks, which Maris had overlooked at the frontier. It would even be possible, she realized now — if she could come back occasionally and visit — to form a friendship with them, which would give her a sense of proportion, a feeling of security, a focus for her aspiration.

She wished Val were here so she could communicate this wonderful awareness.

When I started up the Valcarlos Pass, I was still living in the Roland legend, she would tell her, but in this narrow defile where he died, I walked out of the legend, into life itself.

"*Merci*," she murmured, as she returned to the car.

She looked back through the rear window at the place where she had stood enveloped in the cloud until it was out of

sight. What she saw wasn't the Chapel or the Cross of Charlemagne or Roland or Oliver, but her own childhood, which
she left up there, at the summit of the Pass.

She'd never retrieve it, not with the Addisons or anyone
else. But she didn't feel sad. She felt amazingly buoyant and
lighthearted. This wasn't the end. It was the beginning: of
what, she didn't know.

5

FARTHER DOWN, AT THE HOSPICE, WHERE THE PILGRIMS FROM western France and England and northern Europe used to spend their first night on Spanish soil, the man stopped the car so Maris could walk around the large, somber monastery and the old church.

It was lunchtime. The place looked deserted, locked up. Nowadays, few people came to this isolated spot.

But Maris could imagine what it must have felt like to arrive here in the Middle Ages, the relief it would have been to reach this haven after the perilous journey from Saint-Jean-Pied-de-Port. Coming over the Pass on foot, a pilgrim would have been guided by the tolling of the church bell, which the brothers kept ringing so that those who were struggling over the narrow mountain trail, encircled by tall peaks or enveloped in mist, as Maris had been, would find their way.

When the pilgrim arrived, his feet were washed for him with charity and humility. His worn shoes were repaired. His clothes were cleaned and mended. He was given soup and white bread and excellent wine, not only during his stay at the Hospice, but to take with him, provisions for the morrow's journey.

179

If he were ill, he was nursed back to health. If he died, he was given the last rites and buried close to the Hospice, with as much consideration as would have been evidenced at home.

At the Hospice of Roncevalles, it was said,

> The door is open to all, in sickness, in health,
> Not only to Catholics but to pagans as well.

Maris felt intensely moved by these gray buildings. Stark and forbidding though they appeared, inhospitable at the noon hour, they bore witness to an age when large communities of men and women devoted their lives to the care of others.

Beside the road, there was a sign: *Camino de Santiago*, the Way of Saint James. It gave the distance to the goal — 787 kilometers. Maris translated this to herself roughly as five hundred miles. She was just about halfway.

She got in the car, but as they were leaving Roncevalles, driving beneath huge pine trees, she asked the man to let her out once more, so she could run her fingers over the lichen-covered stone cross, where the *jacquots* always stopped to pray.

The Belgians didn't just take Maris to Pampeluna; they insisted on depositing her at the door of her hotel.

She tried to explain that she was grateful, not only because of the ride.

"It was a pleasure for us, too," they answered, as they shook hands under an arcade in the Plaza. And the woman added, looking a little embarrassed, "We were reluctant at first. If you hadn't been a pilgrim — You see, with your fair hair, we took you for German and it's hard to forget what we went through during the War. So many of our relations and our Jewish friends — It wasn't till we discovered you're American that we felt easy. One mustn't blame individuals, but we endured too much. At least," she said, glancing at her husband, "we didn't refuse."

They both squeezed her hand affectionately. There were

tears in the woman's eyes.

Now that she was in Spain, everyone began taking care of
Maris, even people who didn't know she was a pilgrim. Wherever she went, she aroused pity and concern, because she was
traveling alone.

"*Sola?*" the chambermaid asked incredulously, when Maris
was getting settled in the hotel.

"*Si.*"

"*Sola!*"

The chambermaid's tone conveyed astonishment and fear.
Clearly, she'd never encountered such a sad situation, a young
girl traveling alone!

She was a pretty, lovable little person, who poured out her
sympathy in Spanish. Maris couldn't understand the words,
but she got the idea. It was the same in the dining room. The
waitress, very fancy in her stiff black silk uniform and berib-
boned white bonnet, asked, "*Sola?*"

And when Maris answered, "*Si,*" she repeated compassion-
ately, "*Sola!*"

Maris wasn't able to translate the menu and even after the
waitress brought her a dish, she wondered what she was eating. But it tasted good. The dessert, called *flan*, turned out to
be baked custard swimming in caramel sauce.

As soon as Maris stepped into the streets of Pampeluna, she
saw that the city was dominated by bullfighting. Posters and
souvenirs glorified this one theme. She remembered what an
American girl she'd met at the Hostel in Bayonne said about
her trip to Spain.

"I loved the bullfighting!"

"What is there to love?" Maris had asked, unable to believe
that any civilized person would choose this form of entertain-
ment.

Having grown up with Ferdinand, Maris couldn't get used

to the idea of killing a bull for sport.

"The skill," the girl answered and, reflecting, "the kill."

Maris had shuddered.

Now, after she left the neighborhood of the bullring and those bloody posters, she began to like the old town, with its warm ochre, almost orange houses.

She went first to San Saturnino and was greeted at the door of the church by Saint James, weathered, tender, with his scrip over his shoulder and his staff in his hand, looking down on a grateful young pilgrim kneeling at his feet, the boy he rescued from hanging.

In the Cathedral, examining the stone basin where the pilgrims of the Middle Ages washed themselves, Maris suddenly realized how little she could actually identify with them, for there was running water in her hotel room, not only cold, but hot.

The next morning, she took a bus to the village of Puenta la Reina, where the pilgrims from Italy and eastern France used to join those who'd come down from the North or from England by way of Roncevalles or the Basque plain. It was only fifteen miles to Puenta la Reina, yet the bus took an hour because the driver stopped for errands and conversation at every hamlet.

First, the road mounted steeply to cross the Sierra del Perdon. Then it dropped into the Valley of the Arga.

This was one of the clearest days Maris had had. The colors were intense — tangerine houses, bright cornfields and neatly laid out vineyards. On the horizon, mysterious, violet mountains rose and fell away.

When she left the bus at Puenta la Reina, she felt elated. She had read descriptions of the streams of pilgrims coming from all over Europe and joining here, at the Bridge. They banded together against loneliness and robbers and other perils of the road. While they might not be able to talk to each other in any language, they could pray and sing together in Latin.

They had the same objective, they endured the same hardships. From Puenta la Reina onward, they traveled in a unity which overcame national and racial differences.

"One needs a companion," the Swiss fellow had said, "but only to share the experience."

Maris's soul was as thirsty for this companionship as her mouth was for the mineral water she bought in a grocery store near the head of the Bridge. A crusty little loaf and an orange would keep her till she reached Longrono.

She settled down to this meager lunch in the porch of the Church of Saint James. While she ate and drank, she read the *Pilgrim's Guide*.

> At Puenta la Reina the Arga and the Runa flow together. At Lorca, take care, for the water is deadly. On our way to Santiago, we found two Navarrese seated on the bank, sharpening their knives. These men skin the beasts who die from drinking the water. They said in a deceitful way that the water was good. We therefore gave it to our horses. Two of them died at once and were skinned then and there by the Navarrese.

After lunch, when Maris went into the church, she saw the loveliest Saint James she'd seen yet, a Fourteenth Century wooden statue. He was a travel-stained pilgrim going to his own shrine. There were three shells on his hat. With the hand that held up his cloak, he carried a book. In the other, he held a staff.

His expression was thoughtful, as if he were still the fisherman who'd left his nets in the boat when Jesus called him and he had some foreknowledge of the hard road ahead.

When Maris crossed the ancient Bridge, she felt very solemn. From the other side, she looked at the wide stone arches that spanned the water coming down from the Pyrenees and she thought of all those tired feet which, century after century, had passed this way.

Thousands of pilgrims had crossed the Bridge in their time. Today no one but Maris went over. Not a single person would accompany her to Santiago. She felt desolated.

This wasn't the same as the loneliness she'd suffered from in Orléans. There, she was afraid of staying in a hotel or walking into a restaurant by herself. Like a baby, she wanted her mother. She had got over that. She rather liked being on her own.

It was a different sort of loneliness that beset her now — the absence of someone to share her experience, as the Addisons had done during those brief, wonderful days.

When they spread the cloth in a field of an afternoon, when Val brought the teapot crowned with its cosy out from Elsie and the children followed, carrying the boiled eggs upright in their little cups and the square plates, heaped with thinly sliced bread and butter, with watercress and radishes and cake, when they all settled down crosslegged on the grass and made a ring of hands for that meaningful moment of silence before they began the meal, Maris felt part of a circle of love.

But she had been only a waif looking in through the window of a lighted house. The Addisons made her part of their circle for a time, yet she had had to go on alone. The love she was seeking lay elsewhere.

How will I ever find it? Maris wondered, as she stood near the Bridge, waiting in the noonday sun for the bus to take her to Longrono where she was spending the night. It was still thirty miles away. The scrip and knapsack weighed a ton. The bus was already an hour overdue. Maris began to suspect that it didn't run.

The loneliness of spirit and the heat became unbearable.

Yet, the bus didn't come. The only thing in sight, kicking up a cloud of dust as it rolled over the bridge toward Maris, was a bright red Volks.

Instead of accelerating after it crossed the river, the car

stopped.

Music sounded softly in the quiet road, some plaintive folk song, almost drowned out by the beat of drums. A fair-haired boy poked his head through the window.

"Want a ride?"

An American! Going her way! Maris could hardly believe it. But naturally — a pilgrim! Hadn't strangers met here for a thousand years and continued on together?

Too happy to speak, Maris stood staring at the boy.

He had a nice face, the kind one seldom finds in real life, only in ads. And he was familiar. Not that Maris had ever seen him; she'd simply seen dozens of boys like that, though less handsome, at High School and College. To find one here, in a strange country, going to Santiago!

"Want a ride?" he repeated, as if he thought she hadn't heard.

6

THE BOY OPENED THE DOOR OF THE VOLKS AND JUMPED OUT, uncoiling himself to such a height that Maris wondered whether he could get back in again.

"How did you know I'm American?" she managed to ask.

He grinned. "Just the way you look," he explained, on a note of approval.

His voice was resonant.

As if Maris had agreed to ride with him — she certainly hadn't — he picked up her knapsack.

"Wait!" she cried. "Are you a pilgrim?"

He broke into a loud guffaw. "That's the last thing anybody'd call *me!*" he exclaimed. "The very last thing."

"Then, where are you going?"

"To Portugal."

Maris was hardly able to conceal her disappointment. "Thanks," she muttered, trying to grab her knapsack.

But the boy held it beyond her reach, looking down on her and smiling, as if they'd just been introduced at a party and the whole point of the occasion was to make friends. And again, Maris had that uncanny feeling that she already knew this person she'd never laid eyes on.

186

"Come along," he urged. He turned and heaved the knapsack onto the back seat of the Volks. "Don't just stand here in the blistering sun. You'll get tetched. Jump in and I'll take you down the road a piece."

"I'm waiting for the bus to Longrono," Maris murmured, still not committing herself. But her knapsack was already in the Volks.

"I'll take you there. Where is it?"

That made them both laugh — the eager way he promised, when he didn't even know how far he was offering to go.

Maris hesitated. The bus might never arrive. Still, to hitchhike, if this was hitchhiking — No, she hadn't wagged her thumb.

Would it be better to refuse, stay here and get sunstroke?

Dragging her feet, Maris nevertheless walked around to the other side of the Volks and opened the door. She couldn't get in; there was no room. A portable record player occupied the seat, spinning out Bob Dylan or stuff like that.

The boy reached over from the driver's side to stop the record, lifted the player tenderly and set it next to the knapsack, taking up the song himself where he had broken it off.

"You put your eyes in your pocket and your nose on the ground," he sang, as they both got into the car. Then he spread a map over the steering wheel.

Maris leaned toward him so she could read the fine print. Inadvertently, her chin skimmed the shoulder of the boy's shirt.

"We're here," she explained, pointing to Puenta la Reina, which was too small a place to be marked. "This dot is the town I'm heading for, Longrono. Is it in your direction? I don't want to take you out of your way."

She looked up at him anxiously.

He had stopped singing, but he tapped his foot and nodded his head from side to side, as if he still heard the music.

"You're not," he assured Maris. "It's right on the road to

Burgos, where I'm spending a couple of days."

Maris settled back into her corner. Even then, the car was so small, they were almost as close as before.

"Burgos," she repeated. "I'll be there tomorrow myself." Then she added, disillusioned about public transportation, "that is, if the bus runs according to schedule."

"What time is it supposed to get to Burgos?"

"Eleven thirty."

"A.M. or P.M.?"

"A.M."

Why did he have to know?

When he set the map down between them on the seat, his hand brushed lightly against Maris's skirt. He started the car.

The air began to circulate. Maris took a deep breath. It was nice in the Volks, like being in a little playhouse on wheels.

"Where you from?" the boy inquired, without taking his eyes off the road.

"Massachusetts."

"No kidding! Boston?"

"Neville."

He grinned, as if what Maris had just said was the most wonderful thing he'd ever heard. "I live in Concord," he explained. "I haven't met a soul who speaks English since I left Barcelona. Suddenly, here you are, standing in the middle of nowhere, looking helpless, and you come from Neville, which isn't more than an hour from where I live. Isn't that fantastic?"

"Yes." It seemed just as marvelous to Maris. "But I'm not helpless," she told him firmly.

Laughing good-naturedly, he asked where she went to college.

"I'm going to the Sorbonne."

He looked impressed.

Maris had never heard of his college. She didn't tell him so.

He was meeting a couple of classmates in a fishing village on the southern coast of Portugal.

"What are you doing this far north?"

"Collecting material for my thesis on Hemingway. Naturally, I had to see Pampeluna. It wasn't that much of a detour. Don't you think *The Sun Also Rises* is a great book?"

Maris· hadn't read it. To cover her ignorance, she asked, "Why Portugal?"

"It's beautiful. You can live on next to nothing and swim all day. Though," he assured her hastily, "we're not beachcomber types. We'll all three be working. One guy's writing a novel — powerful. The other's going to paint."

"And you?"

A little pucker formed between the fair eyebrows.

"Explore."

"In Portugal? What is there left to explore?"

"My psyche. I want time for thinking. All these happenings at school never leave you a minute to yourself. Did you ever feel like you were whizzing along faster than the speed of light, not having the foggiest idea where you're going?"

"Yes!" Maris cried. "Yes, I know. That's why I'm here myself — to find direction."

She told him about her pilgrimage, feeling such instant kinship with this stranger that she confided freely all she hoped to discover.

He listened to her gravely.

"When you were in Pampeluna," she asked eagerly, "did you see the lovely statue of Saint James at San Saturnino, the one with the young pilgrim he rescued from hanging?"

The boy shook his head. Between the fair eyebrows, the pucker was forming again.

"There's another magnificent Saint James in Puenta la Reina," Maris went on. "And in the Portico of Glory at Santiago —"

"But what do these old statues have to do with a girl like you?"

"Their idealism — What you said you were going to work

on — exploring the psyche. Isn't that the soul? A pilgrimage is the same sort of thing; mine is, anyway."

"But I don't see that it's the same at all! Going to those churches, expecting statues to turn you on — that's too passive, docile. This age calls for action."

Maris felt so disappointed at his lack of understanding that she was almost angry. "What action is there lying on a beach all summer?" she retorted.

"Plenty," he answered patiently. "Like I said, I'm going to explore my psyche. Plenty of action. Digging down through the unconscious, stripping away layer after layer. What's your name, anyhow?"

Maris told him.

"Mine's Bron, Bronson Shaw. Look, Maris, what are you planning to do in this place we're heading for? Visit friends?"

"Oh, I don't know a soul in Longrono. I'm going to look at the Cathedral."

"And then?"

"Walk around, I guess. There isn't anything to do in a little Spanish town. I'm staying at the Inn."

"Why don't you stick with me? I'll take you to Burgos tonight."

Maris felt a tingle of pleasure. He wanted her with him!

"You were planning to go there tomorrow anyway," he argued, when she didn't immediately accept.

She nearly did. They could spend an hour in Longrono, see the Cathedral, cancel her reservation at the Inn and drive on. It wouldn't be a very drastic change in plan. Not to have to travel alone — And he was so nice!

But something held Maris back, a certain fear. Was it that, if she went with him, she might become helpless, passive, docile? Sticking to her itinerary assured her independence.

He didn't press her.

They passed through beautiful countryside, vineyards and cornfields set in folds of undulating earth. Then, suddenly, they encountered sheer, red cliffs.

"Isn't it lovely!" Maris exclaimed.

"What? The landscape? Oh yes, very. But when you think of the history of this area — the Inquisition, the expulsion of the Arabs and the Jews, the Civil War —"

"I know," Maris murmured. She didn't like to think of this aspect.

In Longrono, Bron stopped the Volks before the Cathedral. He twisted his neck to look up at the facade. At the very top, a warlike figure sat astride a charger with his sword upraised.

"Who's that up there?" Bron asked Maris. "Do you know?"

"Yes," she admitted, wishing he hadn't noticed the statue. "That's Saint James as the Moor Slayer. He's credited with having slaughtered, singlehanded, sixty thousand Moors around here. Not personally, you understand. He'd been dead for centuries. But at the height of the battle, he was seen performing this miracle."

Bron turned to Maris with an expression of deep revulsion. "A saint," he exclaimed incredulously, "an apostle, guilty of mass murder, genocide?"

Maris looked down into her lap. She felt ashamed of her Saint.

"In recognition," she felt forced to admit, "he got tribute from every farmer in Spain — so much corn for every ploughed acre, so much wine for every vineyard."

"Since he was out to perform a miracle," Bron reasoned, "why couldn't it have been a moral one instead of military? Why didn't he win the victory by peaceful persuasion, instead of letting his horse trample people? That would have been worthy of him. Might have changed the whole course of history."

"He didn't really do it," Maris cried miserably, defending her Saint. "That's just a legend people made up."

She turned to Bron, her eyes begging forgiveness, but she could tell that he didn't intend to excuse Saint James.

When Maris looked up at the statue again, she had the crazy idea that, in contrast to his behavior, the Moor Slayer's expression was benign, faintly apologetic, as if he were murmuring to the victims beneath the hoofs of his horse, "Sorry! This hurts me more than it hurts you."

"Well," Bron was saying, "you've seen it now. So, how about coming on to Burgos with me?"

Maris hardly had the strength to resist again.

"No," she managed to say, aware that her voice betrayed her regret, "there's another little place I want to go to before I reach Burgos, Santo Domingo de la Calzada. When Saint James held up that innocent boy who was hanged, the boy's father ran to the judge to tell him his son was still alive. The judge was having his dinner, just about to carve. 'It's no more true,' he said, 'than that this hen should stand up and the cock crow.' Whereupon," Maris told Bron, giggling, "the hen stood up on the platter and the cock began to crow! Ever since, they've kept live fowl in the church at Santo Domingo."

Bron was not charmed by the story.

"You're kidding!" he cried. "You don't mean you'd go out of your way to see a hen and a rooster cooped up in a church?"

"Every pilgrim stops to see them. There's even a verse describing the place in an ancient French marching song. Listen,

> When we were at Saint Dominic,
> We went into the church
> We heard the cock crow!"

While Maris sang, Bron beat time with his foot. When she finished, he said gently, as if she were a child he felt bound to enlighten, "Maris, man is no longer rooted in these legends. His destiny is determined by the technology of the future."

"I've heard all this before," Maris muttered, thinking of Jim.

She reached for the handle of the door and squeezed it hard. But she didn't twist it.

"That hen and rooster aren't going to turn you on," Bron

argued. "Skip them and come with me."

Inside Maris's head, a voice was whispering, If you don't go now, this second, you never will.

Still squeezing the handle, still hesitating, Maris made a great effort and opened the door. As fast as she could, she jumped out, afraid Bron would be hurt.

He wasn't. Sad, yes, and disappointed. But not hurt.

He held the knapsack up behind her while Maris put her arms through the straps. Then he spun her around by the shoulders and bent down and kissed her.

Before Maris knew what was happening, Bron had manipulated himself into the Volks again. He was driving off. She stood at the curb, watching the little red car disappear before her eyes.

"Wait up!" she wanted to shout after Bron. "I'm coming with you."

It was too late. He'd gone.

7

As Maris walked through the town, hunting for the Inn, she passed a pump, where women had come with jars to fetch water.

Other women stood in doorways, looking up and down the road. Their housework was done; the day held little more of interest for them. Their husbands, Maris had heard, spent the evenings in the cafe together. Apart from their children, these women had little companionship.

Many of them were beautiful, but rather sad. They stood, framed by the doorway, holding a child in their arms, while a slightly larger one clung to their long skirts.

Maris tried to make contact.

"*Buenos noches,*" she called, smiling.

But there was seldom a reply, or it was so soft that she couldn't hear it. No one had the courage to speak to this strange creature.

I must look like a monster to them, Maris thought, striding by alone, with my yellow hair falling loose on my knapsack.

What did they think of her impudent independence? Did they envy her? Or were they critical, because she didn't even have the modesty to cover her arms?

194

What was she going to do with this freedom, which was denied to others?

"*Buenos noches*," Maris called to an older woman, as she passed another house. This time, her brave, phrase-book Spanish brought a response.

Added to the already heavy knapsack, Maris felt the weight of her culture, which she carried with her. Burdened down by all this, she could barely stagger up the steps of the Inn.

The hospitality of the lady who ran the Inn was unbelievable. She acted as if Maris were her daughter, although, the landlady intimated gently, no daughter of hers would be allowed to make a pilgrimage alone. The nuns would take her with her class and they would stay at convents. Nevertheless, since Maris was in this fix —

Nobody spoke a foreign language, here in the country. Maris took out her phrase book. When she sat down to supper at nine o'clock she ordered *tortillas, cocido* and *torta*. She got what she expected: omelet, stew and cake.

After supper, the landlady offered her coffee candy.

"*Gracias*," Maris said. "*Me gusta muchisimo.*"

In bed, she tossed and turned, asking herself why she had left Bron, when he was so eager to have her come with him. Plenty of Americans traveled around in couples. Why was she so driven to preserve her selfhood?

Toward morning, she fell asleep and dreamed she was being trampled on by white hoofs. Saint James, sword in hand, grinned down at her over the flank of his horse and said, "Sorry!"

Inside her skull, bones were cracking. The sound was so terrible that Maris woke up. Never had she felt more thankful to discover she'd been dreaming. The bedsheets were drenched.

She jumped out of bed and opened the curtains. It was a sunny day. Leaning her elbows on the windowsill, Maris waited to recover from the nightmare. Her heart was still pounding.

So that was how it felt to be one of the vanquished, a Moor, a Jew, a Protestant, a non-believer!

Bron was right. Any saint who allowed such things to be done in his name, worse, who did the trampling himself —

Did she have to give up Saint James, too?

Was her maturity conditional upon this surrender? Did she have to give up Saint James, the way she'd had to give up Roland and, before him, Jim? Couldn't she have *anybody*, not even a saint?

Bron. She could have had Bron for a couple of days. On what terms? Would he, sooner or later, have asked, like Jim, Why not?

Suddenly, Maris had the feeling that she was being watched.

Yes. From an upper window across the way, a boy of fifteen or so, dressed all in black, was looking at her through spy glasses. The next thing Maris knew, there were boyish black figures with spy glasses in all the windows. A seminary, probably. This was as near as these strictly segregated boys could get to a girl, peeping at any who might be staying in the Inn.

Maris quickly closed the curtains.

Sex, she decided, was the same everywhere, whether your culture permitted or forbade it. The instinct was stronger than any training.

The bus which was to take her to Santo Domingo de la Calzada didn't disappoint her. She found a seat by a window. As soon as she was settled, two friendly priests across the aisle offered to share their sandwiches. Where was Maris going?

She explained, without regard to Spanish syntax.

A young nun sat next to Maris. She had a beautiful, thoughtful face. As the conversation between Maris and the priests continued, she listened and smiled but took no part.

Directly in front of them sat a mother with a baby in her arms. Although the baby was only a few months old, her ears had already been pierced and she wore tiny pearls.

Another little girl, about two, ran up and down. She was fascinated by the beads hanging from the nun's waist. Warily, she approached them, her little hand outstretched, looking up with large, dark eyes to see whether she dared. The nun sat perfectly still, drawing the child to her, yet not saying a word. Reassured, the child took hold of the beads. She looked up at the nun, enchanted.

Maris felt drawn to the quiet person beside her, almost like the child. There was something powerful in her serene silence. It must be wonderful to have such security, to know what you wanted to make of your life.

But to submit to that discipline, to wear those clothes, to own nothing, never marry —

How did they do it?

Turning to the window, Maris watched the passing scenery, thinking how different this nun was from the girls at College, who dreaded being called virtuous, who feared inhibitions more than the consequence of an action.

Looking out at the arid cliffs, with sun-topped mountains in the distance, Maris puzzled over these two extremes. Most Freshmen had to scrap the code they brought from home. What had been right for them before was labelled square at College. A Freshman had to choose — either she gave up her parents' standards or she wasn't with it.

Not everyone surrendered, Maris had to admit, noticing the lemon-colored houses with their red tiled roofs. A few girls stuck by the tradition they'd been reared in. Oddly enough, the others respected them.

But whichever way she played it, almost every girl felt that her security depended on wearing groovy clothes and having a man.

Maris recalled how desperate she was before she met Jim; how she looked out of the window and wondered, What's wrong with me?

Yet, this young nun expressed more security than any girl

Maris had ever known.

But I have it too, now, Maris said to herself, surprised. I have security.

Ever since she started the pilgrimage, people had suddenly shown respect for her, even her parents, even Lonsie. Those she'd met along the Way seemed to say, We're glad you came. You brought us something.

Her security didn't depend on a man anymore. It was in her.

Now that her pilgrimage was nearly finished, she felt what she could only describe as a proud humility.

Yet, that essential thing, that insight — when she reached Santiago, would it be there? Suppose, after all this, she didn't find it and she returned to Paris still confused about the future?

The bus drew in to the town of Santo Domingo de la Calzada, Saint Dominic of the Causeway. Maris put on her knapsack.

The priests said goodby regretfully. The nun smiled. The little girl dropped the nun's beads and waved. The mother and the baby were asleep.

Walking toward the church, Maris felt in no mood to sing the French marching song. Bron had taken all the charm out of the legend which drew pilgrims here. She looked dutifully at the cock and the hen caged inside the church, but the cock wouldn't crow for her, it just fluttered.

Had Bron broken the spell which held Maris? Was she like the Sleeping Beauty, to whom a stranger's kiss —? She felt only pity for the poor creatures who belonged in the sunlight.

I belong there myself, she thought, running out of the building.

But when Maris was in the next bus, heading for Burgos, she suddenly thought of Saint Dominic of the Causeway, whose town she had just left. How stupid she was! She'd missed the whole point of the place. So taken up was she

with the childish legend of the cock and hen that she forgot
the Saint, who dedicated his life to the Jacobean pilgrims. He
gave them shelter at his hermitage in the forest, fed them,
nursed the sick, protected them from robbers. Seeing their
distress, when they were obliged to cross the River Oja, he
built a causeway for them.

There was something very noble about this Saint. He did
nothing spectacular, performed no miracles to prove himself.
He simply spent his life helping the people who passed by
his door. He was the great thing in the town that was named
for him, not the folktale.

No wonder Maris hadn't been moved there! She'd over-
looked the whole importance. She wished now that she'd told
Bron about Saint Dominic instead of reciting that silly Saint
James legend. He might have been more sympathetic.

The bus for Burgos made good time. When it reached the
terminal, Maris slipped on her knapsack and jumped out.

Instead of landing on the pavement, she was caught in a
pair of strong arms. The breath was squeezed out of her.

"Bron!" she whispered, "Oh, Bron! I never expected to see
you again."

"You didn't think," he said, laughing, "that I was going to
let you get away?"

8

THE LITTLE RED VOLKS STOOD BY THE TERMINAL. MARIS'S knapsack took its old place, next to the now silent record player. Bron held the front door open.

This time, Maris didn't hesitate. Jumping in, she felt instantly at home. But she was still knocked off center by the surprise.

"Where you staying?"

Maris gave the name of her hotel.

"I know that place. It's not far from mine."

They drove through ancient, crooked streets. There were almost as many priests and nuns on the narrow pavements as lay people.

Stopping at an intersection, Bron turned to Maris and smiled happily.

Their whole relationship was different. They were old friends now.

Maris told herself this was ridiculous. Twenty-four hours ago, they hadn't even met. But her reserve was crumbling.

When she checked in at the Hotel, the room clerk handed her a card, postmarked, Bordeaux.

"It's from the Addisons!" Maris exclaimed. Then she re-

200

membered that Bron didn't know. "I'll tell you about them later."

They had all signed the card, even Periwinkle, who wrote in painstaking block letters, with great dignity, *Sarah*.

A little bellboy stood near the reception desk, waiting to show Maris to her room. But she had to read the message to Bron first. It was in Peter's handwriting.

"Our anthropologist friend wonders whether, on your visit to Chartres, you saw the wampum belt presented to the Virgin in 1691 by the Abenaki Indians. Isn't that the tribe you told us about?"

The Abenakis! At Chartres! How unbelievable!

"My grandfather will be fascinated."

As Maris spoke, she had the funny sensation that she was living two lives at one time or one life on two planes. Bron knew nothing about people at home or even about the ones she'd met only a week ago. Superimposed on her past was this present encounter, a sudden wonder, charged with unpredictable excitement.

"A wampum belt at Chartres," she said slowly, trying to recall. "I don't remember that. How do you suppose it got there? Was it through the French missionaries, who followed Champlain to Maine? Maybe they told the Indians about the Virgin at Chartres and the Indians sent her a gift. Does that make sense?"

Bron shrugged, indicating that he not only knew nothing about this but he couldn't care less.

"Well," Maris said, seeing that he wasn't interested, "I can't figure it out till I go back to Chartres. Soon as I get to Paris —"

"Paris? I thought you were going to —"

"After Santiago, I'm returning to Paris."

"I thought," Bron repeated, looking surprised, "you were going to Portugal with me."

"I never said that," Maris cried.

She was furious. What did he take her for? They'd only

met yesterday.

The bellboy was still waiting.

Without another glance at Bron, Maris walked off. The bellboy led the way up a circular staircase.

Bron followed Maris to the foot of the stairs.

"Hurry," he pleaded, looking up eagerly, while Maris spiralled over his head. "I want to show you Burgos."

She pretended not to hear.

In the room, she had the awful feeling of being trapped. If she went back down, he'd work on her some more. She'd have to keep convincing him that she didn't intend to go to Portugal. The only way she could handle this situation was to stay locked in the room the rest of the day. When she didn't appear after a few hours, Bron would get the message. After all, it wasn't as if they had a date. She hardly knew him.

She threw herself across the high bed and buried her face in her arms. Did he really believe she would give up the pilgrimage now, so near her goal? Maybe he was only joking — testing her.

No. The way he caught her in his arms when she jumped down from the bus, squeezing the breath out of her — he wanted her to come.

I want to go, she cried out to herself. Not for keeps, just a week or two, long enough to take the edge off this unbearable loneliness. He's very attractive.

But she didn't love him. How could she, this soon?

He needed her. Wasn't that reason enough to go with him? Not that he'd given any indication of need. Maris just had that feeling.

She sat up and reread the Addisons' card. Each signature recalled the personality of the writer. Maris was overcome with homesickness for everyone, including Elsie.

What would Val think if she got a card from Portugal explaining that Maris had quit the pilgrimage and teamed up with some fellow who picked her up on the road?

To Val, sex meant marriage and family. Maris had always believed in this, too, not because of any moral code she'd been taught, but instinctively. There was something in her that wanted to make a total commitment. She still couldn't give a rational explanation for this. But she felt it in her bones, or had, until just this minute. Now, suddenly, she was considering — But only for a week or two. What was there about Burgos that made her see things differently?

She got up and washed her face, reasoning with the still reluctant girl in the mirror, who scowled back at her over the old-fashioned basin.

Is pushing on to Santiago alone the only way a person can grow up, for goodness sake? Wouldn't it be better to break out of this isolation? Wouldn't welcoming him give me more maturity than all the pilgrimages in the world? Until I open that door, like Lonsie, willingly and freely, I'll always be a child.

What makes you think that's in his mind? the girl in the mirror inquired, mockingly. He didn't suggest anything. It's a long drive to Portugal, that's all. He wants company. Maybe he even has a girl back home.

Returning to reality, Maris put on a fresh blouse and combed her hair.

At the foot of the circular staircase, Bron was waiting. He didn't mention Portugal again. His happiness in going around Burgos with Maris seemed to be enough. How superior he acted, showing her the sights, as if he were an old settler, instead of just another tourist, who'd arrived a few hours earlier!

And Maris felt silly for having imagined — Thank goodness, she came downstairs!

They walked along the river, passing a statue of the Cid, who was for some girls at College, those majoring in Spanish, what Roland had once been for Maris.

It was beautiful by the river. They were actually in a long park with statues and fountains and huge box bushes clipped like urns. At the end, they passed beneath an old city gate, the Arch of Saint Mary, and stood before the magnificent Cathedral.

"High Gothic," Maris said, feeling out of her element. "It's so ornate."

Inside, they went from chapel to chapel, overwhelmed by the riches, the carvings and paintings and statues and ornamental grilles.

When at last they reached the chapel of Saint James, they saw through the iron leaves of the grille that he was just another Moor Slayer, riding his white charger, busy trampling the faces and bodies of his enemies. His sword had fallen out of his upraised hand, but he still held his banner.

"Not again!" Bron groaned, turning away. "That does it!"

They wandered into the cloister.

Suddenly, Maris stopped and confronted Bron. She had to stand up for her Saint.

"Isn't he still the same man?" she asked angrily. "Isn't he still the peaceful fisherman who followed Jesus? He can't help it, if later generations misrepresented his character. That makes it harder for us to understand him, but it doesn't make him different. Isn't it *how* one looks at him that determines who he is?"

"I don't like him," was all Bron would say.

Out on the sunny street, they watched a little lamb being led to market. Old ladies with black dresses and headcloths and stockings padded by on flats, carrying shopping bags full of vegetables. One had a goose, whose sad neck dangled from the bag. Its lifeless head bounced on the cobblestones.

In a plaza surrounded by ancient houses with porticoes and galleries, a blind woman stood, selling tickets for a lottery.

Bron took Maris to a nice little restaurant. They had a good lunch, without talking very much. It was almost as if they had nothing to tell each other. Maris remembered that she had promised to speak about the Addisons, but she doubted if he'd really be interested. The thing he seemed to care most about discussing was himself. Then he surprised her.

"What does it all add up to?" he asked cynically, inclining his head in the direction of the Cathedral.

And Maris thought miserably, How can I tell someone like him, when I'm not sure myself?

She changed the subject.

"Are you going to be a Senior?"

"Yes. Well, depends. After this exploration, I may not go back. Who knows?"

"Not go back for your senior year!" Maris exclaimed, shocked.

Then she laughed. For her, of all people, to say such a thing! But it was different. She had three years left.

"You ought to be able to stand one more year," she argued.

He gave her a look of scorn. "You talk just like everybody else."

"Well," she murmured, getting up and placing *pesetas* on the table to pay for her lunch, "thanks for the ride. I'm going out to Las Huelgas."

"What's that?"

"A Twelfth, Thirteenth Century convent, a couple of miles from here."

"I'll take you."

He seemed so little interested in antiquity, why did he offer?

They drove to a village that looked completely medieval and passed under a crenellated arch.

"Kings and queens were married here," Maris told Bron, as they drove up before the Convent, "were crowned and buried here; knights received the accolade in the Chapel of Saint James."

"So what?" Bron muttered.

The nuns were in the Main Chapel. A crowd of tourists waited in the anteroom. Although the nuns weren't visible, their beautiful voices, singing in unison, came through a little grating in the wall.

Bron's whole expression changed. He looked transported.

Standing there, listening to those almost heavenly voices, Maris wondered what it would be like to be cloistered here, amongst the dead and the glories of the past. A shudder went through her.

"Now that," Bron said, when the singing ended, "that turns me on."

A guide led the tourists from chapel to chapel.

"It's modelled on the abbeys of France," Maris told Bron, "with Spanish and Moorish influence."

She felt relieved when they came to Saint James, for he was quite harmless, a Thirteenth Century wooden statue, polychrome and gold, seated on an altar with sword raised. But he wasn't hacking up enemies. His job was to dub knights. He had this visionary look, which characterized most of his statues. His arms were articulated, so that he could bring the sword down and whack a man into a knight.

"Bugs me," Bron remarked.

But Maris thought that this movable statue must have seemed miraculous in early times. Perhaps even today, the doll-saint delighted little nuns coming here from the country, younger than Maris, to be cloistered the rest of their lives.

The guide led the tourists out of the Chapel and into the Museum. They were shown cases of funerary objects uncovered not long ago, when some of the royal tombs were opened. It was a marvelous collection of woven and embroidered clothes in Moorish and Byzantine designs, still superbly colorful. Even the little nails taken from the coffins were displayed.

"Look, Bron. The nail heads are shaped like scallop shells! Aren't these brocades and tapestries magnificent? Wait a minute. I want to copy this design."

Maris reached down to take her notebook out of the scrip

hanging from her shoulder. It wasn't there!

"Bron," she cried, "my scrip — I've lost it. My money, my passport! I'm stranded!"

"You can't get into Portugal without a passport," he said gravely. "And you've got to have money."

Disregarding this, Maris tried to think. When had she last seen her scrip?

Oh! She'd put it down, for a minute, while she was studying Saint James. Against the base of a pillar —

She rushed back, her heart pounding.

Bron followed her.

"With all these tourists about," Maris cried hysterically, "someone has surely — I'll never find it."

But she hadn't reckoned with Saint James. When she reached his chapel, she saw her blue scrip lying at the base of the pillar, just where she'd left it. The Saint was keeping a watchful eye on it, waiting for Maris to return.

She picked it up.

"Just the way he upheld that innocent boy," she said to Bron, giggling with nervous relief. "Remember that one I told you about, who was unjustly hanged?"

9

"YOU LIKED THE SINGING, DIDN'T YOU?" MARIS ASKED, WHEN she and Bron left the Convent and drove back to Burgos.

"You bet! That resonance and clarity. The nuns must be young, judging by their voices. You know what I was thinking while they sang? That I'd like to blow the doors off the place, let them all out, so they could take a trip." He grinned. "Wouldn't that be great? I don't go for this chastity."

"The nuns I've met seemed very happy."

Bron turned to Maris almost in anger. "People should be free to communicate with anyone who wants to communicate with them," he told her flatly, "at every level, mental and physical."

"With *any*one?"

"Don't you believe in communication?"

"Yes. But —"

"Well, of course," he conceded, "if they happen to be married — then, maybe — But people like you and me should go all the way with no sense of guilt, no involvement or investment or commitment. Just, they meet, couple, and split when they get bored. No hard feelings on either side. That's how it should be — beautiful."

As he described his ideal, his face lit up.

"Without involvement or investment or commitment," Maris repeated slowly. "But I — I want to throw my whole self into such a relationship, not just mentally and physically, but with all my heart. I want to invest everything I have. How could I go away later saying I didn't really care? I *want* to be committed."

He turned to her in such astonishment that Maris suspected she might be the first girl he'd ever met who wasn't a push-over for his argument. He was so attractive! Had the others really gone away without hard feelings, or did he just choose to think so, avoiding responsibility?

They drove around town until dark and then ate.

"How about the movies?" Bron asked after dinner.

"No. I have to write home. And I'm leaving for Léon early in the morning."

"What time?"

She wouldn't tell him.

He took her to the hotel.

"Goodby," she said, drawing back when he tried to kiss her. "And I mean good-by."

There was something not quite honest about that. She meant it and she didn't. But if she wasn't firm, she'd never shake him.

After she climbed into the high bed, Maris had so much to think about, she couldn't go to sleep. In one afternoon and evening, she had seemed to live a lifetime and she was ex-hausted. First, briefly, she'd been an idiot and had indulged in that fantasy of going to Portugal with Bron just for a week or two. Only a few hours later, she felt revolted. "They meet, couple, and split when they get bored."

Maris was so hung-up on loneliness, she was in danger of succumbing to anything. Now she saw that there were worse things than loneliness. Going with the wrong person, for in-stance. She wanted someone who cared, who'd continue to care.

Bron had so much — looks, brains, education and a Volks. But she was lucky to be rid of him. Who knows what might have happened, if he'd worked on her another day or two?

When she went down to breakfast the next morning, there was Bron, waiting at the foot of the circular staircase.

Her first reaction was one of pleasure. He was snowed. But then she thought, I mustn't let him hang around any longer.

"I thought you were leaving for Portugal," she said aloud.

"Not without you."

"I'm not coming. I told you. I'm going in the other direction, to Léon."

"I'll take you there."

"It's out of your way. You're going south."

"I can go south later."

"But your friends are waiting for you. They'll worry when you don't turn up."

He laughed at that. "None of us ever worries."

He was like a bright balloon sailing through the atmosphere with its string dangling, unattached to any finger.

"I wouldn't like it," Maris said, "if someone didn't worry about me, when I was days late."

She thought gratefully of her father's insistence on a detailed itinerary, so they could always be in touch, and of the reservations he had made for her at hotels. She was free, on her own, but the string she trailed led back to Neville.

"Come on! Why struggle with trains, when you have the Volks?"

"After we get there, you'll go right on to Portugal?"

He nodded.

"Promise?"

He nodded again.

"It's a long way," she cautioned.

But after breakfast, she met him outside the Hotel. She stood by the car while he stowed her knapsack. He had a record on the player.

"I can't get no satisfaction,
I can't get no satisfaction
And I try and I try and I try and I try.
I can't get no, I can't get no —"

They drove off in jerks and bounces. Bron tapped his foot on the accelerator in time with the singing and nodded his head from side to side. If such a thing were possible, he was high on music.

Like the plainsong at Las Huelgas, which affirmed with heavenly sweetness the glory of God, this cacophonous defeat had moved him. He looked almost hypnotized.

Maris felt relieved when they got out of town without hitting anybody. The record stopped. They rode on in silence.

Maris thought about Jim. How they had talked and talked when they first met! They wanted to know everything about each other. After two dates, Maris could have recited the names of all Jim's uncles. He knew about her grandfather and life in Meddybemps.

But this boy wasn't interested in Maris as a person, nor anxious to tell her anything about himself. He seemed to have just one thing on his mind.

Shepherds with homespun blankets slung over their shoulders shooed goats off the road. In one small, sun-baked village, the goats were all over the place. Bron had to stop the car. He turned to Maris with an expression on his handsome face that she found both wonderful and frightening. He looked as if he'd fallen in love, deeply, truly in love.

But love isn't the same for him that it is for me, Maris warned herself.

"Let me tell you about this fantastic spot we're heading for," he said, when the goats were finally dispersed and the car could go on. "It's a little fishing village —"

"I'm going to Santiago! I've been looking forward to getting there for months."

"Why does it make that much difference?"

"What?"

"Whether you go there or someplace else? Have you taken a vow, stuff like that?"

Maris laughed. "No, I haven't taken a vow. But I started out to do this and — well, I want to finish."

"That's no reason."

"Maybe not. I can't give a reason, just that it's important to me."

"But me," he exclaimed petulantly, "don't you think I'm important?"

When Maris said nothing, Bron turned cold. "Up to you," he muttered.

After that, there seemed to be nothing for either of them to say.

The excitement they had shared only a day or two ago, when they discovered each other, so far from home; all that bound them together in these strange surroundings couldn't relieve the tension that Maris's determination set up.

She could hardly bear it. As they drove into the outskirts of Léon, she took refuge in the ancient pilgrim marching song, singing at the top of her voice until Bron broke out in a grin and hummed along.

> "When we reached the town
>   Called Léon
> We all sang together
>   This song.
> The ladies came to their doors
>   In a throng,
> To hear the pilgrims sing,
>   The children of France."

There were not many stanzas left. Léon was the last stage of Maris's pilgrimage. Tomorrow, she'd be in Santiago!

10

"Where you staying?"

"At the Monastery."

He rose to this. Maris knew he would. She giggled.

"The knights of Saint James built it in the Twelfth Century to protect pilgrims from robbers. Don't get excited! The monks have died out. It's a hotel now, still serving pilgrims."

"Can other people stay there?"

Maris caught on.

"Now, Bron," she exclaimed, determined to have it out, "You promised you'd leave when we got here."

"After all that driving?"

"Only a couple of hundred kilometers," Maris argued.

"I need food and a good night's rest."

Maris felt frightened. She'd thought it had all been settled in the car, when Bron muttered coldly, "Up to you." Now — Of course the Monastery took people who weren't pilgrims! How could she stop him from staying there?

A smiling Civil Guard with his hand on his holster gave Bron directions: keep left and go straight along the river.

"Wow," Bron exclaimed, when a huge, ornate facade appeared before them. "Is that it? Looks expensive. Oh, what the heck? One night —"

Maris was caught. Staying in the same place —

Inside, the Monastery was awesomely luxurious. The old simplicity was smothered by tapestries, oriental rugs, overstuffed furniture.

Checking in with Bron beside her, Maris felt embarrassed. If only there were some way to signal the room clerk!

But she was in Spain, a young girl, traveling alone. The room clerk had his own method of dealing with her predicament. He put Bron in another wing of the building, separated from hers by a courtyard.

As soon as she saw her room, Maris forgave the modern extravagance. Attached to it was a sumptuous tiled bath — in the old pilgrim cell! The bedspread was handwoven. There was even a telephone.

Bron was waiting when she came down. "Let's walk," he said.

How could Maris refuse to go with him, after accepting all those rides?

The moment she stepped into the streets of Léon, she was charmed. It was a small city. Roman ramparts still circled it. The Cathedral stood back from the bustling center. By the West portal, two or three old ladies gossiped in the sunshine. Apart from them, the place was deserted.

"It was built in the Thirteenth Century," Maris told Bron, "when pilgrims thronged down from France, bringing their stonemasons with them."

The West front was a warm rose in the afternoon sun. And there, part of the heavenly crowd by the door, stood Saint James, wearing Maris's grandfather's sailing hat! She was so pleased to see him, she could have thrown her arms around the stone neck. She remembered that evening at Meddybemps, when her grandfather showed her a picture of this very statue. At last, Bron was seeing one that did the Saint justice.

But Maris must shake Bron, once and for all. She wanted

to walk the last few miles by herself, up Mount Joy and on to Santiago.

"I'm skipping Portugal," he announced. "More fun going with you."

"No! No, you can't do that. I want you to leave me alone."

Maris's heart began to thump wildly. Instinctively, she looked around for help. There was no one, only Saint James.

What could *he* do? She didn't believe in the supernatural. Those old legends were made up by people in trouble, who had no weapon but their imagination. The legends hadn't saved them from disaster, but faithfulness had kept their spirit whole. Faithfulness to what they considered worthy of reverence invested the Saint with power, not magic, simply faithfulness. The Saint himself, drifting a long, long way in that tiny boat — even he, with his body chopped in two, remained whole to this day.

If only I — Maris cried out silently, pleading.

Her heart still thumped. But there was something in those gentle, far-seeing stone eyes that reached out and held her in secret understanding. And suddenly, it was as if Bron weren't there.

Just the two of them, Maris and this beckoning vision —

Slowly, calm and awareness returned to Maris. She looked around. *Bron wasn't there!* He really wasn't. He'd left her, at last.

Still bemused by that secret understanding, puzzled by Bron's sudden departure, feeling like a prisoner released, Maris walked around the Cathedral and discovered another statue of Saint James. He was wearing a different hat, very much like that funny one of her mother's, with an exaggerated crown and no brim. On the front was a large scallop shell. There was a large shell on his scrip, too. Smaller ones ran down the front of his robe, like a row of buttons.

His face was pensive, but strong and, above all, kind.

Inside, the Cathedral was superb, uncluttered, with marvelous stained glass. Entering, Maris felt the repose, the mystery, the celestial order which had moved her at Chartres. The windows were like pages of a huge, illuminated Bible.

Ethereal light was streaming down through the Western Rose, shining on Maris as she stood in the Léon Cathedral, thinking now about a distant country church, where the Virgin and Saint Anne had the features of Abenaki squaws.

She turned to study the rose and there was Bron, coming across the street with a coke. He hadn't left, after all! He entered the Cathedral and stood still in a pool of color, tipping back his fair head so he could look up at the clerestory and take a swig of coke at the same time. Then he joined Maris and offered her the bottle. She refused it.

When they left the Cathedral, they followed the ramparts to Saint Isidore, the Romanesque Pantheon. Maris looked at the frescoes dreamily. She didn't really focus on them. She was still far away, on an Indian Reservation in the Maine forest, seeing the faces of those living children, not the dead ones painted on these walls.

"Bron," she said, when they returned to the Monastery, "this really has to be the end. I mean it. It was great of you to bring me this far but I have to go on alone." She held out her hand and he shook it, looking as if he didn't really believe her.

She turned and rushed upstairs.

At nine o'clock, when she went down to supper, he was nowhere in sight. But as Maris entered the diningroom, Bron came toward her and escorted her to his table.

After dinner, he stuck so close that Maris couldn't speak to the hall porter about trains for Santiago. She didn't want Bron to know which train she was taking. That would be fatal.

The telephone by her bed — she could call from the room in privacy!

With another farewell speech, Maris took leave of Bron again, only too aware that he'd be waiting for her right here, at breakfast time.

As she started up the stairs, he said something that almost stopped her. "You've turned me on."

The handwoven bedspread had been removed. Maris curled up on a beautiful, soft blanket and telephoned to the hall porter. He answered in elegant English.

She was, she explained, making the pilgrimage to Santiago. At what time did the train leave tomorrow morning? Where should she get out so that she could walk the last lap?

The hall porter answered regretfully that it would be impossible to walk by the time Maris arrived at Lavacolla, which was on the road to Mount Joy. It would be dark. The train didn't leave Léon until afternoon. She would have to change at Monforte. By the time the local reached Lugo and Maris caught a bus — She must go straight to Santiago.

Maris thought she'd burst into tears. To arrive at Santiago without having climbed Mount Joy! Her first sight of the Cathedral must be from that hill.

"I wish to walk the last lap," she insisted. "Isn't there a morning train?"

No, only the four forty-five, which was much too early. The *Senorita* wouldn't get breakfast and at that hour none of the hotel personnel would be available to accompany her to the station, which would be necessary, since it would still be dark.

How far was the station?

A ten minute walk.

"I'll take that train," Maris announced. "Please have me called at four o'clock."

The hall porter tried to dissuade her. Very emphatically, Maris repeated her request.

She washed practically every stitch she owned and stood under the hot shower a long, long time.

Am I ever getting my money's worth out of this bathroom! she said to herself, as she spread her laundry on the heated towel rods. It would dry in no time.

When the telephone beside her bed woke Maris at four o'clock she almost turned over and went back to sleep. Coffee was what she needed. Maybe on the train —

The night porter was waxing the floor in the vestibule. He gave Maris the bill and she paid it.

"*Adios,*" Maris said to him, as she left the Monastery.

There was no one else about this early, Sunday morning. Maris almost lost her nerve. Here in Spain, a young lady wasn't supposed to travel alone even in broad daylight.

As her eyes became used to the dark, she found that the stars were intensely bright. She recognized Orion in the East, with Sirius just clearing the horizon. Cygnus, the Northern Cross, was already half lost behind the Cantabrian Mountains.

Maris wiggled her knapsack into position on her shoulder and set out boldly for the Bridge of Saint Mark, which every pilgrim who ever came this way had had to cross.

But as soon as she reached the bridge, her heart sank. On the parapets, deep bays jutted over the piers. Robbers used to hide in such bays, pouncing on unsuspecting pilgrims as they trudged past. Bron might be lurking there, waiting for Maris. As she came alongside, he'd spring out and, before she knew it, she'd be speeding toward Portugal.

That was ridiculous! Bron had no idea Maris was leaving. And he couldn't make her go with him, if she didn't want to. There might be a robber crouching in one of the bays, but Bron was still asleep at the Monastery. Hours from now, when he came downstairs and began searching for her —

Each bay was a little harder to walk past. It took more and more courage. Maris tried to concentrate on the pilgrims who had braved this bridge before her. She was, she reminded herself, only one in a long procession, part of history. Her feet were following thousands, maybe millions of frightened, weary feet. Still others would follow hers.

Safely over at last, Maris drew a deep breath. All that remained was a short walk along the river. It was still terribly dark, but she could already see the lights of the station.

She looked down at the water flowing under the arches of the ancient bridge and glanced back at the huge facade of the Monastery, outlined against the stars.

Imagining Bron's disappointment, when he discovered she was gone, Maris felt sorry. She knew what it meant to have someone you cared about desert you. She felt really sorry for Bron, but she owed him nothing.

It wasn't like Jim, who owed her everything, when he rode off on his Honda, out of her life.

Jim had treated her badly.

As she walked on, Maris wondered suddenly whether she had treated Jim just as badly. This surprised her. She'd always thought he was entirely to blame. But perhaps she — Was it possible that she was responsible, too? This had never occurred to her until now, as she walked in fear through the dark streets of a Spanish city.

With Jim, she had certainly been living in a legend, trying to make it a reality by insisting on its coming true. Yet, that special quality Val had called essential, that ageless vitality was missing. Deep down, didn't Maris know all along that she and Jim couldn't stay together? Their objectives were too divergent.

He wanted to make her into the girl he was looking for; she wanted to become herself. She longed to be committed forever; he for a while. He'd been quite honest about it.

Jim had never suggested that their relationship was for keeps. Maris was the one who kept talking about marriage. Even if she had gone to his room that afternoon, a time might have come when he would have ridden off on his Honda, anyhow.

Knowing this, why had she rocked his universe, going so far, unwilling to go further?

He had begged for sexual satisfaction and she offered him

a scallop shell. It signified all her aspiration, it was the greatest gift she could have given him. But it was not what he desired. And when she finally acquiesced, he sensed that it wasn't with all her heart. She was grateful to him now for not taking advantage of her when, for the moment, her defenses were down.

What she regretted was that she had made Jim suffer. Not intentionally; she'd simply been stupid. Yet Jim's suffering must have been as acute as if she'd meant to hurt him.

When you're dealing with another human being, to be stupid is as bad as being bad, isn't it? Poor Jim!

All at once, it seemed that Maris had a great deal to account for; that she was unconsciously carrying a burden far heavier than her knapsack. Exactly what was in the other leaden bundle, she didn't fully comprehend, but the weight became so crushing that, at the entrance to the station, she had to stand still.

She couldn't take another step. She wondered how she could go on living.

Standing there, she saw that overhead, Capella, the giant amongst stars, was riding high. And there was her old friend, the Milky Way!

Maris was gazing through it, like Charlemagne in the window at Chartres. Suddenly, her eyes plummeted earthward, energy galvanized her, she rushed into the station. The train, she mustn't miss that train!

For the Milky Way was drawing Maris westward to Santiago, drawing her as irresistibly as it had drawn Charlemagne, almost twelve hundred years earlier.

part 5

I

THE TRAIN WAS CROWDED.

Maris found a seat by the window in a compartment full of sleepy men and one woman, who clung miserably to her husband's shoulder.

Day was breaking. The people tried to rouse themselves, but the compartment was so stuffy, after they'd slept in it all night, that Maris almost went back to sleep herself.

In her scrip, she had some bread left from yesterday's lunch. Breakfast was clearly not going to be served on the train.

Eating her last crust, Maris was reminded of one of the miracles in the *Golden Legend*.

> There was a man went to Saint James and his money failed him by the way. And he had shame for to beg and ask alms, and he laid him under a tree and dreamed that Saint James fed him. And when he awoke, he found a loaf, under ashes, at his head. He ate sufficiently twice a day of the same loaf and always in the morn he found it whole in his satchel.

This morning, a hungry pilgrim's pathetic hallucination had real meaning for Maris.

It was light now. Everyone was beginning to sit up.

Submarine sandwiches, stuffed with sausage, issued from newspaper. They were pressed on Maris with touching generosity. She was so thirsty that she almost took a sip from somebody's wineskin.

Everyone talked, except the clinging wife who, it appeared, was carsick. She sat opposite Maris, by the window, where she could lean out quickly, when necessary. Between bouts, she was quite attractive. Obviously very interested in Maris, she did her best to sit up and converse.

"*Sola!*" she cried incredulously, like all the other Spanish women. But then she turned green again.

The jolly little man beside Maris began playing his harmonica. Another one had a portable player with scratchy jazz records.

Maris thought of Bron. He'd be waiting for her now in the breakfast room at the Monastery. Or maybe he'd already discovered what happened and he was driving to Portugal. No, Bron was still asleep.

The carsick lady must be feeling better. She was getting talkative. Maris had visited Léon? Had she seen The Virgin of the Way, that magnificent new church? Such uplifting modern architecture! Her eyes shone.

Alas, Maris had been so taken up with the medieval and with Bron that she'd overlooked it. A late Twentieth Century church on the Way of Saint James! It would have been interesting.

At Lugo, Maris had to leave her new friends. They said farewell as if they'd known her forever.

Lugo was an ancient, walled town with a Gothic cathedral. Maris would have liked to see the statue of Our Lady of the Large Eyes. The name intrigued her. But she had no time for sightseeing. She only just managed to pick up a bottle of mineral water.

When she got on the bus, someone, seeing the shell on her

beret, jumped up and paid her fare. Maris felt embarrassed. It wasn't the first time this happened. There were still people who felt obliged to help pilgrims.

Leaving Lugo by the Gate of Santiago, the bus crossed the River Mino and climbed a steep hill.

How glad Maris was to have that mineral water! She felt lightheaded. No breakfast, no lunch. Leaning back with her eyes closed, she seemed to experience a strange clarity. Something was unfolding within her, like the opening of a bud in sunlight, promising to transform her when it reached maturity.

She didn't try to hurry it. The mysterious thing had to develop on its own. Maris was so tired, she couldn't concentrate, right now.

Dozing off, she came to for a minute. She'd been dreaming of writing to Jim, telling him she was sorry.

Once, when the bus stopped abruptly, she realized that she'd been dreaming she was back at Chartres, looking at the Roland Window, studying the medallion in which the angel spelled out Charlemagne's secret sin — a sin so terrible, he couldn't bring himself to confess it. But when the angel waved a scroll in his face on which was inscribed the name of the sin, Charlemagne repented and was pardoned. Charlemagne didn't know how to read, but this inconsistency didn't trouble the Thirteenth Century glazier.

Over the years, people were curious about the nature of this sin. They speculated that it must have been sexual.

No, Maris thought. That's too personal. It would have had to be something universal to be commemorated at Chartres.

Wasn't it more likely that, at the end of his long life, Charlemagne suffered secretly because he'd killed all those infidels? At some point, he must have recognized that they, too, were people. Even in the Middle Ages, man must have known, deep in his heart, that to kill in the name of Christ was the worst sin of all. Charlemagne simply hadn't loved.

To the glazier, God's mercy appeared so great, it could

pardon even that.

God forgave Charlemagne, Maris thought sleepily. Did Charlemagne forgive himself?

Although it was only sixty miles from Lugo to Lavacolla, the bus took three hours. When it reached Arzua, Maris woke up, regretting that she'd slept so long. She'd missed seeing the place where, according to the *Guide*, pilgrims used to pick up a stone and carry it as far as Castaneda. There, it was made into mortar, when the Cathedral at Santiago was under construction. Thus, every pilgrim, however poor, had a little share in the building.

The country Maris was passing through was extremely beautiful, full of chestnut trees and oaks and grazing cows. The road crossed narrow valleys with vineyards, undulating toward the horizon, like waves in the sea. It went by Romanesque churches and ancient ruins overgrown with ivy and gorse. The ploughed earth was red. Then they came to stretches of orchards and larks flew out of the trees.

The bus driver pointed to the Pico Sacro, outlined now against the horizon — the Sacred Peak, which Maris had read about, a counterpart in nature to those spires in Santiago.

Seeing the Sacred Peak, Maris knew they were nearing Lavacolla. She took out the *Guide* and read.

> A certain river, flowing near Santiago, waters a wooded country called Lavamentula, because it is there that French pilgrims, for love of the Apostle, are in the habit of washing their chins. Also, after stripping off their clothes, they cleanse their whole bodies.

The modern name of the place, Lavacolla, evidently signified that, in later times, the pilgrims also washed their necks!

The driver stopped the bus and let Maris off on the main road, before he turned off to go to the Airport.

Now she was walking to Santiago! A mile from here, she'd

stop to climb Mount Joy. The driver had told her to keep on
the main road till she saw an ancient fingerpost pointing left.
It was marked San Marcos, the modern name for the Mount.

The weather was marvelous. Shouldn't Maris be singing
now?

But she was depressed, maybe because she was hungry. And
she was still thinking of Jim, not of what she'd done to him;
what she'd done to herself. She had allowed her self to become
so absorbed in herself, she couldn't see anything else. She was
plenty old enough to take her place in the world. She wanted
to. Yet, she was disengaged, wrapped up in her own preoc-
cupation.

And she was homesick, not lonely. She was thankful Bron
wasn't here or even Lonsie. But she was deeply homesick.

It was curious that she should be thinking about her parents
and George and Jack, wondering what they were doing today; wishing she could see her grandfather. At College, in
Neville, all Maris had dreamed of was being here.

Yet, now, in the very act of fulfilling her dream she thought
of home. She hoped there were letters waiting for her in
Santiago.

Would the place fail her? If, after all this, she didn't find
answers to those questions —

There it was, the ancient fingerpost, just as the driver had
said, pointing to Mount Joy!

Maris turned off the road and started up a steep lane, which
was so darkened by heavy pines, it was a little scary.

But this was a momentous occasion!

She thought of the *jacquots*, who'd walked all the way from
France, trudging up here for their first view of the Cathedral
spires, of how, when they finally reached the top, they turned
to each other, shouting, "Joy! Joy!"

She passed farms with stone walls, which reminded Maris of
New England, only that the roofs of the barns were of red tile
and **the corn cribs** were built in a style characteristic of Galicia,

this province of Spain, with a cross at the gable of one end
and a fertility symbol in the other. The tradition must go
back to pre-Christian times. The hay stacks were rounded,
beautiful golden mounds.

Maris passed an old lady pulling a cow by a rope, and a girl,
about her own age, being followed by sheep. The old lady
spoke to Maris in a dialect that was quite unintelligible, but
the girl was too shy to give a greeting. They looked very poor
and more like a part of antiquity than like people living in the
present.

The knapsack and scrip were growing heavier and heavier,
although Maris had only walked a mile. She had three more
to go, before she'd reach the Cathedral in Santiago.

When she came to the top and actually saw, in the valley
below, the three spires, blazing in the afternoon sun, she forgot
her fatigue. She began singing to herself the next-to-last stanza
of the French pilgrims' song:

> When we reached Mount Joy
> We were joyous.

There was nothing up here but a deserted little chapel and,
all around, a ring of mountains. Gazing at those three spires,
Maris felt such excitement that she couldn't get her breath.

But her excitement fell flat as, looking around, she saw that
she was alone, that there was no one to hear her, if she shouted,
"Joy! Joy!" There was no one to whom she could announce
her dramatic arrival, no one to marvel at her coming all the
way from America, no one to share the joy. She was the only
living soul on this hilltop.

Beyond the windswept trees, the violet mountains encircled
all Maris could see of the world.

Yet, unlike Charlemagne, on the other side of Compostela,
hurling his spear into the sea at Finisterre saying, "Farther
than this, no man can go," Maris knew there was much more
to the world than the little that was visible from here.

No one to share her joy with? *No one?* Why, she had the whole universe, if she could only make herself heard. If she could learn to express this elation effectively enough, a great many distant people who were now desperate could hear her and, hearing, would respond, "Joy! Joy!"

The realization shook her. She felt she was on the edge of a great discovery.

And it came to Maris, like the urgency of the breeze blowing in from the Atlantic and lifting her hair, that she didn't have to give up Saint James in order to act like an adult. Just the opposite. She had to dedicate herself to him with fresh intensity, more mature understanding, through service that only a grown-up can render.

Because she knew suddenly — this minute she knew — what she wanted to do with her life.

It was to present the Saint as he really was — the humble fisherman who went out to preach the brotherhood of man — not the legendary figure, created centuries after his death, encrusted with as many superstitions as cockle shells, transformed into a little hero for one exclusive race, one nation, but an irresistible cosmic force, present in every person, no matter what his skin or his allegiance, no matter what name he gave his god.

Maris couldn't make a statue of this saint out of stone or wood; she couldn't construct a translucent portrait from hundreds of little pieces of glass. Who knows what he looked like, anyway? She wasn't an artist. But somehow, if she poured all her energy into it, she could translate his essence into her own action.

She opened her scrip and took out the shell she'd picked up, three thousand miles beyond Finisterre, on the other side of the Atlantic, and held it in the palm of her hand, looking at it a long, long time.

"This is for you," Maris had said solemnly, when she offered it to Jim, that day at the beach, "the badge of Saint James."

But till this moment, on Mount Joy, Maris hadn't really known what the badge of Saint James signified. It meant a great deal more than a pretty little keepsake, a kind of talisman. It was an obligation.

Turning to the three spires in the distance, that looked like candles burning in the afternoon sun, Maris suddenly felt a rush of impatience, an eagerness to run down the hillside and begin her life.

Why spend a year knocking around Paris? Medieval geography and Romanesque architecture wouldn't, of themselves, do anybody any good. Maybe later —

I don't have a minute to waste, she thought. Paris would be a lot of fun, but, right now, I've got too many other things to do.

She'd go home and prepare herself to interpret what she'd experienced. Val had known this all along — that, whatever Maris planned to take up, she'd have to finish College first.

How she wished Val were here, so she could tell her! Val would cry, "Joy! Joy!"

There was something else Maris would say to Val, if she were here: that she'd decided to give up this shell. That night, when Val suggested giving the shell away, Maris had thought she couldn't part with it.

"Not now," Val had said, "but when you reach the end of your pilgrimage, you may wish to."

Maris wasn't quite at the end of her pilgrimage, yet she already knew that the moment had come to separate herself from this particular shell, which Jim had once grabbed as she was gazing into its silvery cup and had pitched savagely across the sand. It was indeed the badge of Saint James, but to Maris it also represented James Grant. Because of this, she didn't really want it anymore.

She closed her fingers over it hard. If she didn't keep squeezing, if she looked at it again, she might change her mind.

How to set about finding this outsider Val had spoken of —

someone who, like Maris, wasn't a *bona fide* pilgrim and therefore didn't rate a shell from the Church, but who was also looking for the meaning of life?

This could turn out to be very difficult. When Maris reached Santiago, it would be late. Where was she going to begin hunting for such an odd person?

Every other pilgrim arrived without a token of pilgrimage and returned bearing one. Maris Miller was bringing one and she would fly home empty-handed.

As she started down the hillside, so impatient that she almost ran, she held the shell tightly, cherishing it for the last time.

2

WHEN MARIS CAME DOWN FROM MOUNT JOY, ELATED AND
eager, she found the Pilgrim Cross, which marked the place to
which Saint James brought the dead man from Lorraine and
his friend, who nursed him in the Pyrenees. The Cross stood
by the wayside, in front of a cornfield.

Maris remembered how that story from the *Golden Legend*
had positively scared her, when she was in the Pyrenees herself, standing on the bridge between France and Spain, not
knowing whether to go on or turn back.

How glad she was now, that she had gone on!

If only she could have believed in the miracles of the
Golden Legend, she wouldn't have been so scared, because
when the pilgrim who stayed behind to care for his sick friend
was

> . . . sore afraid, for the place which was solitary and
> for the cruelty of the strange people, and for the
> darkness of the night that came on, anon Saint James
> appeared to him in likeness of a man on horseback
> and comforted him and said: Give me that dead body
> tofore me, and leap thou up behind me on my horse.

232

And so they rode all that night fifteen days journey, that they were on the morn to see the sun rising at Mount Joy, which is but half a league from Saint James.

The sun rising on Mount Joy, Maris repeated to herself ecstatically, *which is but half a league from Saint James!*

It was mid-afternoon, but Maris had seen her sun rising on Mount Joy. She could hardly wait to rush forward and greet her new day, to experience and savor whatever it might hold.

She wasn't scared of anything now, not even the Dean at College. Thinking of him, as she continued along the main road, she laughed out loud.

Wouldn't that fathead be surprised, when Maris turned up to register!

The first thing he'd demand to know was, What did she plan to major in?

But this time, Maris wouldn't be put off by him. It didn't matter, really, which courses she elected. Almost any field would prepare her for teaching — not subject matter, but a way of looking at life. Maybe, when she graduated, she'd go to some developing nation and help, to Africa or South America.

Developing nation! she thought then. What is the United States, finished?

It's developing, too. Those Indians. I don't have to go to Africa or South America. There's plenty left to develop, right at home.

Those children who'd so haunted Maris in Léon that she hadn't been able to concentrate on the antique frescoes she was looking at — suddenly she knew how much they needed her.

Maybe she could learn Abenaki and study their history, which no one seemed to know much about. She could give those children an awareness of their tradition, pride in their inheritance. Her grandfather had told Maris, when he took her to the Reservation, that this pride was the first step, the essential impetus, if the Indians were ever to extricate themselves from a seemingly hopeless situation. A sense of identity —

I know how to find old things in libraries, Maris thought, striding along the Way of Saint James with new energy. I could look up Champlain's voyage — see what happened when he found the Indians on the coast of Maine, in the first years of the Seventeenth Century. The missionaries must have kept records, too. They'd tell about the Abenakis.

Those smudgy blond children, whose white fathers copped out, needed to know about their Indian heritage. The tribal folklore must be full of good stories. But it would be important to tell the stories well. The children must be excited by them, come to *care*.

So many possibilities! Maris hardly knew where she'd begin.

All her fatigue left her. She was raring to go. Even before reaching Santiago, she'd found her direction. If it weren't for that Twelfth Century statue in the Portico of Glory, she wouldn't even stop to visit the Cathedral. She'd rush right home.

"Who knows what I'll discover?" she had asked her father, when he insisted that she have a definite plan to carry out after the pilgrimage.

Remembering that, Maris laughed again. It struck her so funny. This was the last thing she'd expected when she left home, dreaming about climbing Mount Joy: that the lane going up there would lead back to College!

Oh, she thought, suddenly troubled, I have a reservation at that hotel beside the Cathedral, the place Ferdinand and Isabella built for pilgrims. Father wrote them I was staying a week or two.

They'd have to release her. The minute she arrived, she'd explain that her plans had changed and she was leaving tomorrow for the United States.

No, she'd have to return by way of Paris, pick up her stuff and Lonsie's, inform Mlle. Berthe that she wasn't going to spend the winter, after all. Then she'd hop the next plane for Boston.

She couldn't wait to see everybody, to announce her decision about College, to have as much fun with George and Jack as she'd had with Selwyn and Ian. She'd ring up Lonsie and ask her to share a room again. She'd go to Meddybemps and explain to her grandfather about the real Saint James. And when he heard that she was going to help his Indians —

Now, it was downhill all the way, into the setting sun. When Maris reached a bridge, she knew she was crossing the Sar, that river which, according to the *Pilgrim's Guide*, lies between Mount Joy and Compostela. She was nearly there!

Ahead, the road was suddenly full of men, women and children, wearing their Sunday best, carrying gourds and ears of corn. They were going to the Cathedral, too, but undoubtedly they brought certificates and when they got there, they'd be given a shell.

Maris had traveled a thousand miles over the Way of Saint James, yet these were the first pilgrims she'd seen.

Evidently local people from some outlying parish, they hadn't made the detour up Mount Joy. To them, seeing the spires from the hilltop wasn't the emotional climax that that first sight of the Cathedral was for pilgrims who had traveled all the way from France or England or Germany and the Low Countries, even from America!

These people, who looked poor, whose faces were weather-beaten and lined, had walked this road all their lives.

Even the children were solemn, as they trudged beside their parents.

Coming up alongside the group, Maris gave the ancient pilgrim password.

"*Dios ajuda y Santiago!*" she cried excitedly — God and Saint James help me!

Either these people didn't know the password or they couldn't understand Maris's Spanish. They didn't reply, as pilgrims would have done once, *"Dios ajuda y Santiago!"*

There was something paradoxical about this that troubled Maris. She didn't mean the words literally, only historically, even playfully; she wouldn't have said them in prayer. These pilgrims, who undoubtedly did ask God and Saint James for help, said nothing. The discrepancy needed to be thought out — not now, at a future time. Maris had to be careful to say only what she actually meant.

She was greeted with reserve, in contrast to the easy friend-liness she'd encountered in trains and buses. Country folk, she realized, were everywhere suspicious of strangers.

But Maris herself felt a curious kinship with these simple people who, bearing their primitive offerings, were walking her way.

A boy brushed past her. He was holding a stick with a gourd tied to the tip. The gourd bobbed up and down with each step he took.

This was the calabash, the medieval pilgrim's canteen. In the old days, it had carried water for the long, thirsty march. Now, the gourd was chiefly a symbol, since the modern pilgrim carried his drink, more apt to be wine than water, in a goatskin.

Maris thought the boy ought to be singing the ancient French couplet,

> My calabash is my lass,
> My pilgrim staff's my friend . . .

But, like all the rest, the boy was silent.

Maris came abreast of an old lady, who was all in black, even to the kerchief tied under her chin.

The old lady's lips kept moving. She must be saying prayers. In her brown, work-worn hand, she carried a stick from which hung an ear of yellow corn.

Didn't Maris have an offering, too? She clutched it tightly in her fist.

She had earned the right to walk shoulder to shoulder with these pilgrims. Like them, she was moved by one desire, to reach a place from which to start out again, fresh.

When they arrived at the Cathedral, the pilgrims and Maris would do things differently. Over the centuries, a whole ritual evolved, which was peculiar to the veneration of Saint James, beginning with the fitting of one's hand into the five-fingered groove, when one entered the Portico of Glory. These rites, which had so much meaning for the others, were only of historical interest to Maris. Yet, she came reverently.

This was what people hadn't been able to understand, when she announced her intention of making the pilgrimage and they exclaimed, "You're not a Catholic, are you?"

What difference does that make? Maris wondered. Why do people create a block?

Throughout history, so-called religious devotees had insisted on raising these artificial barriers, willingly sacrificing their lives and, even more willingly, the lives of others, in defense of hair-splitting doctrines. But now, at last, the world was entering on an era of new insight. In Maris's own lifetime, religious men were raising themselves above these petty differences, reaching out to one another in the recognition of their common humanity.

For thousands of years, enlightened people must have yearned for this marvelous moment in history. It hadn't arrived until Maris's time. She could build on their hopes. What a trust! It was sobering, but glorious.

She felt like a pioneer, walking this road, one who came, not bearing the name of any particular sect, but unchurched, open in heart and in mind, going to Saint James.

In the doorway of bleak farmhouses, surrounded by hens and goats, women stood, watching the pilgrims go by. So, over the centuries, in these same doorways, their forebears must have stood, watching this never-ending procession.

And Maris was part of it, certificate or none.

They reached a crossroad. The open fields were left behind. Suddenly, they were in town.

The old lady turned to Maris and announced, *"Puerta del Camino."*

Maris felt a thrill of excitement. *The Gate of the Way!* She was entering the walls of Santiago de Compostela!

3

The town was beautiful.

It had narrow, winding, ancient streets. The gray stone houses, softened by lichens, were crowned with red tiles. Some of their portals were surmounted by coats-of-arms or garlanded in sculptured fruit. Arcades with magnificent, weathered capitals bordered the shops.

The pilgrims, with whom Maris had walked the last two miles, seemed impatient to reach the Cathedral. But Maris was diverted by the shop windows. While she stayed with her companions, following them beneath the arcades, she went more slowly, stopping to peer in through the glass at an interesting bookstore, at the display in another window of uncomfortable-looking shoes, and, next door to that, at mounds of shellfish — half alive or completely dead — crabs and shrimp, octopus and goose barnacles.

Maris was starving, but these didn't tempt her.

Neither did the tripe in the next window, which lay on a platter beside a heap of pigs' feet. But farther on, there was a bakery with little cakes in the window. Maris wondered whether these were the ones she'd read about, that they made around here, out of pine seeds.

Turning from the bakery window, she found she'd lost the old lady. There was the ear of yellow corn, way up ahead! Maris was straggling at the end of the line.

Suddenly, bells broke out, all over town. They were somber, with a haunting, cracked resonance, that clutched at the pit of Maris's empty stomach.

She remembered how, in the Tenth Century, when the Moors conquered Santiago, they destroyed the Church of Saint James and took its treasure, placing the bells on the shoulders of their Christian prisoners, who had to carry them to Cordova. Then, three centuries later, when the Christians conquered Cordova, they placed the bells on the shoulders of their Moorish prisoners, who had to carry them back to Santiago.

How were those Christians any more Christlike than the Muslims? Maris wondered.

All at once, she stood stock-still on the cobblestones, letting the pilgrims pass out of sight. She couldn't go on. These haunting bells reminded her of something — bells she used to hear, when she sat on the window seat at College, waiting for Jim to round the corner of the Quad on his Honda. Those New England bells, tolling a long way off, sounded muffled and mournful, like these.

Hearing the distant ones echoing in her memory, Maris had had a sobering thought, which made her stand still: if she went back to College, wouldn't she, sooner or later, bump into Jim? Wasn't that really why she decided to leave?

She hadn't recognized it till this moment, though Val must have, when she asked whether Maris had run away. Yes, she did. She ran away.

She stood beneath the arcade, overwhelmed by the sudden revelation.

Could she go back and face the possibility that in some class or at some party or just crossing the Quad someday, she might bump into Jim? Would she run away again?

She felt so faint, she couldn't go on. Then she pulled herself together. What she needed was something to eat. She must find a restaurant and order a meal. Now she was in a town. At last, she could get some food.

But it would take too long to sit through one of those Spanish menus. Like other pilgrims, Maris was impatient to reach the Cathedral. She wanted to greet Saint James in the Portico of Glory, tell him she'd arrived, coming all the way from Massachusetts to behold him, face to face!

Besides, Maris couldn't relax till she'd parted with her shell. That was the first thing. If she put this off, she might weaken, not because it hurt to give up the shell — she didn't really want it anymore — but because she was afraid the person who got it wouldn't appreciate it. After all, hadn't Jim pitched it savagely across the sand?

A snack would take away this all-gone feeling. Maris went back to the bakery. It smelled nice. Those pine seed cakes weren't particularly appealing. Maris bought some chocolate covered cookies and munched them greedily, while she looked out through the open door of the bakery at the people strolling under the arcades.

In her left hand, she still clutched the scallop shell.

How was she going to find that strange person — the one who deserved it, who came without a certificate, making the pilgrimage according to his or her conscience? It seemed impossible.

You can't just go up to people in the Cathedral and ask about their religion! Maris thought.

Selecting a second — a sponge cake with white frosting — and standing by the counter, consuming it, she saw in a flash that finding this person would actually be amazingly simple.

When *bona fide* pilgrims reached the Cathedral, they didn't enter the Main Chapel right away. They stood out in the Portico of Glory, at the feet of Saint James, and pressed one hand against the marble column on which was chiseled the

Tree of Jesse. So many faithful hands had been pressed against that column, by centuries of pilgrims who arrived exhausted and had to steady themselves while they prayed, that a five-fingered groove had been worn into the marble.

With time, that act of steadying had become a rite, which was practiced down to the present day. Even those who came in cars, feeling fresh and rested, fitted their fingers into the groove and prayed.

Maris herself wouldn't do this. It seemed irreverent, a mockery, to go through the motions without believing in them. And the person she was trying to find, who wasn't a *bona fide* pilgrim, but who came, as she did, earnestly seeking truth, wouldn't press a hand against the column, either.

So, all Maris had to do was to stand beside the statue of Saint James in the Portico of Glory and watch everyone who arrived. The first person who failed to put a hand against the Tree of Jesse would be offered her shell. She hoped it would be somebody nice, somebody who'd appreciate it.

Hurriedly stuffing the last of the cake in her mouth, Maris left the bakery and walked on beneath the arcades, feeling stronger, even victorious. All the way to Santiago, she had, like a child, harped petulantly on the token of pilgrimage she wouldn't receive. Now, she was concentrating on the one she had to give.

But the Cathedral was hidden by buildings. She didn't know which way to go. Without the pilgrims to follow —

Ask somebody! Whom?

There were so many people! Pedestrians spilled over from the narrow sidewalk into the middle of the street. That woman with a tall milk can on her head and pails in either hand — much too big a load for anyone — she'd know. But Maris wouldn't ask her to stop.

Then, a class of boys, headed by a priest, caught up with Maris. Maybe they were pilgrims. She tagged along. Down a flight of stone steps, mellow with moss, under an archway and suddenly — yes, they were nearing the Cathedral.

She hurried around the corner and found herself in the enormous Plaza, facing the Town Hall. There on the roof, like Santa Claus, but riding a white charger and flashing his ugly sword, was that Moor Slayer!

Maris turned her back on him. She stood before the Cathedral where, way, way up, between two gigantic towers, above baroque windows and spiral columns, under a massive granite cupola, a more peaceable James awaited her, dressed like a pilgrim.

So that was how he spent the money which every farmer in Spain had been obliged to pay him annually, in return for his having trampled on the Moors! In the Eighteenth Century he built this fabulous facade.

It was the most gigantic, ornate edifice Maris ever beheld. But she knew that, once inside, she'd find Master Matthew's simple Twelfth Century Portico, its glory preserved.

She looked at those flights and flights of steps, leading to the Main Portal, and wondered how she'd ever make it with the knapsack.

Near the corner, a fat woman sat beside a little pushcart, displaying souvenirs and post cards. There were quantities of plastic shells in all sizes.

For tourists, like me, Maris thought wryly. She couldn't imagine buying a plastic shell.

At the far end of the Plaza stood her imposing hotel. Maris recognized the highly decorated facade from the picture on the prospectus, which the manager sent her father, when he confirmed the reservation.

Shouldn't she walk over there, check in, leave her knapsack and return?

No! That would take too long.

Maris started up the stairs of the Cathedral eagerly, but halfway up, she had to stop and get her breath.

Out of a clear sky, she exclaimed to herself, as she stood

there on the landing, I've forgiven him!

In that instant, she saw for the first time how angry she'd been with Jim, secretly hurt and bitter. Now, she held nothing against him anymore.

Suddenly lighthearted, Maris started up the last flight of stairs. She wasn't afraid to go back to College. She could face Jim now, be friendly, detached, kind, even.

It's not all that simple, she said to herself, slowing up again. I've forgiven Jim, yes. But have I forgiven myself?

Erase the record, begin over, with greater awareness. Like any pilgrim, Maris came for pardon. She had never dreamed of that, when she set out.

As she neared the top, she sang to herself triumphantly the last stanza of the French pilgrim's song. Weeks ago, she'd sung the first one for the Swiss fellow in the South Porch at Chartres.

Streams of people were going up the stairs, but no one made Maris want to sing out loud. Everybody's eyes were lowered, concentrating on each step, wearily anticipating the next one in that long flight. Or, perhaps, these people were meditating, gravely preparing their souls for the encounter with Saint James.

There was no one to sing to. If Maris had kept up with the old lady, she might have sung for her:

> When we reached Saint James,
>   By the grace of God,
> We entered the Cathedral
>   To pray
> To God and that glorious martyr,
>   Mister Saint James,
> That we might return to our country
>   And have a good journey.

Those old French pilgrims were just like Maris! All they thought about when they finally reached here was going home.

4

Puffing, Maris reached the top of the stairs.

But when she passed through the massive old doorway and entered the Portico of Glory, the whole weight of the journey, the fatigue, the loneliness fell off her shoulders, like the knapsack she laid at her feet.

There, in the central arch high over her head, sat Saint James, welcoming the entering throng. His chair stood on two little lions. He looked just the way Maris had dreamed he would, only more wonderful, more other-worldly.

Of heroic proportion, he rested one hand on his staff. Behind his head was a metal halo studded with rock crystal. His locks and his beard and the folds of his garment were magnificent. He wasn't burdened with a single shell.

It was the vision that held Maris, the eyes which seemed to be gazing beyond this place, westward, to a splendor unimaginable here.

Above the Saint sat Christ in majesty and angels led childlike figures toward the Arch of Glory. The little lions were perched on the capital of the beautiful old column, which was incised with the Tree of Jesse. And there, shoulder-high, very plain, was the five-fingered groove, worn into the gray marble through the centuries.

The underworld of monsters at the base of the column was almost hidden by a crowd of people who were lined up, waiting to fit their fingers into the groove and pray.

Maris squeezed her shell. She must stand here, watching each person till she saw someone fail to observe the rite. Only after she'd found this person and had placed the shell in his or her hand was she going to enter the Main Chapel.

Would she say something, explain that the shell came from the other side of the Atlantic? How could she possibly convey its significance in Spanish, or even in English?

The person she gave it to would take her for a kook. She'd say nothing.

She noticed that many of the people who entered the Cathedral wore ugly plastic shells, like the ones she'd seen on the pushcart outside. Maybe the custom of bestowing a token of pilgrimage on those who arrived with a certificate had gone out and the pilgrims had to buy shells themselves.

These plastic things were only symbols of symbols, Maris thought. Hers had once housed a living organism. It had been washed by the ocean and dried by the sun. It was a real symbol.

Taking the modern guide book out of her scrip, she identified the statues on either side of Saint James. They stood on beautifully decorated columns. To the left were the Old Testament figures: Moses, Isaiah, Daniel and Jeremiah. Daniel was grinning.

Maris read with amusement,

> It was said that he smiled at Queen Esther opposite, whose ample curves were reduced by order of an archbishop.

To the right were the Apostles: Peter, Paul, James the Less and John.

These were magnificent Twelfth Century sculptures, but

Maris's attention was drawn back to Saint James. She put the guide book away. Later or tomorrow, she'd look at everything. Now, she must dispose of her shell.

She stood on the edge of the crowd, gazing up at the superb statue, then down at the people who streamed into the Portico, anxiously scanning every face, searching for that rare individual who was not a *bona fide* pilgrim, yet who came to Compostela reverently seeking the meaning of life.

Several people looked like possibilities, but then they joined the line, waiting their turn to press against the column.

Out of the crowd, one figure emerged that made Maris hopeful. It was a girl about her own age, very colorfully dressed, who looked much more like a tourist than a pilgrim. She could be European or American.

She wore a crimson kerchief, a pink blouse and a short blue skirt. In her left hand she held a little wicker hamper and her jacket.

When Maris saw her white shoes, she was certain that the girl must be a tourist.

But then, the girl stepped up to the column and pressed her right hand against the Tree of Jesse, bowing her head. So Maris knew this was a *bona fide* pilgrim and not the person to receive her shell.

As she waited, Maris glanced through the Arch into the Main Chapel, down the longest nave she'd ever seen. It was dim, lit only by candelabra, which were suspended from towering Romanesque vaults.

On the High Altar, enthroned amidst incredible splendor and profusion, sat Saint James. He was so far away that Maris couldn't see his features clearly.

People sat on benches facing the High Altar. Some knelt before the confessionals along the side naves or simply on the bare, checkered pavement.

Maris couldn't wait to go in and sit down. She was feeling lightheaded. As soon as she'd parted with the shell —

Hopefully, she looked at a young man. Seeing what a nice face he had, Maris hoped fervently that he wasn't a *bona fide* pilgrim. She'd be glad to give her shell to him. If he just didn't get on line to press the marble column!

Unable to bear the suspense, Maris began to move toward him through the crowd, grasping her precious offering so tightly that it dug into her palm.

This must be very near to praying, the way she hoped and wished and willed that she might find someone who'd value her badge of Saint James.

The young man moved suddenly and took his place at the end of the line.

Overcome with disappointment, Maris felt she'd drop if she didn't sit down a minute. She'd have to give up her search for the time being. After a little rest, she'd come back and try again.

Lifting the knapsack, she walked into the vast Main Chapel. She felt faint and downhearted.

Who would think, she asked herself, as she collapsed on one of the back benches, that it would be so hard to give away a little scallop shell?

5

Sitting in the enormous Cathedral, Maris felt homesick again, not for Neville, this time — for Chartres. She longed for the radiance of those bright windows. They had illuminated her soul.

This nave, with its clustered columns supporting a deep triforium, was somber.

Yet, there was something else here. In place of overwhelming beauty, there was aspiration, reaching back to an age before the memory of man. Perhaps even in prehistoric times people had come here to worship. For some obscure reason, this spot was thought to be holy ground. By their coming, by their aspiration, men had hallowed it.

Maris looked at the rounded arches towering over her head, at the bronze pulpits and battle flags. Way, way down in front, Saint James was sitting under a fancy canopy on the High Altar. He was holding a silver pilgrim's staff topped with a golden gourd. Although the statue was ancient, it had subsequently been so covered with silver and diamonds and other precious objects that none of its initial personality remained.

How different from the statue out in the Portico of Glory,

whose utter purity made it seem almost divine! This one was more an idol than an ideal.

The monks of the Middle Ages believed that the sparkle of jewels and the glitter of precious metals reflected the glory of God. But Maris felt revolted. She could only think of the effort and privation which this wealth represented: the farmers who had been forced to contribute part of their meager harvest — a bushel of corn from each acre of land, so many casks of wine from every vineyard to support this edifice. She could only think of the slaves in the mines of Africa and, later on, America, whose lives had been squeezed out of them that this statue might sport jewels.

What connection was there between all that show and the young fisherman who left his nets when Jesus called?

Neither Jim's arguments nor her father's pleading, "Try for a minute to live in the Twentieth Century, Maris," not even Lonsie's prediction that she'd "get over" the Middle Ages, had made Maris feel so much a part of her own time as the display on the High Altar of Santiago Cathedral.

The unnecessary sacrifice filled her with shame.

Because she was still lightheaded, she was glad that the *botafumeiro* wasn't being swung right now, that giant censer suspended from the dome. The swinging would certainly make her dizzy.

She had read how, at great celebrations, eight men in scarlet cassocks pulled on a rope, hurling the censer from side to side across the transept, farther and farther above the heads of the congregation, creating in the worshippers a kind of ecstasy.

The censer wasn't swinging but, behind the Altar, there was continuous movement from South to North. Pilgrims were mounting a hidden stairway at the back of the statue in order to kiss and embrace its silver-caped, stone shoulders. After that, they went down to the crypt to venerate the Saint's supposed remains.

This was the climax of a *bona fide* pilgrimage.

Maris would do none of these things.

Opening her fingers, she gazed for perhaps the last time into the cup of her shell, recalling those words which still held enchantment for her:

> Give me my scallop shell of quiet,
>> My staff of faith to walk upon,
> My scrip of joy, immortal diet,
>> My bottle of salvation,
> My gown of glory, hope's true gage;
> And thus I'll take my pilgrimage.

As Sir Walter Raleigh walked in faith and hope to his execution, pilgrimage became the symbol of an even larger life. Like Saint James, like Roland, he turned defeat into victory, death into immortality.

The little rest on a back bench of the Main Chapel helped. Maris felt better. Eager to see the transept, she got up and walked slowly toward the front.

There was the Moor Slayer in a blood-red mantle, riding his white charger over the High Altar, having a time for himself, trampling heads!

Another, harsher word had breathed here too, so distinctly that it had not the power to die, either — a denial of the brotherhood and charity which the Church stood for, a twisted inhumanity not yet redeemed by all the sacrifice.

Bron was right. Saint James still had to perform a miracle: victory, not by fighting but by persuasion. He still had to convince men that the heads they placed beneath the feet of his charger — all heads, of whatever race — were, in a truer sense than they were willing to acknowledge, their own.

The whole thing was one great big contradiction.

Still, people kept on trying. They streamed through the Main Chapel and knelt on the hard pavement, facing the High Altar or one of the confessionals. They had come from who knows what part of Spain, traveling all day, perhaps, to spend an hour in the great Cathedral.

For the foreign pilgrims, there were signs at the confessionals, indicating where they would be understood. *Pro linguis germanica et hungarica*, it said in one; *pro linguis britannica et gallica*, in another. These went back to the time when there were a great many foreign pilgrims. Looking at the faces of the people about her, Maris doubted that there were very many now.

But the Chapel was crowded with visiting priests and nuns.

Maris thought of that Sister on the Indian Reservation, a long way from here, one of those who taught the Passamaquoddy children. She'd always wished to make the pilgrimage to Compostela. Maris, she felt, was standing in for her.

The Passamaquoddy children, halfway across Spain, haunted Maris. Now it came to her with surprise that the farther she'd gone, the more she'd been drawn back by those children. She'd gradually waked up to their desperate needs.

As soon as she got home, she'd do a lot of research on the tribal handicrafts that had died out. She'd look up the shapes and designs for basket work and show these to the children. Maybe later, she could find an artist who'd come to the Reservation and teach the Indians woodcarving, so they could make beautiful things again, the way that old man did, long ago, giving to the Virgin and Saint Anne the features of his people. Some day, there might even be an Abenaki Saint James!

Excited by the enormous possibilities, Maris left the Main Chapel.

But as she was about to return through the Arch to the Portico of Glory, she stopped before the statue of Master Matthew, the Twelfth Century stonemason, who created all this beauty. Just inside the Arch, he had left his own likeness, kneeling, facing the Main Altar.

It was a tradition — not a religious rite, but a fun sort of thing — for students to bump their heads against Matthew's, in the hope of knocking some of his intelligence into their skulls. Now that Maris was going back to College —

Giggling to herself, she bent down and bumped her forehead against the stone one.

Out in the Portico of Glory, pilgrims were still lined up before the Tree of Jesse.

And Maris was still clutching her shell. Tomorrow morning, when she wasn't so hungry and tired, she'd return here and wait until she'd found the person she was looking for. Then she'd fly back to Paris and start home.

How was she going to wait for that wonderful moment? Impatience pushed her out through the massive doorway.

Running down the steps of the Cathedral into the setting sun, with her face turned toward the New World, Maris put the shell in her scrip. Tomorrow morning, first thing, she'd be back.

For she was about to embark on still another journey, longer and more difficult, perhaps, than this pilgrimage. She had to start out unencumbered.

6

As Maris crossed the Plaza, she saw that people were sitting at little tables on the Hotel terrace. The tables held tea and coffee pots, tall glasses and platters of cake.

Coffee! At last!

Even before checking in, she sat down at one of the little tables. A waiter appeared. In no time, Maris was devouring a delicious chicken sandwich.

Is it ever welcome! she thought, feeling satisfied for the first time in twelve hours.

The coffee, served in a dainty cup with a proper napkin, was the best Maris had had since she left home. It cost more, too, than she'd paid elsewhere in Spain. But money didn't trouble Maris now. All that really mattered was her life work.

From where she sat, she could see the whole facade of the Cathedral, turned rose by the setting sun. It was a most fantastic, pompous edifice, yet Maris was getting fond of it.

Looking in the opposite direction, she saw, spread out below the terrace, beyond the red tiled roofs, a panorama of green fields with purple hills in the distance. According to the *Pilgrim's Guide*, the River Sarela flowed down there, to the West of the Town.

254

For a moment, Maris had the idea that here, amongst the tourists, she might find the person she was looking for. But a glance at the people sitting at the other tables told her there wasn't one who'd appreciate her shell. They were cosmopolitan, sleek, rather arrogant. Those fancy cars, parked out in front, undoubtedly belonged to them.

How different from the people she had seen in the Cathedral, the priests and nuns and humble country folk!

As soon as she finished the sandwich and coffee, she left the terrace.

Above the portal of this elegant hotel, which Ferdinand and Isabella had built for sick pilgrims, stood a row of stone figures in niches, surmounted by shells. At the top was Saint James, dressed like any other pilgrim, with his staff and broad-brimmed hat.

The interior of the old hospital was luxurious now. But it was furnished in excellent taste.

Maris startled herself by announcing boldly to the room clerk that her plans had changed. She was flying to Paris tomorrow.

He took the news without reproaching Maris because her father had made a reservation for a week. He even offered, in faultless English, to get her tickets. She'd have to fly from Santiago to Madrid and from Madrid to Paris.

"The bus for the Airport at Lavacolla leaves here at eleven o'clock in the morning," he told Maris.

The shell, she thought, panicking.

Would she find someone to give it to by eleven? She'd get up early. Surely, with nearly the whole morning to stand beside the Tree of Jesse — If she didn't see the right person, she simply wouldn't leave.

But she wanted to go home. She couldn't wait. An extra day would be unbearable.

The room clerk had disappeared. He returned with a stack of letters, which he handed to Maris. What a mail! She clutched the big pile joyfully.

A bellboy showed her to her room, leading the way past an iron grille to a courtyard with a magnificent fountain in the middle. There were flower beds bordered with box bushes and, at the end, a sculptured cloister.

When they reached her room, Maris decided that, though it was very Twentieth Century, the comfortable furnishings retained some of the austere dignity of the ancient hospital.

The bellboy retreated.

Maris kicked off her shoes and threw herself across the bed, rolling over on her stomach. She laid the letters out separately on the green damask spread.

From her mother, from Lonsie, from her grandfather — very fat and typewritten, which was unusual — from George! Imagine George writing to her! And a postcard with an Italian stamp and a picture of a Sixth Century mosaic, very beautiful blue and gold. It was signed, *Augusta Key*.

What a surprise! Mrs. Key remembered Maris. With ninety-nine other girls in the Hall —

The postcard, mailed in Ravenna, had gone to Neville and Maris's father had readdressed it. Mrs. Key had no idea that Maris was in Europe, too.

Seeing these marvelous old mosaics, she wrote, *I was reminded of you who, more than anybody else I know, love antiquity. I'll miss you next year but I like thinking that you are happy at home, pursuing your true interests. Do write in September and tell me how things are going.*

Nice Mrs. Key!

Maris could already picture her Housemother beaming with delight when, instead of writing to her, Maris appeared at College in person, a Sophomore!

She opened Lonsie's letter first. It was overflowing with congratulations. By the time this reached Maris, the pilgrimage would be finished. Lonsie was tremendously impressed. She knew, she wrote, from firsthand experience what hardships

Maris had endured.

That amused Maris. Hardships, in *Paris!*

Lonsie admired Maris but honestly, she was glad she herself wasn't in Santiago. Her parents were giving her an engagement party, a real blast. She was busy choosing silver and china patterns. Maris had no idea how much was involved in getting ready for a wedding.

George's letter touched Maris. He'd never had a good word for her before. Now, he was completely snowed. Maris might have been a football player.

Her mother was also exultant, but the praise was tempered by anxiety. Was Maris all right? The neighbors kept calling up to ask whether she'd arrived yet. They were all very proud of her. Maris had done something possibly no other American girl had ever achieved.

Maris's father even added his message. To Maris, this was the greatest tribute of all. He never wrote to her.

I trust you have arrived without incident. I admit, I have been very fearful for your safety all these weeks, but if this reaches you and all is well, I shall be glad that we did not stand in your way.

That stanza of the French pilgrim's song, the one she sang for the Swiss boy, echoed in Maris's mind:

> When we departed from France
>   In great desire
> We left behind our father and mother
>   Sad and forlorn.

It was the very first stanza of the song, yet Maris hadn't realized until now, when her pilgrimage was over, that it accurately described the feelings of her own parents.

We seem to talk of nothing but your pilgrimage, her father wrote. *It is a big thing for Neville. The News had a write-up about you last night. I am going to get some extra copies and I shall send you a clipping to Paris. Your mother will not let me enclose the one we have. She is too busy showing it to people!*

It's as if I'd won a race or something, Maris thought.

This sudden admiration on everybody's part gave her a big lift. But she didn't feel she'd done anything. She had merely gone from place to place till she got here. She hadn't achieved anything. She'd *found* it, up there on Mount Joy. It was waiting for her there.

If she had allowed the hall porter in Léon to dissuade her from taking that early train, she would have missed walking into Santiago by way of Mount Joy. She had been terribly hungry and that had been what Lonsie would call a hardship. But Maris didn't see that she should be congratulated for getting here.

Tomorrow morning, first thing, she would send her parents a cable. That would really please them. She had intended to wait until she returned to Paris. Then she could have told them the exact date of her arrival. It might take some time to get a flight. And she was determined to go to Chartres to see the wampum belt the Abenakis sent the Virgin. But it wouldn't cost a fortune to send two cables. After reading these letters, Maris felt she had to let her parents know that she was here and that she was coming home.

Her grandfather's letter she had left for the last. In every mail she received, all along the Way, his was her favorite. His personality came through in writing more than anyone else's, because of his elegant old-fashioned style. The strange bulk of this letter, sent expensively airmail, made Maris curious.

She tore the envelope. Folded inside three typewritten sheets of onionskin — why typewritten? — was a little package, carefully made of taped cardboard. What would her grandfather have sent her, all the way to Spain?

When Maris pulled off the tape, tears sprang to her eyes. A scallop shell, the smallest one she'd ever seen.

The token of my pilgrimage, she thought happily, my badge

of Saint James! How like Grandfather to think of that! I must have told him they wouldn't give me one. He sent this so it would be waiting for me, when I arrived.

It was paler than the shell Maris had found that day with Jim, almost honey-colored, except near the hinge, where the radiating ribs suddenly became a warm brown. Turning it over, Maris looked into the creamy cup, wondering about the little animal who once was protected by it. Had some starfish overpowered the scallop, wrapping its long arms around the valves, forcing them open, eating the soft inside?

Maris shuddered. She'd never considered this until now. What was the fate of the poor animal whose house this had been? These shells had more and more meaning.

Where did Grandfather find it? she wondered.

She didn't think there were scallops in his part of Maine. Too cold.

This shell she'd keep always. After she'd given the old one away, she'd still have this one, the emblem of her new life.

Laying it lovingly on the spread, Maris unfolded the letter. In the upper righthand corner it was dated: Meddybemps, Maine, August 15th.

The day I was at Roncevaux, Maris thought, the anniversary of the Battle.

Hi Maris. That was the salutation.

It made Maris jump.

Doesn't sound like Grandfather, she thought, a little alarmed.

But, though he invariably wrote longhand, this was certainly written on his machine. Maris had used it often enough to know. Anyhow, nobody else in Meddybemps would write to her. Still, *Hi.* Her Grandfather would never say that!

Maybe you'll think it funny, me writing to you now, the letter began, *but I have something very important to say.*

That's not Grandfather!

Maris separated the sheets, searching for the signature. There it was: *Jim.*

7

J IM WHO? M ARIS WONDERED. J IM — IT COULDN'T BE — IT wasn't Jim Grant? After all these months of silence?

Her heart started pounding.

How did he know she was in Europe, in Santiago? What was he doing in Meddybemps?

But that large, easygoing, almost childish scrawl — that was Jim's, all right! Once, the sight of it had stirred tremendous emotions in Maris.

It still did, she discovered with surprise. Her hands were shaking so, she had trouble getting hold of the first sheet again.

To begin with, the letter went on, *I guess I ought to explain why I never phoned.*

When I left you that day, I was burned up. After I'd worn down your resistance, I didn't want you. I was scared I'd be drafted before I had a chance to live. That's why I was in such a hurry. Later, I began to think you were right, only then I didn't have the nerve to call. When I read about your Prize in the Daily, it seemed like a great excuse — congratulations and all that. But I didn't dare.

Didn't dare? Maris thought, stunned. If he only knew how I —

She hurried on.

Just as I was leaving for Wyoming, my orders were changed and I was sent to the National Seashore on Cape Cod. They were short a lifeguard. I sat perched above the beach all day, looking at the Ocean and thinking how I'd messed things up. There were all those couples making love. It isn't so great, when you're not the one and you have to watch somebody else. Makes you think.

Maris was impatient. What was Jim doing in Meddybemps? Why didn't he tell her?

Last Wednesday, I was walking on the beach at sunset, not where I work but a little cove near where I room, Pleasant Bay. It's beautiful. But I was hung-up. Suddenly, there in the sand was this little scallop shell, made me think of the one you gave me that day. Remember, I threw it away?

Remember? Yes, Maris remembered. But not with the bitterness she'd felt before. She had forgiven Jim.

This shell seemed to say, You ass, quit feeling sorry for yourself and DO something. I thought, What? Phone? I wanted to explain. But I was afraid you wouldn't speak to me. That's when I got the idea of trying to see you. While we were going together, you said you'd be visiting your grandfather in August. You told me the name of the place and no one could forget that. I asked for three days off. It's a long way from Cape Cod to the eastern end of Maine. And on the Honda! It isn't built for that kind of ride.

He'd gone all that distance, just to explain to Maris! All that distance on the Honda and the whole time, she'd been thinking he didn't care!

I had trouble finding the place and I was scared you'd give me the gate. Then, what a letdown! Your grandfather came to the door and said you weren't around. He was just getting supper. He invited me to share it and spend the night.

Which room did he sleep in? Maris wondered. Was it the one at the top of the stairs, which looks out over the lake, the one I love?

Was I glad! I was pretty well racked from that ride and so disappointed. I'd wanted to give you this shell that I found. Anyway, here it is now.

So Jim had sent it, not her grandfather! Jim sent Maris the token of her pilgrimage!

She picked it up and gazed thoughtfully into the cup. Then she went back to the letter.

What a guy your grandfather is, Maris, what a great guy! At supper, he told me about you and Lonsie going to Europe and how she came back. Later, he got out the maps and showed me your whole route. He had books, too, with pictures of the things you're seeing. Was I impressed! I'd never really understood you before. All that medieval stuff. I was out of my depth. Instead of trying to understand, I kept wanting to make you over, more like me. I was a dope.

But I was to blame, too, Maris thought. I'll have to tell him that.

Yesterday morning, Mr. Maris asked, Why didn't I stay, the breeze was just right for a sail? It was great, out on the lake all day. He talked about his law practice and the Indians, about your grandmother and you — said he hoped you'd return to College some day. That was the first I heard about you dropping out and it threw me. After you'd won the Prize and all! I knew it was my fault. I wanted to jump in the lake.

So that's why I'm writing. To say, Come back to College, PLEASE, Maris. I won't try to date you, if you don't want me to. But come back and finish.

Maris felt the tears stream down her cheeks. She'd write to Jim immediately and tell him what she'd decided, just today, on Mount Joy.

I'm starting for the Cape right after I mail this letter. Here's my address, in case you want it.

Box 498, Orleans, Mass.

*One more thing. I read a lot of Pascal this summer for my
Junior Essay. Not just his scientific work, which was all I
cared about before, but his thoughts. One night, a sentence
jumped out at me from the page and, Maris, it was about you.
Remember how I kept asking, Why not? And you couldn't
seem to give any reason? This is what it said: "The heart has
its reasons, which reason knows nothing about."*

Come back.

Jim

What does it mean? Maris wondered, dazed. When I get
to College will we —? What does it mean?

She laid the letter aside and dropped her forehead on her
arms. Her face was wet. She must have fallen asleep instantly.
The chambermaid woke her, coming in to close the shutters
and turn down the bed. All the letters were strewn on the
green damask spread, which the chambermaid was waiting to
remove and fold up for the night.

It was nine-thirty, just the right hour to be getting ready
for dinner in Spain.

In the elegant, long dining room, Maris had a terrific meal.
The waiter attended to her gravely, expressing no surprise
that she was *sola*. He treated her like the equal of any grown-
up.

So did the man sitting by himself two tables away. He kept
trying to catch Maris's eye and she pretended not to notice,
but she saw that he was pretty old — thirty, maybe — and a
little on the fat side, though not bad-looking. He surely was
interested in her!

She felt very grown-up, taller, even, as she walked out of
the dining room and onto the terrace. It was a perfect evening.

Across the Plaza, the Cathedral stood, silvered by moonlight, no longer a mass of sculptured stone, but something
ethereal, a minstrel's haunting song made visible.

Maris took Jim's shell out of her pocket. Touched by the

moonlight, it glinted like the rock crystal on the Saint's halo in the Portico of Glory.

How should I your true love know
From another one?

We're like Aucassin and Nicolette, she thought dreamily, those medieval lovers who were always losing and finding each other again. I'll tell Jim that in my letter.

But when Maris looked up at the Cathedral once more it troubled her. It was beautiful in the moonlight, yet eerie. She actually felt a little afraid of it.

She remembered how she had told her father that there was some mystery here. She was facing it now.

Some have turned defeat into triumph, death into immortality, the minstrel's haunting song seemed to be saying. It is also possible to turn triumph into defeat, life into —

8

THE BELLS OF SANTIAGO WOKE MARIS. THEIR SOMBER, CRACKED resonance clutched at the pit of her stomach.

This was like the fear which overwhelmed her last night, when she stood on the terrace, looking at the Cathedral in the moonlight. For one short moment, she had imagined herself blissfully tearing around with Jim next year. She had made believe Jim and she were like Aucassin and Nicolette, those medieval lovers.

Then, glancing at the eerie Cathedral, Maris had suddenly known that she was in peril, that it was possible to throw away her triumph.

Shivering, she had run across the courtyard, through the cloister, as if she were being chased. She ran till she reached her room and locked the door.

"Are you afraid?" the Swiss fellow asked in Chartres, when he predicted that Maris would come face to face with a new person in herself.

"A little," she had answered.

But now she was very much afraid, terrified — not of the person she had encountered. She rather liked her. What she was afraid of was losing her again.

She recalled how she'd felt before her last date with Jim, when she stuck the point of the compass into her notebook — the awful desire to escape because she was so helpless, dependent on Jim, on her parents and profs, a prisoner.

Now she was free. She was making her own decisions, based on the insight she had won for herself.

I am a different person, she realized with surprise. If Jim saw me now, he probably wouldn't even care for me.

What frightened her so last night, when she looked at the Cathedral, was its uncertainty in the moonlight, its divine aspiration interlocked with human failure.

She was capable of the same aspiration and the same failure. Just getting a letter made her dream of surrendering all she'd won.

Orléans, she repeated to herself, giving it the French pronunciation. That's where I was so lonely, I almost ran home. I in the Loire Valley, Jim on Cape Cod — each of us struggled in a place called Orléans.

Loneliness had nearly defeated Maris there. But, like the defeat at Roncevaux, it turned to triumph. To throw away that triumph now — start hacking around again, daydream on the window seat, cut classes, when there was so much to do —

Last night, in bed Maris had composed a lot of letters for Jim. None of them sounded right. Either they were too grateful and eager or too cold. If she wrote she was coming back to College, wouldn't Jim think it was because he begged her to? How to convince him that she'd reached this decision herself? She'd have to describe the whole pilgrimage, leading to her discovery on Mount Joy.

She jumped out of bed.

She had no time to write anything now. Until she'd gone to the Portico of Glory and had parted with the symbol of her old, uncertain self, she wouldn't feel free to leave here and she couldn't wait to go home.

As she was combing her hair, she noticed her arms in the

mirror. They were tanned and the down was bleached. But it wasn't all that horrible. Anyway, it was part of her. Why had she let it make her so miserable?

Grandfather likes it, even, she thought.

He hadn't written. This was the first time. Probably, he figured one letter from Meddybemps was enough. What did he think of Jim? Maris would have to wait to find out. She already saw herself, curled up on the couch by the fireplace, telling her grandfather all about the pilgrimage. How pleased he'd be, when she unfolded her plans! She pictured him, the way he looked that evening, before she left.

"*Au revoir*," he had whispered, when he gave her the shell pin and she threw her arms around his neck. "Make a good pilgrimage. It's the hardest thing anyone can do."

Had she? Was it a *good* pilgrimage?

Yes! she thought, as she left the room and passed through the cloister. She stopped to admire the fountain in the court-yard and the flower beds.

Yes! It was a good pilgrimage.

She was impatient to get home, to start working. She'd spend every spare minute in the College Library, finding out about the Abenakis. Maybe there were courses in the anthropology of the American Indian. She'd begin at once, learn the language, spend next summer on the Reservation.

Will they let me come? she wondered suddenly. If Grandfather speaks to the Governor —

She wasn't the first student to go there. Last summer, that group spent their vacation helping the Indians patch up their houses, tutoring the kids, playing with them —

In the dining room, there were only two or three people. Businessmen, no doubt. When you finish dinner around eleven in the evening, you don't have an early breakfast unless there is important business to attend to.

Mine's important, Maris told herself gravely.

She wondered where the stranger was right now, who

would receive her shell this morning. Still asleep? Or trudging along the Way, having seen the sun rise on Mount Joy?

Suppose he or she didn't get to Santiago in time? Maris would miss her plane, the only one out of here today. She wanted so much to get back to Paris, to secure her flight home.

Please hurry, she implored the unknown person.

It was eight-twenty when Maris finished breakfast.

She walked across the Plaza. In the morning light, with the sun behind it, the Cathedral loomed gray.

Standing still a minute in the center of the huge Plaza, Maris counted four Saint Jameses: one above the Town Hall — that Moor Slayer; one on the portal of the Colegio San Jeronimo, one in the gable of the Cathedral and one on the facade of the old hospital, which was now her hotel.

As she neared the long flight of stairs leading to the Portico of Glory, Maris saw that the grille at the bottom was closed and locked. Too early!

Maybe one of the side doors —

She passed the Bishop's Palace and, at the corner of the old hospital, she started up a flight of stairs covered by an ancient arch. Pigeons scattered before her. The North Portal was closed, too.

Maris remembered how the *Pilgrim's Guide* described this side of the Cathedral in the Twelfth Century:

> When we, the people of France, wish to enter the
> Basilica of the Apostle, we go in from the North.
> Near the door, at the side of the road, stands the
> Hospice of the poor pilgrims of Saint James.

In many respects, the place hadn't changed. But the magnificent fountain, which, the *Guide* claimed, had "no equal in the entire world," was gone.

Opposite, surmounting a monastery, was a statue of Saint Martin on horseback, sharing his cloak with the beggar. Maris thought of the little Addisons in Tours.

Continuing around the back of the Cathedral, Maris descended some steps and arrived at the East Portal. But this, she knew, was the Holy Door. It was never opened, except in the Jubilee Year, when July 25th, the Saint's Feast Day, happened to fall on a Sunday.

In a niche above the doorway was one of those statues of Saint James dressed as a prosperous pilgrim, carrying a long staff.

The sculptors of the Seventeenth and Eighteenth Centuries cast Saint James in these theatrical roles — as a pilgrim, as a warrior. He wasn't meant to be himself, the Biblical character. He was acting a part these men wanted him to play.

When Maris reached the Plaza of the Silversmiths, on the South side of the Cathedral, she saw the famous Horse Fountain in the center, spouting water, with ferns issuing unexpectedly from ancient cracks. And there, at the top of the fifteen stairs, with its door still shut, was the beautiful Romanesque South Portal, which she had studied in photographs, back home, when she didn't think she'd ever get here.

God was creating Adam by laying His hand over his heart; Jesus was healing the blind; David was playing his harp; the mysterious woman was holding the skull of her husband or lover in her lap; angels were blowing trumpets, devils and strange beasts crawled over the pediments, a mother was nursing her baby.

These were Maris's old friends, even the beasts and the devils!

Above the door, between two stone cypress trees, stood Saint James. In the Portico of Glory he was barefoot. Here, he was wearing "sandal shoon." His expressive, long-fingered hands held a tablet saying, *Peace be with you.*

He was a very different personality from the one in the Portico of Glory, but equally genuine and forceful, a man of heroic character and vision, a giver of peace.

Maris stood looking at him, reaching up with her eyes, with

all her heart toward this perfection, longing to draw a portion of it unto herself.

No, Santiago had not failed her.

Directly overhead, in the Clock Tower, the bells struck nine.

They were just as cracked as before and much louder here, at the base of the Tower. They shook the Plaza of the Silversmiths. But they didn't frighten Maris. Peace was with her.

When she lowered her eyes, she saw that the door of the South Portal had been opened.

9

When Maris mounted the fifteen steps leading to the South Portal and entered the Cathedral, she was overwhelmed, as she'd been yesterday, by the vastness of the interior. Soft light streamed down through the arches of the galleries, enveloping her like that mist at Roncevaux.

She was almost alone. A few people were coming in through the Portico of Glory. Perhaps one of them was that person Maris looked for. But, although she was pressed for time, she wanted to sit down for a minute on one of the benches in the nave.

Could one girl, still very young, really accomplish anything? Could she bring to neglected people the riches of the spirit?

Yes, Maris thought. And what better place to start than here, where beauty had outlived the centuries? Here, the spirit in one era spoke across time to the spirit in another. It was almost possible to hear a continuum of hosannas reverberating through the ages up in that dome.

But Maris could never belong to a confraternity, like the pilgrims who came here together. If she was to become a member of any community, she'd have to have a part in creating it.

That's a pretty awesome thought, she said to herself.

271

She got up and walked down that long nave till she passed through the Arch into the Portico of Glory, thinking, as she went, that this pilgrimage had turned out to be something quite different from what she'd expected. It had turned out to be not to a place but to a vision, one so infinite that it couldn't be contained in any cathedral or embodied in any sculpture.

Her coming here was what mattered and the people she'd met: the Swiss fellow, the Addisons, the Belgians, those Spanish border officers, the waiters and chambermaids who felt responsible for her — a young girl *sola* — her fellow-passengers in buses, who paid her fare when they saw the shell pin in her beret, or the strangers she appealed to when she was lost, who left their own road to walk part of the Way with her. Even Bron —

Poor Bron! She wondered whether he ever got to Portugal.

Standing in the Portico of Glory, waiting for that person she was looking for, Maris gazed up at Saint James in gratitude. If it hadn't been for his drawing her on to Santiago, she might be in Portugal herself now.

There was nothing supernatural about this. Her faithfulness had kept her from doing something she didn't really want to do.

People were beginning to arrive, but no one who ought to be given the shell. At least, Maris didn't think so. They either pressed the Tree of Jesse or they looked as if they'd be annoyed if a strange girl came charging up and presented them with a scallop shell. They'd think she was asking for money.

Why did she have to do it? Nobody was making her. She didn't want that shell anymore; she could just throw it away. Why miss her plane, delay her return home for the sake of a stranger who probably wouldn't even understand what the shell represented? When Val suggested this, she never dreamed how hard it would be to find that person who wasn't a *bona fide* pilgrim, yet who was earnestly seeking the meaning of life.

But Maris wouldn't give up yet. Someone might still come.

She'd recognize the right person immediately.

She held one shell in each hand. Jim's was smaller than the old one. She had to clench that fist tighter to feel the scallops.

How sweet of him to send it! She wouldn't fly home empty-handed, after all.

Standing so far below the heroic statue, Maris felt very small. But that only seemed to intensify her proud humility — proud because she'd won her freedom which, in turn, demanded such great things of her that she was filled with humility: the willingness to listen and learn.

No! she told the Saint, shocked to think that she'd been so obtuse. I'm not going to the Reservation to teach the Indians what I think they ought to know. Grandfather doesn't have to speak to the Governor for me. I'll wait till I'm asked. I'll prepare, study subjects which might give them pride in their heritage. But then I'll wait. I'll visit them, listen to what they have to say, learn from them. It takes time to make friends. When they find I'm interested and have something to give, don't you think they'll invite me?

Before Saint James had a chance to answer, the bells began to ring.

Maris jumped. So soon! The bells reverberated in the Portico of Glory and, beyond the Arch, up the nave, along the high vaulting, through the galleries, in the dome. Ten o'clock! Time was running out.

Maris wasn't paying enough attention to the people who arrived. Her mind was on the Indians and on Jim.

When Jim kept asking, "Why not?" that day at the beach, Maris couldn't explain because she hadn't been free. Now she was cool. She could choose, weigh, use her head, not be driven by feelings that she couldn't control — her own or some boy's.

The Saint, sitting up there, relaxed, with his hand resting on his staff, looking westward farther than Maris's eyes could see was certainly cool.

Could she keep her cool, when she got back to College?

I hope I can, I do hope so, she told Saint James.

Maris wondered whether he had any idea how hard it was, whether he guessed what almost irresistible pressure threatened this resolve. Way up there, with his eyes on eternity, with his stone limbs — how could he know what people had to cope with, down here?

But surely in his lifetime, a young man, coming ashore of an evening with his catch, surely even he had had to wage this struggle.

You know, Maris said to him, now that I'm cool, anything might happen when I go back. I might fall in love with someone else, someone I haven't even met yet.

I don't want partial union! she blurted out. I made this pilgrimage alone; I had to. Until I can be completely joined to someone, married, I'll go on alone. Not, she explained to Saint James, because I believe partial union is wrong — who am I to judge? — but because it isn't perfect.

She wished she could tell Jim the answer to his question. But it was too late. He wouldn't care for her the way she was. He still thought of her as the old Maris, the pushover she'd been at College. He didn't know how much she'd changed.

He's changed, too, she told the Saint. Or was the Saint telling her? Jim rode all that way on the Honda, just to explain. Doesn't that mean, to be forgiven? At any rate, to forgive himself?

Jim had made a pilgrimage, too — a pilgrimage to Meddybemps! It sounded funny, but he had gone there, carrying his shell, as Maris had carried this one to Compostela. He had responded to the nobility in her grandfather, as she responded to the art and idealism here.

Suddenly, she found the person she'd been looking for.

Isn't he the one? Saint James! Listen! Isn't Jim the one who should have this shell? He made a pilgrimage, too. I'll have to hurry. That Airport bus —

She didn't wait for the Saint's answer. She already had it.

10

With a last, loving grateful glance at Saint James, Maris turned and flew out of the Portico of Glory, down the steps of the Cathedral. Carrying a shell in each hand, she ran across the Plaza, across the courtyard, through the cloister to her room.

The taped cardboard Jim had mailed his shell in lay on the bedside table, next to the pile of letters. It was all the wrapping Maris had. Her fingers shook, as she tried to make the cardboard reach.

But the shell was too big. She simply couldn't manage to enfold it in this tiny piece of cardboard. It would get smashed in the mail.

The hall porter helped her, not personally. He didn't undertake such menial jobs. But he dispatched a little bellboy with the shell.

Maris scribbled a hasty note. After all those letters she'd composed in her mind last night, this was all she said:

Thanks for the token of my pilgrimage. Here is yours, the badge of Saint James. It's the same one.

Maris

275

By the time she had addressed the envelope, the bellboy returned, carrying a small, tissue-wrapped package on a salver. Maris put the package and the note into the envelope and sealed them, thinking that if she and Jim ever saw each other again, it would be as strangers. They would begin over, getting to know these new people, who'd returned from Santiago and Meddybemps.

The hall porter insisted on having the letter mailed for Maris, but she wanted to do this herself.

"It's half past ten," he warned her.

Then, smiling knowingly, as if to say he understood the shell had sentimental significance, he gave Maris directions for finding the Post Office: cross the Plaza, pass the Colegio San Jeronimo and the Colegio de Fonseca beyond it, turn right beneath the arcade.

Maris hurried.

It's going to cost a lot if I send it airmail, she thought, as she followed the hall porter's directions with the envelope in one hand and Jim's little shell in the other.

But Jim was waiting for an answer.

He wouldn't pitch the shell away again, would he? Now that he'd changed —

Maris wished Val could know how gladly she was relinquishing the old shell and the identity of this pilgrim, who so earnestly sought the meaning of life.

When the bulky envelope was weighed, when the expensive stamps were stuck on and the shell was dropped into a box, gone forever from her grasp, Maris went to the telegraph window to send her parents a cable.

She had just had a wonderful idea.

A beautifully designed Spanish calendar, hanging on the wall of the Post Office, informed Maris that if she pursued this idea, she'd only have about ten days at home before the opening of College and she certainly wanted to go to Meddybemps to see her grandfather. She was cutting it pretty fine.

Nevertheless, this was what she cabled:

*Everything marvelous returning to College home
in about a week stopping to visit Peter Addisons
Queen Elizabeth School Southampton.*

She sent a second cable, asking the Addisons to let her
know in Paris whether it would be convenient if she arrived
on Thursday. They'd surely meet her at London Airport in
Elsie.

She felt so happy and lighthearted, it seemed to her she
could easily spread her own wings and fly to Madrid, to Paris,
to London, across the Atlantic without setting foot in a plane.

She rushed to the Hotel.

As she was stuffing her belongings into the knapsack, before
she had a chance to hoist it onto her back, she heard the bells
break out all over Santiago. Their cracked resonance almost
clutched at the pit of her stomach. *Eleven o'clock!* Would
the bus wait for her?

She slung the scrip over her shoulder, sticking the little shell
in it while she was streaking through the cloister and across
the courtyard.

Yes! The bus was still there, standing on the Plaza.

Those businessmen who'd eaten breakfast early were already sitting in it, nobody else. They expressed relief when
Maris appeared. Evidently, they'd been worrying about missing the plane.

I'm not more than ten minutes late, Maris thought. In Spain,
that's nothing.

But the businessmen weren't Spaniards. Maris didn't know
what language they were speaking. Now that she wasn't holding them up anymore, they paid no attention to her.

The bus went up the street that Maris had walked down
when she arrived with the pilgrims. She saw the bakery where
she'd stopped to eat. Those pine seed cakes were still in the
window. The tripe and pigs' feet were still on display next

door and, beyond them, the octopus and goose barnacles. As
the bus moved cautiously through the crowd of people walking in the middle of the street, Maris saw everything.

Leaving Santiago by the Gate of the Way, the bus crossed
the Sar. On the open road, heading for Lavacolla, it picked
up speed.

Maris looked back at the red tiled roofs of the town. The
three spires weren't visible. Only from Mount Joy —

They passed the Pilgrim Cross, where Saint James set down
the dead man from Lorraine and his friend, who nursed him
in the Pyrenees. For a poor fisherman, Saint James certainly
was a great one for getting around on horseback! He had
miraculously covered in that one night the distance of a fif-
teen-day journey.

But Maris would reach Madrid in an hour and cross the
Atlantic in seven! She was pretty miraculous herself.

That ageless vitality in these legends, what Val said she as-
pired to in her actions —

All my life, Maris thought, I want to hold fast to that.

When they came to the lane of dark pines and she saw the
old fingerpost pointing the way up to Mount Joy, she started
singing, silently but with gusto.

It was the song the French pilgrims used to sing in prepara-
tion for their journey, the one she herself sang as she went
around the house in Neville, getting ready to leave. The verse
she had sung then was:

> The things that are needed
>   I have to prepare
> As the Fathers before me
>   Went well furnished there
> With a staff and a scrip,
>   With a hat broad of brim
> And a cloak to protect
>   From winds that are grim.

That wasn't the verse Maris concentrated on today. The one which came to her mind as she was leaving the Field of the Star had completely escaped her at the time. Now she realized that it was the most vital:

> Before going off
>   I must think of myself
> I must shatter the wall
>   Which holds me in myself . . .

She hadn't thought of her self, hadn't shattered the wall before going off on this pilgrimage. But that didn't matter now.

She was about to start another.